ALL SOULS' DAY

JJ MARSH

PREWETT
BIELMANN

All Souls' Day

Cover design: JD Smith

Published by Prewett Bielmann Ltd.

All enquiries to admin@jjmarshauthor.com

First printing, 2020

ISBN 978-3-906256-01-6

To Lorraine Mace, Barbara Scott Emmett, Anne Stormont
and Amanda Hodgkinson
who helped nurture the early seeds of Stubbs

Chapter 1

"Beatrice Stubbs speaking."

"Hi, Beatrice, it's Theo. I'm calling from a phone box because I need to look at my mobile at the same time. I think I found our guy."

"Have you? How come?"

"For someone who's just done a runner with a wodge of his company's cash, he's not trying very hard to hide. He just posted a picture of a canal on Instagram. I found the spot and it's in the centre of Bruges, not more than an hour away from Brussels. He's also using a running app and shares data on his best times, speeds and so on. He went for a run around Bruges early this morning, starting and ending at the same spot. It's a hostel within walking distance of the main train station. Do you want the address or just the phone number?"

"Both, please. I'd better go in person and get photographic evidence of the man. Good work, Theo. I'll go get some snaps, report to the client and return to London. That was one of the easiest jobs yet, thanks to my brilliant assistant."

"All part of the service. See you when you get home."

The train to Bruges was half-empty, a fact which pleased Beatrice. She spread out her paperwork at a table of four, not because she needed it, but just to deter anyone from joining her during the next hour. Her first task was to make a call.

"Banque Franck et Schneider, Christopher Sheldon speaking."

"Mr Sheldon, Beatrice Stubbs here. It seems the missing item has turned up."

"Just a minute." He put her on hold. "You still there?"

"I am," she confirmed, eyeing her tuna and egg sandwich.

"You found Das?"

"I believe so. My colleague managed to pinpoint his physical location via some kind of running app. I don't have proof he's still there, but I do know he was at a hostel in Bruges earlier today."

She heard an intake of breath. "Bruges? Do you have an address?"

"Yes. I intend to travel there this afternoon."

"No need. Where are you now?" he asked, his tone terse.

"At the train station. Why?"

Sheldon dropped his voice. "I'll take it from here. Send me the details via message then delete it from your phone. I'll pay you the rest of your fee this afternoon. Thanks, you did a good job."

Beatrice frowned. "The job is not yet complete. I can't be sure he's at the same address. I will check in person and send you photographic proof."

"As I said, no need for that. Just send me the details and take the next Eurostar to London. Gotta go, thanks again. Please remember what I said about discretion."

The train was already pulling out of Brussels Centraal and Beatrice quite fancied a potter round the mediaeval town of Bruges, so ignored the man's advice. She sent him the details of the hostel and proceeded with her plan. First point of action, eat her sandwich. With nothing to sustain her since the full English on the Eurostar earlier that morning, she was absolutely starving.

The walk to the one-star accommodation was inspiring, like being in a Hans Christian Andersen story. All the pretty little canals and gabled roofs were exactly as she'd pictured and she dallied on a bench for several minutes to watch the autumnal sunshine play on the water. Climbing plants dipped tendrils on the canal's surface, rippling with the wash of passing boats and screening a pair of swans. The skyline presented a hotchpotch of chimney pots, spires and turrets while a bridge's reflection in the now-still water gave the illusion of a perfect ellipse. She found it completely charming, but the October air was chilly and she pressed on with her mission, reaching Hostel Herribert forty minutes after leaving the train.

It was a bleak-looking building, in dire need of a paint job since the shutters leaked varnish or paint, so that each window looked as if its mascara had run. It gave the place a sad, unloved air and would put most people off. Unlike most of its neighbours, not a single light showed the place was inhabited. Beatrice walked past twice, assessing its size and potential number of rooms. There was no movement either in or out, and most windows had net curtains, meaning she could see precious little of the interior or its inhabitants. Nothing for it but to go inside.

Reception was a recycled bar plonked in front of an office. She cleared her throat several times to announce her presence, but to no effect. An unpleasant smell permeated the air, like compost or rot, and she made up her mind to act and get out. It seemed as if the place was abandoned until she caught sight of an elderly lady in the sitting room. She was positioned so she could see out of the window and into the corridor simultaneously. Beatrice nodded and attempted to make her enquiry in French. "*Bonjour, Madame. Je cherche le propriétaire.*"

The woman nodded in return and pointed with an unsteady hand down the corridor. From the rear of the ground floor,

Beatrice detected a voice. She thanked the little lady and followed the sound. Through the frosted glass of the kitchen door, she saw a man pacing and talking on the phone. She couldn't understand a word and assumed he was speaking Flemish. Intent on his conversation, he sounded furious but maybe that was the nature of the language. She retreated into the shadowy corridor. Behind the reception desk was a ledger, so old-fashioned it could have come from a Dickens novel. Making sure she stayed out of sight of the elderly woman and with one ear on the voice at the end of the corridor, Beatrice leaned over for a closer look. Six rooms: two downstairs, three up and one in the attic. Reading upside down, Beatrice was puzzled to see the attic room was significantly cheaper than the others, but what interested her most was the name of the occupant – S. Das. *Found him!* The voice from the kitchen grew angrier and the sound of a fist thumping some kind of surface reached her ears.

She climbed the stairs, noting the stink was less offensive the higher she got. On the first floor, she stopped to listen for any noise behind these less-than-stout doors. Total silence. The shouting man had gone quiet, so Beatrice tiptoed up to the attic, aware she was trespassing. As she ascended, she assessed her situation. She needed a photograph of Sonny Das to prove she had located him. At the same time, if some strange woman knocked on his door and snapped his image, he would immediately guess who she was working for and take flight.

Her best option would be to pretend she was a maid and offer to clean his room. If he was in situ, he'd most likely send her away. Then in lieu of a photograph, she would have to call her employer and give a physical description as the next best thing. If Das wasn't in residence, she'd go outside and wait somewhere inconspicuous until he returned, catching a shot as he entered the building. Maids didn't carry handbags or wear grey trouser suits, however. She would need some sort of disguise.

Before she had even stepped onto the second floor, she could see the door to the attic room was ajar, light spilling in a parallelogram onto the floor outside. She stopped, eyes and ears alert. Apart from traffic noise rumbling from the street below, all was silent. She took two paces closer, leaning to the right to see further into the attic. A corner of the bed, a window and some ratty carpet told her nothing. Then she saw the chair, fallen on its side. Beatrice's training as a detective with the Met enabled her to jump ahead, preparing her for the most likely explanation. She steeled herself and pushed open the door with the toe of her boot.

Even though she expected it, the sight caused her to catch her breath. Sonny Das, wearing only a vest and underpants, dangled from the ceiling, a rope suspending him by the neck.

She'd seen worse. This must have been recent, as there were no signs of decay. It was even feasible the man was still alive. She ran into the room, righted the chair and stood on it to check his pulse. Nothing. Although his body was still warm. This man had died less than an hour ago.

Her running footsteps must have alerted the shouty bloke downstairs. His laboured breathing announced his approach. Beatrice went on the attack and met him on the landing, brandishing her ID.

"Beatrice Stubbs, Private Investigator. We have a suspected suicide in this room. Seal the staircase immediately and call the police."

The man wore a shabby brown cardigan. His hair was white and tissue-thin. Watery blue eyes stared at her without comprehension.

"Do you speak English? Police! *Polizei*! *Policía*!" She mimed picking up a telephone. "Emergency!" She pushed open the door and pointed at the dead man.

Cardigan-Man's eyes widened in horror and he backed away, clutching his hands to his own throat. Beatrice gave up on the useless old duffer and called the police on her mobile.

"Police, please, I'd like to report a death. Hostel Herribert, on Vestingstraat, top floor. It seems someone has committed suicide. Sorry? Oh, yes, of course. I'm a private investigator. My name is Beatrice Stubbs."

Chapter 2

It was very inconvenient to make three different statements to the Bruges police, particularly as she was missing lunch. Once at the scene, a second in the less-than-fragrant B&B dining room and one more time at the police station. At the third recital of her explanation, a young officer interrupted to say he had finally managed to contact Sheldon, who corroborated her story. She signed her statement and left the building. Her intention was to go straight back to Brussels and catch the Eurostar to London. She glanced at her watch. With luck, she could be having dinner with Adrian and Will by seven o'clock.

On the train out of Bruges, she called Theo and explained how their job had ended. He was shocked and asked several pertinent questions. However, the fact remained that Sonny Das was dead, the private bank would pay them in full and she was on her way home. In response to her enquiry about any other job offers, Theo's tone was despondent. She was about to wish him a good weekend, but made a spontaneous decision. She invited him for a drink at Dionysus Wine Bar for a chat before she headed off for dinner. He agreed and she made a mental note to cheer him up somehow. He'd been thoroughly miserable ever since his girlfriend in Mallorca had dumped him. The lack of business at the agency didn't help. Work had been thin on the ground since the summer. She would need to focus attention on publicising the services next week, if this job was over. That was a big 'if'.

Her timetable indicated a train leaving for London in forty minutes or another in two hours. Rather than stress herself rushing from Centraal to Midi, Beatrice decided to take the later train and to pay a visit to Sonny Das's flatmate. The young chap had been so very accommodating that morning and was clearly quite distressed. Better to hear the news of his friend's demise from her, than an impersonal police officer. In the taxi to the apartment, she rehearsed a kinder way of breaking the worst kind of news.

"Hello again, Mr Ghosh. We spoke earlier?"

The man's furrowed brow furrowed still further. "Yes, I remember. But as I said this morning, I really don't think I have anything else to add. He left here on Wednesday evening and I haven't seen him since. I don't know what more I can tell you."

Beatrice clasped her hands together and gave him a sympathetic smile. "I'm here to bring you answers rather than ask questions. May I come in?"

He took several steps backwards, his face filled with concern. "Is Sonny…? Is he OK?"

Beatrice came into the apartment and with a gesture to the sofa, encouraged Bikram Ghosh to sit down. He did as he was bid, his arms tightly folded as if he was holding himself together.

"It's not good news, I'm afraid. After I left you this morning, my colleague located Mr Das via his telephone. He was staying at a hostel in Bruges and I travelled there to gain photographic proof. Unfortunately, before I arrived, Mr Das took his own life. I'm truly sorry to break such upsetting news, but my gut instinct told me you were friends as well as sharing the apartment. The police will undoubtedly contact you with regards to his effects, so I wanted you to know what had happened before having to deal with the practicalities. Mr Ghosh, can I get you anything?

A glass of water?"

The young man's face seemed to age in front of her eyes. His gaze remained on his bare feet, his eyes shielded by his long dark eyelashes. Arms wrapped tightly around himself, he rocked slightly back and forth.

Beatrice waited, only too aware of how much time bad news took to process. The only sound in the apartment was the whirring of a laptop on the coffee table.

Bikram Ghosh lifted his head, his expression dull. "I imagine you look at me and Sonny and think, how nice, two young Indian men must have so much in common. Everyone makes the same assumption. The reality is that Sonny and I come from completely opposite regions, speak different languages and our backgrounds are two castes apart. It's like assuming you, a Brit, would automatically find common ground with a coalminer from Iceland, for no other reason than that you are both European. Mrs Stubbs, in a theoretical sense, Sonny and I should have been at one another's throats." He swallowed and Beatrice noted the imprints his fingers left on his upper arms.

"I'm not comfortable with risk. That is one reason Belgium suits me. I'm happy to be here and all I want to do is work hard, earn a good salary and live a safe life. Sonny is different." He pressed his fingertips to his forehead, massaging it in circles. "Sonny *was* different."

Something in his tone focused Beatrice's attention. "That's the impression I got from his employers. He gambled with clients' money and lost a great deal; triggering him to abscond with whatever cash he had managed to embezzle."

Ghosh shook his head like a horse dislodging a fly. "No. I know who's paying your salary and what story they told you. Nevertheless, I assure you, I am prepared to stand up in court to say that is false. Sonny Das was investigating fraudulent accounting at Banque Franck et Schneider. I didn't want to know. His intention was to blow the whistle and unveil corruption at the bank. Had the situation been ordinary, I doubt he would have told me much about what he was trying to prove. We work long hours, under normal circumstances, seeing each other for a short spell before we go to bed. Then I got sick. Burnout, nervous breakdown, whatever you want to call it, the company gave me three months' leave. That changed our relationship. We talked more and he confided in me what he was planning. I discouraged him. It was dangerous and to be honest, it scared me. I'm no whistleblower, Mrs Stubbs, because I haven't got the guts Sonny had. When I went back to the office, he persisted with his enquiries and didn't share them with me. Look where that got him."

They sat in silence for several minutes, both occupied by their own thoughts. Sheldon had shown her documents demonstrating how much Das had funnelled into secret accounts and she had taken that at face value. She and Theo had located the fleeing fraudster; she'd told Sheldon the address and arrived to find the young man already dead. There had to be a reason Sheldon wanted her to delete the message containing the details of Das's whereabouts from her mobile.

Eventually, she spoke. "Do you have any proof of that, Mr Ghosh?"

Ghosh looked up with a start, as if he'd forgotten she was there. "Um, no. Everything Sonny found he stored in a secret file on his computer. He was strict about security. Although I'm IT savvy, I'm not sure I'd be able to find it, even if I was given access to his laptop."

She got up and paced the room. "May I make a suggestion? Don't tell anyone else what you just told me. By making an accusation you can't prove against your employer, you're putting your job on the line and possibly yourself in danger. I'll make a few discreet enquiries and report my findings to the detective in charge of investigating Sonny's death."

"Why would you do that?" Bikram watched her as she paced.

"You're a PI and no one is going to pay you for this."

"It's a bad habit of mine. I have a compulsion to get at the truth. Time is getting on and I have a train to catch. You have my card and if I learn any more, I'll get in touch. I'm really very sorry for the loss of your friend."

He acted as if he hadn't heard her, moving towards the kitchen. "The day we returned to the office, he gave me something. I was leaving the apartment early, trying to avoid crowds, and he passed me a note. He said to keep it safe in case I ever needed it. I was a bit stressed about going to the bank, so I put it in the kitchen drawer and forgot. That was the end of July, so three months ago." He rattled under some cutlery, brought out an envelope and handed it to Beatrice. The name on the front was Bikram Ghosh.

"You open it," she said. "It's addressed to you."

He hesitated, and then slipped a pen under the corner, tearing open the letter. His eyes scanned the contents and his brow wrinkled in consternation. "I have no idea what this is supposed to mean." He showed Beatrice the neatly written message.

Bikram, if things get terminal, you'll need this. Whether you want to use it or not is up to you. Unlike me, you're not keen on being in the middle of things. All the best, mate. Sonny.

9920 - 668390

The message, to Beatrice's eyes, contained some kind of communication only Ghosh would understand. Except he didn't.

"Two numbers you would need. He must have thought you'd know what it referred to. Perhaps a code to access his secret file? A pass code to his mobile?"

Ghosh's gaze flickered from left to right, as he searched his memory. "It's not his phone. That's only four digits and likewise with bank cards. I doubt that's a master password as they're all numbers and you'd need a mixture of letters, special characters and so on. It's not an entry code to the bank either because we all have individual swipe cards."

"What about the six digits? Perhaps some sort of dates?" She tried backwards, upside down and alternate numbers, but no combination made a coherent date, either DD.MM.YY or using the American system.

"I honestly don't know what it means, Mrs Stubbs. Maybe I need to think about it for a while. If anything comes to mind, I'll contact you."

"I'd appreciate that. I must go. The Eurostar leaves in an hour."

"The Eurostar? At this time of day, I'd advise a taxi to Midi-Zuid ... oh, wait a minute."

Beatrice peered at him while he read the note again.

He spoke slowly, his face thoughtful. "On a couple of occasions, Sonny and I made use of a locker at the train station. This was a matter of convenience. If Sonny was going to London for a weekend and had forgotten something, I would leave it in a locker at the Midi-Zuid terminal, to save him coming all the way home. Twice he did the same for me when I went directly to work from the airport. He would text me the locker number – four digits – and the combination – six digits."

Beatrice read the note again.

Bikram, if things get terminal, you'll need this. Whether you want to use it or not is up to you. Unlike me, you're not keen on being in the middle of things. All the best, mate. Sonny.

9920 - 668390

"His use of the words 'terminal' and 'middle' speaks for that theory. Perhaps we should have a look. Shall we take a cab and check? I don't have much time so we'd better dash."

Ghosh scratched his goatee beard. "Sonny said it's up to me. He's right. I don't like being in the middle of things. You take this, Mrs Stubbs, and do what you think is best. I really don't want to be involved. I'm sorry."

Beatrice examined his haunted expression. "If you're sure that's what you want. Once again, my sincere sympathies and I'll keep you informed. Goodbye and thank you."

Outside the building, she hailed a taxi and began her journey home.

At Brussels Midi-Zuid, she stopped on the edge of the concourse, watching the swell of travellers surge and weave in patterns, like swallows preparing to fly south for winter. She turned to stare at the wall of left luggage lockers, each with a keypad, and read the instructions. As a precaution, she took out a pair of gloves. One paid the fee, entered a code and stashed the rucksack or whatever one wanted to leave behind. Then no one else could open the locker unless they knew the code. Each locker was numbered and the system logical. Within two minutes, she found locker 9920. She put down her bags and entered the numbers 668390 into the keypad, feeling excited and embarrassed in equal parts. To her astonishment, the locker clunked open. She stood there, staring into the dark interior, until she remembered that someone somewhere would be watching her via a security camera.

She reached inside, took out a leather folder, checked there was nothing else inside in the darker recesses, then tucked the folder in her handbag and cleared the code for the next person. Once she'd shut the door, she hurried off to check in. The train was delayed by twenty minutes. With some relief, she grabbed a spicy chicken wrap, a bottle of water and two packets of Belgian chocolates from the kiosk as presents for her hosts later that evening. Then she strode onto the train and found her seat. Again, few fellow passengers occupied the business class compartment. Nevertheless, she waited till the train was well clear of the Brussels suburbs before opening the folder to see what Sonny Das had hidden for his colleague.

Chapter 3

The clock ticked towards five and Marianne stopped even pretending she was hard at work. She closed down her machine and opened her phone. To her relief, there was a message from Beatrice, already on her way home from Brussels. That meant Marianne only had to do Dad duty tonight, but the rest of the weekend was free. She wasn't the only one eager to escape the office. On a Friday night in October, everyone had somewhere they'd rather be.

She went to the bathroom for no reason in particular and prepared to leave the accountancy practice. When she came back to wish her colleagues a good weekend, something had changed. Her bosses stood in the centre of the room, their faces grave.

"What is it?" she asked. "I'm in kind of a hurry tonight."

"Sit down, Marianne," said Josephine. "There's no good time to do this and a Friday night is possibly the worst. Nevertheless, the newspapers have got the story. They'll run something tomorrow, full of guesses and hearsay and the usual crap. That's why we have to tell you now. Young and Bundy Financial Advisory have called in the administrators. Everyone is to be made redundant with immediate effect. I'm sorrier than I can say."

Robert took over, quoting statistics, slow growth and the

impact of bigger companies' consolidations on small businesses. He spent several minutes praising their work. Marianne heard one word in ten. She had just lost her job. It was two months before Christmas. She was single, unemployed and had sod-all in the way of optimism. Robert repeated his regrets to a wall of a stony silence, apologised again and guided a tearful Josephine into their office, closing the door.

The team comprised ten people. Two were crying, three were exchanging expressions of shock, one was on the phone – *you're not going to believe this* – and three sat frozen as statues, staring at the bosses' office. Marianne snatched her coat from its hook and glanced back at her desk. There was nothing she cared enough about to take with her. The urge to get out of the building overtook her and she ran, tears flying, down the stairs and into the car park.

When she arrived at Dad and Beatrice's cottage, Tanya's car was parked outside. Best possible scenario. She could cry on Tanya's shoulder, handing her the role of carer for their father until Beatrice returned. Hopefully Luke was at home with Gabriel. Kids tended to occupy everyone's attention which was infuriating when she had a drama to discuss.

Her father and sister were in the kitchen eating scones. Huggy Bear gave her little dance of delight on seeing a visitor, but as it was only Marianne, the terrier returned to sit at Matthew's feet.

"Hi! Dad made scones. Come and have one. Totally delicious. We've got jam and cream too." Tanya saw Marianne's expression. "Are you OK?"

Marianne collapsed into a chair and sobbed out the whole story. Matthew and Tanya listened with concerned expressions to her account and she reached for a tissue to stem her tears.

"So that was one hell of a year. In summary, I lost a boyfriend, a job and ..." She glanced at Matthew, who was pouring her a cup of tea.

Tanya shot her a threatening look.

Marianne avoided that subject. "... survived my sister's wedding. On top of all that, it's nearly the end of the year. What am I going to do?"

"Drink some tea, for starters." Matthew pushed over a cup. "I should say a scone wouldn't hurt either. You're in disarray, dear girl. Just adjust your expectations. You're well-educated and highly skilled. Someone will hire you in no time. You certainly won't starve."

Marianne stirred the tea and tore off a piece of scone. "Unemployment rates are soaring, accountancy firms are relocating and I'm stuck in a backwater with no prospects of either a job or a man. God knows why. It's all right for you." She stabbed a finger at Tanya. "Selling houses is always going to be an option. Plus Gabriel's job brings in a decent salary. Whereas I'm left high and dry and single. Again."

The phone rang in the hallway and Tanya got up to answer it.

Matthew chewed, shaking his head. "I really don't know. Sultanas do add moisture but I can't help feeling they sully a scone. What do you think?"

"Dad, Beatrice is on the phone." Tanya stood in the kitchen doorway. "She's just got into London. Go and have a word."

Obediently, Matthew put down his scone and went into the hallway. Tanya closed the door behind him. At first, Marianne assumed it was to give him some privacy until she saw her sister's thunderous face.

"Listen to me, you self-centred little princess. I'm sorry about the job, but you will find another. Accountants are forever in demand. The reason you are single is because you gave the kind, generous Jago an ultimatum – you or his job. He chose his job and in his shoes, so would I. As for it 'being all right for me', eight years ago, I was a single mother on benefits, raising a kid alone.

I couldn't work because I couldn't afford childcare. I never blamed the world or the universe or my own family. Getting pregnant by that French prick was my own fault and I took responsibility. Time you did the same, Marianne. Sympathy has its limits."

Shocked, Marianne stared at her sister. Part of her wanted to burst into fresh tears at Tanya's betrayal, but that would reinforce the self-pitying accusation.

Tanya sat down and softened her tone. "Why don't you look at this as an unexpected holiday? Just enjoy the break and save job hunting till the New Year. Or you could do as Beatrice has done and set up on your own."

"What you mean?" Marianne sniffed. "Self-employment?"

Tanya buttered another scone. "Why not? I mean, the clients of your firm trust you with their financial records. You could go freelance, work from home. I'm sure could pick up some more custom locally. Maybe get some of your existing customers to recommend you to their connections. You're well-qualified and professional, plus it would give you more flexibility. No more nine to five, just working when it suits you. Either eat that scone or I'm giving it to Huggy Bear."

Marianne began eating, turning over Tanya's words in her mind. It wasn't beyond the realms of possibility that some of her clients would stick with her. She had been working on their books for over ten years now. She was perfectly capable of managing their balance sheets, completing the tax records and advising on investments. Realistically, all Robert and Josephine had ever done as managers was distribute the workload and tout for new custom. She could do that herself.

"It's a lot of work, setting up your own business," she sighed.

"I know. But Beatrice managed it and so did Gabriel. I'm sure both of them would be happy to give you some advice. You'll have to put in a lot of effort at the beginning, but then you're in control. No one can pull the rug from under you without warning. If you did decide to go freelance, you could spend a few weeks preparing yourself to launch. Give it some thought at least."

"Give what some thought?" asked Matthew, coming back into the room.

"Tanya thinks I should set up my own accountancy business," said Marianne.

Matthew put the kettle on to boil. "What a marvellous idea! You've always been very good with numbers. I think that's a capital plan. Your bosses at Jones and Blunkett will be sorry to lose you, I'm sure. When do you plan to break it to them? More tea?"

"Dad, it's Young and Blundy. Anyway, I just told you, they made me redundant. The company has gone bust."

Tanya gave her a warning stare. "I'll have another cup please."

Matthew poured the tea. "Gone bust? Oh dear, that's not a good look for an accountancy firm, is it? Yes, striking out on your own is a jolly good move. Now then, what's the verdict on the scones?"

Marianne ceded the spotlight to her father, with a fond smile. "Usually, I'm a bit of a purist. But in my opinion, the sultanas work. They add a certain sweetness which means they're perfect with nothing else than butter. The plain ones suit the jam and cream. How was Beatrice?"

"Do you know, I think you're absolutely right. My mistake was to put jam and cream on the fruit scones. It all makes sense now. Ah, yes, Beatrice is on fine form and has solved the case already. Don't ask me how; I didn't understand the euphemisms she uses. Seems she's a bit worried about Theo, though. She's taking him out for a drink this evening. Apparently the poor chap is still pining over that yoga teacher."

Marianne shook her head. "Poor Theo. But at the end of the day, there's no use moping around. Plenty more fish in the sea and time to move on. Tanya, pass me the jam?"

Tanya rolled her eyes but handed Marianne the strawberry preserve.

Chapter 4

When Theo walked into Dionysus, Beatrice was already waiting, sitting at the bar with two glasses of white wine. She looked perky and cheerful, considering she had just stumbled across a suicide that morning. He waved and came to sit opposite her.

She gave him a broad smile and a kiss on the cheek. "Thank you for coming to join me. I can't stay long because I'm having dinner with Adrian and Will. But I just wanted to debrief quickly over a glass of wine. This one's for you."

"Cheers. What's the deal with the Brussels situation? The contract was for us to find him. I guess we did that, but too late. Are you sure we'll still get paid?"

"Oh, yes," said Beatrice airily. "In fact, we've already got the cash. Banque Franck et Schneider transferred the money this afternoon. I checked my account on the way here. The thing is, I'm not sure the case is over."

Theo listened intently to Beatrice's account of the conversation with Das's flatmate, the numbers, the locker station and the paperwork contained within the leather folder.

"Can I see?" he asked.

She pulled out a black leather folder from her handbag and passed it to him. "By rights, I should send this to the police in Bruges. But before I do that, I want to know what it is. I can make neither head nor tail of all these spreadsheets and bank statements."

Nor could Theo. He was hopeless with numbers and the sheaf of papers could have been written in hieroglyphics for all the sense they made. "If he went to the length of hiding this and giving his flatmate an encoded message to find it, it's gotta have some significance."

"That's what I thought. I'm going to take the papers with me to Devon tomorrow and pick Marianne's brains. If there's anything to incriminate the bank, I may have to revisit Brussels to pursue it."

For a private investigation agency with almost no paid work for months, Theo thought that was a really bad idea. "You want to investigate our most recent employer? Who's gonna pay for that? And what do I do while you're trying to bring down a financial institution?"

Beatrice sipped her wine. "If there is a case, we'll have to find someone to fund our enquiries. And yes, I do mean 'our'. We should work on this together. I've taken the hulk of our recent jobs and I get the distinct impression that you're bored."

She cocked her head and looked at him for confirmation. Theo revolved the stem of his wineglass between his fingers, staring at the wheat-coloured liquid and trying to phrase his dissatisfaction, which wasn't clear to himself.

"Yeah, I could do with being busier. Now would be a great time to lose myself in work. As it is, I spend a couple of hours on the computer and for the rest of the day; I've got nothing to do. No, that's not true. I run, I go to my kick-boxing class and I put out feelers for work. Even after all of that, I've still got far too much thinking time on my hands." He looked into her eyes. "How long does it last? The painful stage, I mean. When am I going to wake up thinking about anything else but Fae?"

Beatrice studied him, a gentle smile spreading over her face. "I can't remember. It's been several millennia since I lost and found the love of my life. Two pieces of advice. One, move on with lessons learned. Do not, and I repeat, do not hang around trying to analyse what went wrong. She ended it, correct me if I'm wrong, because she felt the relationship had run its course. If that's how she feels, there's nothing you can do to change that. Rather than trying to recover the past, turn your attention to the present. Your dalliance with a Mallorcan yoga teacher was fun while it lasted but didn't work out." She shrugged. "Such is life. It's a waste of time running after people who don't want you, for whatever reason. Especially when there are people who would throw themselves under a bus to get your attention. Move on. Go out on a date but for crying out loud, do not witter on about your ex-girlfriend."

She meant well, Theo knew that. But unless he understood the mistake he had made with Fae, how could he possibly envisage a new relationship? Maybe he just wasn't ready to fall in love.

"You said two pieces of advice?"

"Is it worth it, when you are quite obviously going to ignore the first?" Beatrice eyed him over her glass of wine.

"Try me."

"Work. I want you to throw yourself into investigating Banque Franck et Schneider. Find out if there is any litigation, scandal, rumours or whether any other bodies such as governmental justice departments are looking into their activities. I suspect we've got something on these people, although I don't yet understand it. Then all we need is someone to hire us. That way, we make some money and put a stop to whatever nefarious activities those white-collar buggers are up to. Turn your focus on real life rather than fantasy. Do you see?"

The first time in days, Theo actually laughed. This woman, this infuriating woman, had the determination of a woodpecker. And she didn't care who knew it. "Yes, I see. I'll start tonight. Thank you, Beatrice. I'll think over both pieces of advice and kick myself up the arse. Do you want another glass of wine?"

"I do, but I can't. I said I'd be at Adrian's flat by eight. You know what he's like when he spent the afternoon cooking. Have a lovely weekend and I'll call you on Monday with an update." She squeezed his shoulder, slipped off the stool and bustled out of the front door. Theo surveyed the room, exchanging a smile with some of the members of staff he knew from the old days, and assessing the clientele. Beautiful people with glamorous jobs and trite conversation.

He got off the stool, saluted assistant manager Jed and walked into the wine emporium section, planning to get something Friday-ish to take home and drink alone. Tamsin was behind the counter and offered some smart ideas for a light white bargain. Theo wandered the shop, checking out her suggestions, clocking her in the mirror. Tamsin was a stunning-looking woman. Her black hair was braided into long plaits threaded with bright colours, but it was her face that arrested attention. Her eyes were the same shape as those of a Venetian mask – huge, almond ellipses with long lashes. With full lips the colour of coffee and a figure made to turn heads, she was never short of admirers. But much as Theo liked her, he knew they'd never be anything more than friends.

That was exactly his problem. All his life, he'd been looking for something deeper, more meaningful, and more truthful. He disliked small talk and hated the falsity of everyday interactions. It was one of the reasons he liked Beatrice so much. She was nosy, bossy, domineering and more like a bulldozer when she wanted to get her way. But most importantly, she was genuine, and willing to look at herself in the mirror more harshly than most.

Whereas Theo was a fantasist. He believed in his own emotional depth and sought a partner who felt similar. But the truth was he was as shallow and self-deluded as all the other occupants of the wine bar. He bought a bottle of Chasselas on Tamsin's recommendation and wished her a good weekend. On his walk home, he asked himself when he had become quite so pretentious. Perhaps when trying to be the perfect partner for Fae. He projected transcendence onto her which had turned out to be an illusion. Yet still he persisted in trying to make them an ideal couple, in need of no one else. He was twenty-eight years old with all the maturity of a decade ago.

His idea of love probably hadn't changed since he'd studied Wordsworth or Shakespeare at school. A mind still filled with *A Midsummer Night's Dream*, forest fairies, star-crossed lovers and a naïve belief that his soul mate was circling the globe looking for him. No wonder he'd failed at every job and every romance. If it wasn't instantly magical, it had to be a false alarm. What a fool. He ducked into a corner shop and bought himself a couple of salads. Tonight, he intended to work, as Beatrice had advised.

When he got home, the clock at the top of the stairs showed eight o'clock. Hopefully Beatrice had made it to Adrian and Will's place in time for dinner. A wave of loneliness washed over him and he wished he had been asked somewhere to eat. Or that he'd invited someone over. He thought of Beatrice's words. *Move on.* If he sat here in this apartment, hoping someone would offer a spontaneous invitation, they would find him in five years, a desiccated husk. Just because his last relationship had failed, there was nothing stopping him calling a mate and proposing a drink. He pulled his phone out of his pocket.

"Theo! You all right?"

"Hi, Catinca, am I disturbing you?"

"Nah, mate, just coming out the Tube. What's going on?"

Theo's mouth went dry and he berated himself for not preparing his spiel before he dialled. "Not much. Got some work to do tonight, but I feel like going out tomorrow. Do you want to join me for a drink, maybe get something to eat? If you're busy, no problem." He scrunched his eyes tightly shut in embarrassment.

There was a long pause before she replied. "When some

bloke calls to invite me out on Saturday night, I got some questions. Is it just two old mates going out for curry? Or are you, Theo Wolfe, inviting me on date? Just so I know what to wear, innit?"

Theo laughed, all tension released. "I was thinking along the lines of a sort-of date. Unless you're already committed to one of the celebrities you hang out with these days."

"Stuff the celebrities. What about that Cajun place with live music in Whitechapel? I been fancying that for ages. See you there tomorrow, at seven? Wear that perfume I bought you."

"Great idea, I love Cajun food."

"Sorted! Right, I gotta go. Late for dinner party. See you tomorrow! Can't bloody wait!"

A wide smile spread across Theo's face as he plated his salads and opened the wine. Moving on. It was about time.

Chapter 5

A wriggling black shape dashed out the door and around Beatrice's legs the moment she rang the bell, unlocked the door and stepped into the hallway.

"Hello, Dolly! Good gracious, you're looking sleek as a seal. Come on, let's go indoors. Something smells delicious." She guided the dog out of the communal hallway and into Adrian's downstairs flat. She dumped her bag and rucksack underneath the coat rack and took her bottle of wine and Belgian chocolates down the corridor into the kitchen. One sweeping glance around the living room showed her four guests were expected. Her ears picked up the sound of Will singing in the shower and her nose twitched at the scent of cloves and allspice. Adrian was absent so Beatrice knelt to make a fuss of the moustachioed dog, marvelling at her shiny coat and waggly tail.

"I told you not to bring any wine!" Adrian stood in the corridor, a mock stern expression on his face which softened into affection as he watched Beatrice pet Dolly.

Beatrice opened her arms for a hug, reciprocated by Adrian. "And you expected me to listen? More fool you. We're celebrating! I brought it back from Belgium because that's the only place I've only ever tasted it. Celliers des Dauphins Rosé. It's as if someone made wine from hazelnuts. I adore it and if I had my way I would never drink anything else. Chocs too, just because. Has Will only just got home?"

Adrian took a ladle and poured liquid from a pan into four shot glasses. "No, he got here half an hour ago and took Dolly for a jog. That's why he's showering and she's knackered. Your aperitif, Madame. Mulled wine with cloves as bats and orange slices as pumpkins. What else at this time of year? Chin, chin. If you're back this soon, I assume Brussels was a success. Sit down and relax. I hope you're hungry, because I prepared quite a feast for our brand new detective inspector."

"There's no one who deserves it more. Chin-chin."

The mulled wine was perfection. Spiced, warm, alcoholic and with all the sense of cosy nights. Sitting here with Adrian and drinking this warm glass of liquid seemed like an embrace, a welcome home. She shook her head at her exaggeration. She'd been out of the country fewer than twenty-four hours.

"That is exactly what I needed. Delicious! From now on, I will drink nothing else until spring. I noticed you used the word guests in the plural. The table is set for four. Who else is coming for dinner?"

A door opened and Will emerged, in a lumberjack shirt, his hair still damp. He wrapped her in a fragrant hug. "Your timing, PI Stubbs, is bang on. I'm starving. How did it go in Brussels? Is that for me?" He scooped up his shot of mulled wine and wafted it under his nose.

Beatrice smiled. These men pleased her as friends, as allies and as aesthetically perfect specimens of manhood. Will and Adrian were beautiful to look at.

"Ah yes, Brussels. Let's discuss it over dinner, unless the extra guest is someone we cannot trust? I assumed it was just the three of us."

Adrian glared at Will. "You were supposed to tell her!"

"I forgot! Sorry, I had a lot on my mind today. Anyway, Catinca's part of the family. You don't mind, do you, Beatrice?" Will gave her a beseeching look.

Catinca was family and Beatrice loved her dearly. Her excitement peaked when Adrian did his eyebrow-twerking thing. "Wait till you hear her news. Our friend has just outclassed us all." He pressed a finger to his lips. "No, I'm saying nothing. Catinca gets to tell it her way. Now who wants to see the menu?"

Beatrice and Will took their mulled wines into the living-room. The dining-table was decorated for a romantic feast in navy-blue with a white trim. Police uniform colours with a menu printed in italics.

To celebrate the occasion of William Quinn's promotion to Detective Inspector with the Metropolitan Police, please enjoy a tasting menu fit for The Fuzz:

On the Beat: Caviar and Blini with chives, egg and sour cream

Served with Veuve Clicquot champagne

Shoulder Stripes: Salmon, tuna and squid sashimi, with seaweed salad

Served with Muscadet

Rank and Roll: Vegetable Tempura with two dipping sauces and miso soup

Served with Provençal Rosé

Inspector Morsels: Mixed Yakitori from the grill

Served with Sauvignon Blanc

To DI for: Crème brûlée with a side of blueberry coulis

Served with Sauternes

Coffee and Belgian chocs (if I know Beatrice Stubbs)

Beatrice erupted into a belly laugh.

"You are kidding!" Will exclaimed. "Did you seriously prepare all this for me?"

Adrian brought a tray into the living room, with four flutes of champagne and an assortment of little bowls. "Yes. Because you deserve it." The doorbell rang. "Here she is." He buzzed open the door.

Catinca charged down the corridor to stand in the doorway.

"You ain't gonna believe this!"

"We haven't said a word, I promise," said Adrian. "You can tell Beatrice yourself."

"Eh? Oh, right. Yeah, tell you about that in a minute. But biggest news of all? Guess who just invited me out on a DATE?" Her eyes flashed and her cheeks glowed.

Beatrice wondered if her pep talk this afternoon had taken effect. If so, he hadn't wasted any time. She played dumb. "I have no idea. You mix with so many of the rich and famous, I don't know where to start."

"He ain't rich and only famous in my head, but I been dreaming about him since he walked by me in Liverpool Street Station. So stunned by his looks, I dropped my porridge."

Adrian clapped his hands to his cheeks. "Not Theo! Is it actually a date? A *date*-date?"

Catinca threw off her faux-fur coat and looked less like a chinchilla and more like a blue-point Siamese cat with her beige-periwinkle cashmere tracksuit. "I asked him straight. Date or drink with mate? He said date. D-A-T-E. Theo Wolfe and Catinca Radu are now 'dating', innit? God, I might just reopen my Facebook account to tell the world!" She did a little dance on the spot in her turquoise Converse trainers and went to hang up her coat.

When she returned, all three of them applauded. Her smile was irrepressible as she accepted the glass Adrian offered. The excitement clearly affected Dolly, who lifted her nose to sniff the coffee table, her tail wagging like a brush without a dustpan.

Adrian proposed the toast. "To DI Quinn's promotion and Catinca's hot date!"

"Congrats to Will! Cheers, lovely people! You're all invited to my wedding."

They raised a glass to her triumph and spent twenty minutes on the starter discussing the appropriate attitude to a first date with an old mate. Adrian was insistent she should not fall into bed with him until Will called him out on his hypocrisy.

"You invited me in for a 'coffee' on our first date. Plus you made the first move. I had to leave for the last train home, otherwise we'd have definitely slept together that night."

"That's not how I remember it. You were the one coming on to me! I was the one who wanted to wait until we knew each other better."

"Adrian Harvey, you're a bare-faced liar. Don't listen to him, Catinca. You already know Theo well enough to be sure he's not after a one-night stand."

Catinca tilted her head in thought. "What do you think, Beatrice?"

"If I were in your Converse trainers, I wouldn't set myself any hard and fast rules. See how the evening goes and if it feels right, do it. If it doesn't, don't. Trust your instincts. Theo is a gentleman, that much I know."

"A sodding gorgeous gentleman. Good advice, Auntie B."

Adrian pronounced the sashimi ready and they took their places at the dining-table.

"Shit, I forgot the wakame," said Adrian. "Open the wine, Will, would you? Catinca, tell Beatrice the other thing. I'm sure she knows the people in question." He hurried to the kitchen, Dolly at his heels.

"Yes, I hear you have news?" Beatrice asked, eager to start on her meal.

"Good news comes in threes, innit? Will's promotion, Theo asking me on date and commission of lifetime. Biggest celebrity wedding of next year is gonna be massive. Next summer, Agnessa Trottiscliffe is marrying Baron Simon Kinnloss and guess who's designing her dress?"

"Good heavens, even *I've* heard of him. That railway millionaire chap. His face is in the papers constantly and Matthew approves, so he must be doing something right. The bride's name again?"

Will poured the wine. "Agnessa spelt Trottiscliffe, pronounced Trozley. She calls herself Nessie for short." He caught Beatrice's widened eyes. "Oh, yes. She really is that tone deaf."

"I know you hate her," Catinca said to Will, helping herself to the seaweed Adrian placed on the table. "But her daddy is well minted and I get to pocket just over fifteen grand. Don't have to like her, do I?"

"I don't hate her," said Will. "That would be about as pointless as she is. I find her a facile waste of oxygen, that's all. Still, I celebrate the fact you're liberating some of her unearned wealth by designing something beautiful. That's the difference between the two of you. You have true talent. I mean, why is she even famous? She's never achieved a thing in her life."

They ate and drank and gossiped, showering Adrian's cuisine with extravagant praise. Catinca returned to the subject of Will's new role.

"Should we shut up about it?" Catinca asked. "Don't wanna make you nervous."

"No, I wouldn't say I'm nervous. Just wary. With all due modesty, I should have been promoted over a year ago. They passed me over for a diplomacy pick. That's OK, I'm over it now. But the upcoming cases about to land on my desk are some of the toughest I've seen. Yeah, OK, I am nervous." Will placed his cutlery together on a near-spotless plate. "That yakitori was so good. Into the Top Ten, no question."

Beatrice agreed. "Not only was it delicious, it fits the atmosphere. As does the wine. Thank you both for an exceptional meal. Will, you must project confidence, knowledge, an awareness of their limitations and an assurance that you can handle the politics. Even if you don't feel it. Especially if you don't feel it. You'll be fine, I have total faith."

His face relaxed into a smile. "I hope you're right, PI Stubbs. Want to give me a hand with dessert and fill me in on Brussels?"

They left Catinca and Adrian discussing Agnessa Whatsit and retreated to the kitchen.

"I think the situation was quite the opposite of what I'd been led to expect. This was not an embezzler but a whistleblower. Theo and I tracked him down, I alerted his employers and they got there first. My belief is that they killed him, made it look like suicide and took all his belongings, including his laptop. They must think they've cleared their tracks. Except I have a folder of paperwork he hid, only accessible by his friend."

Only a couple like Adrian and Will would have a crème brûlée torch. Will heated the sugar on each ramekin until it bubbled and cracked. "Can I have a look? You might need a forensic accountant, but I'm happy to make an amateur assessment."

"I'd really appreciate that. Shall I take these two through?"

They lounged on the sofas after dinner, Will and Beatrice poring over the paperwork, Catinca and Adrian scrolling through images of the future Baroness Kinnloss to study her style. Will came to the conclusion that Sonny Das had enough ammunition to sink his employers, but an experienced financial fraud investigator would be required to translate. Adrian labelled Agnessa Trott-is-cliffe (he refused to pronounce it any other way) as a scrawny horse with false eyelashes. He put Dolly on her lead, ready to walk Catinca to the Tube.

They said their farewells, wishing her good luck for her date, and Beatrice followed Will into the kitchen to watch him make coffee.

He continued talking as the machine spat and growled. "One thing we haven't discussed is your domestic situation. Shooting off for a couple of days can be covered by his daughters, but if you throw yourself into a major fraud investigation? What happens to Matthew while you're away?"

An impulse to brush off the question and continue digging into the work of Sonny Das almost won, until she acknowledged

Will was already two steps ahead.

"I'm not sure. Unless I can find someone to fund the enquiry, I might just have to hand it over to the police and stay home to make sure he doesn't burn any more pans of rice."

Will raised an eyebrow. "Talking of torched kitchenware, here's your coffee."

Trust Will to recall the time she'd put the Moka pot on, forgotten about it and taken the dog for a walk. "That was a momentary lapse. You're right, though. I do have to make a decision in the medium term. He's functioning fine, most of the time, but does forget practical details such as where we keep things. Do you know where he stored a dozen eggs last week? In his sock drawer. His rationale was they should be kept somewhere soft."

They sat at the breakfast bar, sipping their coffee; an espresso for him, cappuccino for her.

"What about asking him, when he's having a good day? How would he like his life organised to give him freedom while making sure he doesn't endanger himself, or you, or the animals?"

"Hmm." Beatrice parked that idea for another time. "Maybe I should just give this stuff to the police and stay home. My concern is they won't want to open an investigation. The other reason I want to pursue this as a PI is for Theo. He's had almost nothing to do for weeks and it's getting him down. He needs to be at work."

"You're his boss, not his mum. You just set him up on a date. That's enough for one day. Don't go diving into a pool of piranhas just to keep your employee entertained."

"How did you know I set him up?" she demanded.

Will's face crinkled into a laugh. "Your expression. As soon as Catinca announced it, you were doing a mental victory lap. Those two didn't notice, because neither is a copper. But you and Theo had a drink together earlier this evening. Then Catinca turns up, bursting with excitement after he asked her out. Your fingerprints are all over that one."

She shrugged. "I want them both to be happy. Will, tell me the truth. If you'd found some potentially explosive paperwork, what would you do?"

"Juicy question. Under most circumstances, I'd hand it over to the relevant authorities and ask for an update as the case progressed. In your shoes, that's different. If the Das geezer was trying to blow the whistle, you basically found him and alerted the wolves, who got there first. That's how he ended up dead. It's a conscience thing, I get it. But if you're dealing with a financial institution prepared to kill to keep its secrets, I'd think long and hard about wading into something that powerful and shady. Fraud at the high-finance level is best left to the professionals. European financial regulators, for example. You'd need influence and an understanding of the shitty tricks these banks pull in order to mount a serious investigation. You've got DI nous and an inexperienced assistant. I'd say stand back and leave it to the people who are trained to investigate white-collar crime. This is a lot bigger and uglier than anything you've taken on as a PI."

The sound of the door opening and claws clattering in the corridor announced the return of Dolly. They listened to the sounds of Adrian drying the wet dog, both smiling, until he released her to join them in the kitchen. The young creature scampered and rolled and bunted against their legs, evidently thrilled to be out of the rain.

"I'm so grateful I don't have to go out in this weather," said Beatrice. "Do you think Catinca will be all right?"

Adrian appeared, his hair plastered to his scalp. "It's a hideous night! Dolly and I got soaked. Ten paces down the road to the Tube, it was unbearable. I told Catinca that if she was due 15K for this commission, she should take a taxi and save her cashmere and faux fur ensemble. We hailed a cab and she'll be delivered home to her door. Do I get a coffee?"

"Seeing as you asked so nicely," Will replied. "Oof, that dog pongs like a pond. Dolly, come with me, I'm going to dry you properly. Come, good girl."

Adrian slipped onto Will's stool. "You can relax. Beatrice's Boudoir is all prepared and Catinca will be safely in her own bed in twenty minutes. Now, what do you think of that Theo thing? Last I heard, he was moping over that redhead in Mallorca, and then out of the blue, he asks Catinca on a date? I hope he's serious, because she is mad about him. What I don't get is what provoked him to embark on a romantic liaison now."

"Nor me," said Beatrice. "Who can explain the vagaries of the heart? Could simply be the time was right. Sounds like your coffee is ready. How's business at Dionysus?"

Chapter 6

Grits and Gators was a popular eatery on Plumbers Row. So popular that there was a queue outside. Catinca's heart sank and she released a long sigh of disappointment.

"Never thought to book and I can't be arsed standing around in the cold. Wanna go somewhere else?"

"I reserved us a table for two. We can skip the queue." He led the way past the line of people and addressed a woman standing at a podium. "Theo Wolfe. I have a reservation."

She checked her screen and led them to a table in an alcove, with a partial view of the stage.

Catinca grinned at him. "Not only sexy, multi-lingual and smells gorgeous, but he's thoughtful an' all. Are you actually real and not replicant or something?"

"Would I know if I was a replicant? I might be one of the newer models." His eyes flashed in the subtle lighting.

She'd only seen the film once and fell asleep before the end so decided against taking it further. Instead, she checked out their surroundings. The place was designed to look like a New Orleans street, with murals either side of the room depicting façades of building. Faux balconies jutted out over diners' heads, several lines of washing hanging between them. Crooked, hand-painted signs warned against swimming in the creek and a vintage Cadillac seemed to be parked around the corner, as only the tail fins were visible. Dixieland horns came from the speakers and the ambience worked its magic: a combination of relaxation and anticipation.

"This place is cool! We gonna start with a cocktail?" She grabbed the menu. "Nothing with bourbon, gives me headache. Gin fizz?"

Theo was smiling at her. "Gin fizz is a pretty descriptive name. Sounds delicious. Let's have two of those. As for food, what do you fancy? Before I booked, I checked out the menu online. They can do a vegetarian or vegan version of some dishes. I already made up my mind to try a crawfish *étouffée*. I've been dreaming about it all day."

"Whassat?" she asked. Since arriving in Britain, it had been her mission to try everything she'd never heard of and this was a new one to her.

"Crawfish and vegetables in a thick spicy sauce on a pile of rice. There's a Creole tomato version with no seafood."

"No, I want the original. I eat vegan or veggie when I'm home, but I fall off wagon sometimes, specially when I want to try something new. Draw line at meat, but fishies are OK. If it's spicy and rich, we should drink white wine. Want me to choose?"

"You're the expert." He sat up taller for a second and focused his attention on a waiter. As if the guy had been summoned by remote control, he arrived at their table in seconds.

"Two gin fizzes, please. We've chosen our food, but may need a few more minutes to select a wine."

"Two gin fizzes. Do you have a preference as to which gin?"

"Tanqueray," said Catinca.

"Hendrick's," said Theo, at exactly the same time.

The waiter laughed. "I can make one of each to compare, but I would agree with you," he said to Catinca. "Hendrick's has a floral side which would get overpowered in a cocktail like this."

Catinca lifted her shoulders to her ears. "What can I say? I'm not just wine expert."

"In that case, two gin fizzes with Tanqueray. Thank you."

He didn't seem bothered at his opinion being overridden, just giving her another smile and nod of respect. "You look lovely tonight. I thought so when we met at the Tube, but I hadn't seen your dress. Is that one of yours?"

"Aw, thank you! Yes, trying out new kinda design. Bit too flimsy for this sodding weather, but I need to feel how it flows. Massive commission next year – bridal gown and probably bridesmaids' dresses. If I get credit for society wedding on all gossip pages, I'm laughing. Right, we're having French Chenin Blanc. Should go perfect with … how do you say it?"

"*Étouffée*. It means smothered. Is the wedding dress for somebody famous?" He did his upright thing and targeted his gaze at a nearby waitress, who came over instantly to take their order.

Once she'd gone, Catinca leant forward. "You are definitely replicant. How do you make them staff come running? I know how places this size work. One waiter or waitress takes charge of six to eight tables. They tell demanding customers to wait for own server. How come you get everyone as if snapping finger?"

Theo laughed as the cocktails arrived, along with little sticks of bread-crumbed vegetables and a barbeque dip. "It's a trick I learned when trying to get served at the bar. Make yourself visible, stand still as a statue and project your energy onto that person. It works. Nothing supernatural, more understanding human nature. Cheers and thank you for being here."

She raised her glass and looked into his warm eyes. "Thank you for inviting me. Took a while, innit?"

They drank and he gazed at her. Her stomach flipped at the expression on his face.

"Young wines need time to mature before presented to a connoisseur. I had some growing up to do because you deserve something better than a drifter. Working with Beatrice has given me more of a focus. After the last … what I mean is, I'd like to see if it works, you and me. To be truthful, I think you're out of my league."

He'd been about to say something about that bendy hippie in Mallorca and stopped himself just in time, she knew it.

"Right, listen. Don't pussycat round me. You can talk about your last relationship. I know you been miserable ever since she … you broke up. We're friends first, Theo. I'll tell you all about my Tinder disasters and you can be honest about the Mallorca girl. Deal?"

He shook his head, laughing, his black plaits making a swishing sound like the brush thing those drummers use. "Deal. Beatrice told me not to talk about my ex and the first thing you do is give me permission."

Catinca's hand hovered in mid-air, holding a crispy carrot. "Beatrice? When did you tell her we were going out?"

"I didn't. We had a drink yesterday evening and she told me it was time to move on, to start dating again. That's when she warned me not to drone on about my previous relationship."

Catinca thought back to the previous evening and Beatrice's expression when she announced her date. At the time, Catinca had assumed that wide grin was due to her being pleased. Now, she saw it for what it was – a smug smile from a satisfied matchmaker. She shook her head in disbelief. "That woman! Well, what can I say? I'm glad she kicked you up the backside and I'm glad we're here. A toast! To Beatrice Stubbs. Long may she interfere!"

Theo laughed, lifting his glass. "To Beatrice and her well-meant meddling. You had dinner with Adrian and Will last night as well?"

"Yeah, Adrian made totally mad tasting menu for Will's promotion. You seen their dog?"

The conversation flowed easily, ranging over their mutual friends, Catinca's commission, Theo's broken heart and bruised ego, online dating and the sublime flavours of their meal. She liked the way Theo ate, devoting all his concentration to the plate in front of him when he took a mouthful. He was the same when listening to her stories or telling one of his own. His attention was 100% in the present. His wide smile, strong cheekbones and long black lashes were an irresistible combination and the purple shirt he had chosen for the occasion worked beautifully with his colouring.

"But just because not much work lately, you're not thinking of quitting, are you?" she asked, dragging her attention away from his clothes.

"No! I love this job and it's thanks to you I'm in this position. No, we've just been through a lean patch in terms of cases but Beatrice is optimistic we might be able to get some work out of this Brussels situation. I hope so, for financial reasons and to give me something to do. That food was all I expected it to be and more. Packed full of flavour and so fresh. The wine was a good choice. Would you like a dessert?"

"Nah, I ain't got sweet teeth. What about you?"

"Me neither, I'm full. How about I pay the bill and we stop off at Buonasera for a coffee and a nightcap? Put your purse away. I invited you out so I'm getting this. You can pick up the tab on our next date, OK?" He held her gaze.

She broke into a huge smile. "And when will that be?"

"Whenever you ask me," he grinned. He did his waiter-summoning trick again and within ten minutes, they were out on the street in the biting wind. It seemed absolutely natural to nestle together, her arm tucked in his. He looked down at her as they waited to cross the road.

"I really enjoyed this evening. I'd like to do it again."

An idea occurred to Catinca as the beeps of the pelican crossing sounded and they walked with several other people to the other side of the street. "You know what I always wanted to do? Go ice-skating at Somerset House. To me, that looks romantic and fun and typically London. We could go tomorrow."

"I'd love that. Then we could go all-out traditional and maybe have afternoon tea. Oh, shit, Buonasera is closed. That's a shame. They do the best coffee this side of the city. Sorry."

"Not your fault, mate." She was about to offer an alternative suggestion when he kissed her. She closed her eyes and abandoned herself to the fireworks set off by the touch of his lips. He pulled away, his hand still on her cheek.

"Your nose is cold," he said.

"All of me is cold," she replied. "Apart from my innards. They're on fire."

He laughed and pulled her close. "Come on, let's walk to the bus stop. You should get home and warm up."

She thought back to Adrian's advice, which she abandoned, and remembered what Beatrice had said. *If it feels right, do it.* It felt very right indeed.

"Do you want to come with me?" she asked, her stomach in knots.

He hesitated. "It's not that I don't want to, I do. But you are really important to me and I don't want to mess things up by rushing. Can we take things slowly?"

"Yes, we can. Slowly as you like."

He kissed her again and she relaxed into his embrace. Then he put an arm around her shoulders, she hooked hers around his waist and they walked in comfortable silence towards Commercial Road. Catinca could not stop grinning.

Chapter 7

The sound of opening and closing drawers dragged Beatrice from a profound sleep. She squinted into their brightly lit bedroom and saw Matthew, dressed, shaved and in his jacket, clattering around amid some coat hangers in the wardrobe.

She blinked at the clock. 06.45 am. "What earth are you doing? It's quarter to seven and still dark outside."

"Already? I've spent twenty minutes searching for my wretched ties. Perhaps I'll use the one I keep in the faculty office. I have to go now otherwise I'll be late. Do you think you might walk the dog this morning? I'm afraid I don't have time to make coffee so do help yourself before you leave." He kissed her on the cheek, ruffled Huggy Bear's fur and left the room, closing the door behind him.

Beatrice sat up, blinking, aware that even Huggy Bear was confused about why Matthew was getting up in the middle of the night. She pulled on her dressing gown and hurried down the stairs, just in time to see him pick up the car keys and open the porch door. There was no way to throw cold water on this particular delusion, yet somehow she had to prevent him leaving the house.

"Matthew!"

He turned, his face impatient. "Can't stop, Old Thing, dreadfully late as it is."

"Haven't you forgotten something?" She gave a gentle laugh. "Here you go, tearing out the door as if it's a typical day. The university is closed for Reading Week, remember? So you and I can enjoy a leisurely breakfast, which is exactly what you deserve. After that, I'll help you look for your ties. They must be in a cupboard somewhere. Would you prefer crumpets or pancakes this morning?"

"Reading Week? Is it really? Well, well." He put down his briefcase on the hall table and sat down to unlace his shoes. Beatrice noticed he was wearing brogues, one brown, one black, but at least his socks matched. "That's a blessed relief, to tell the truth. I've no idea where my lecture notes have gone and what I was supposed to say to a bunch of undergraduates in an hour's time. Thank heavens you were here. My preference would be for pancakes. Perhaps I should pick some raspberries from the garden. I'm partial to soft summer fruits on a freshly cooked crêpe."

Beatrice looked out at the bleak and sparse vegetable patch. "Or we could use up those ripe pears in the fruit bowl. They go awfully well with maple syrup. Why don't you change out of your work clothes and into jeans and a jumper so that we are ready for our walk after we've eaten? I'll start on the coffee and feed the animals." She was on her way into the kitchen before the sudden silence made her uneasy. Matthew stood still as a statue, staring at the clock on the wall.

"I don't work at the university anymore. I retired, years ago. You don't live in London now. You live here, with me, Huggy Bear and Dumpling. It's October and there are no raspberries in the garden. I've just done it again, haven't I?"

"Come and sit in the kitchen, it's warmer in there." Before beginning on the coffee, or the pancakes, or chopping up some overripe pears, Beatrice sat opposite the love of her life and tried to seize the moment of lucidity. "We need to think about how to manage this situation. One solution is for me to give up work.

That way, I would be on hand if there were to be an incident. Another is to employ a professional carer during the week, and rely on the girls or Gabriel at the weekend if I'm away. That won't be a frequent occurrence, but something we should still be prepared for. Matthew, what would make you feel most comfortable?"

He spent a long time gazing at his fingernails. Eventually he answered. "I'm not very good with people. Friends, family and you are the places where I feel most comfortable. That said, I don't want you to give up a career that is both stellar and worthy merely to make sure I don't fall down the stairs. It's odd. Sometimes everything is clear and logical, other times I feel as if I'm in a dream. What would a professional carer do, I wonder?"

"Truthfully? I don't know. I presume their services vary according to the needs of their clients. But it wouldn't hurt to enquire, would it? Seeing as the family will be here for lunch, shall we discuss the subject together? Or would you rather not?"

He took her hand and squeezed it. "While I still can, I should like to have my say. I'm going to change and then I expect some fresh coffee, pancakes and pears on this table when I return. Hop to it, woman. Yes, yes, Huggy Bear, we're going out right after breakfast."

All through dog walks and a pint at the pub, Matthew was engaged, alert and his old self. Only on the way home did he ask a random question which made Beatrice start.

"Heather looks very well, I have to say. Things must be going well with Midge for a change. That kind of volatile relationship would never suit me, but those two seem to thrive on the ups and downs. No accounting for folk."

Midge had died some years ago, which might explain Heather's equanimity, but Beatrice moved the conversation on. "She's been promoted to Deputy Head at the primary school. No surprise she's feeling chuffed. As for lunch, I've prepared all the veggies and all we need do is roast the cauliflower and the pheasant. Do you feel up to making gravy?"

The sound of a horn blasted behind them and they started to see Gabriel's Land Rover splashing through the puddles. He pulled up alongside.

"Hop in, it's freezing out there!"

They clambered into the back, Matthew lifting Huggy Bear first. The dog went crazy on seeing Luke, leaping and licking and writhing with delight. That dog and Matthew's grandson had a bond like none other. They were almost at the cottage before Luke tore his attention away from the ball of fur and beamed at his not-quite grandparents. He'd grown up, forsaking hearty hugs, unless it was Huggy Bear.

"We might be getting a dog!" he yelled over the noise of the engine and tyres crunching up the gravel drive.

"Correction," said Tanya, undoing her seatbelt. "We're discussing the practicalities of getting a dog."

"How marvellous!" said Matthew. "A particular breed or a Heinz 57?"

Gabriel yanked up the handbrake. "I'd only want a rescue, but there are circumstances to consider. Ah look, Marianne's right behind us."

With the Land Rover, Matthew's Volkswagen and Marianne's Suzuki parked on the hard standing; there was precious little room left. They squeezed out of the vehicles and after greeting everyone, Marianne made a beeline for Beatrice.

"Got a minute? I'm pretty sure I know why your man in Brussels kept that paperwork. There's a case to pursue here and I had a thought about how to work things out with Dad and all. Leave them to start dinner and we'll have a chat in the study."

Her papers spread all over Matthew's desk and her laptop open, Marianne seemed more prepared for a presentation than a chat.

"Before I start, what did Theo's research turn up?"

"Quite a lot. There's more than one investigation going on and I left a message with a journalist he identified, suggesting a collaboration. She's not called me back yet, but it is the weekend. What I need to know is whether there's anything of value in the file. Otherwise I'm wasting the woman's time. What do you think?"

Marianne brushed her hair from her shoulders and folded her arms. "Executive summary: the folder you found in Brussels is a paper trail proving a series of fraudulent transactions. It shows a system of shifting money between companies, shell accounts and tax havens to escape official governance. Where it gets really interesting is when the money comes back. Not to the bank, but to its board in the form of consultancy payments." Marianne peered at her. "Do you see? In a nutshell, they siphon off profits, launder it to the point where it's stain-free and pay it directly into the pockets of the bank's board, amongst others. This is the trail that guy ..."

"Sonny Das."

"Sonny Das was following. The issue is that the board are lining their own pockets and Das found out. They framed him with that whole embezzlement story and he fled. Not because he was guilty of any kind of misdemeanour, at least in my view. Though that's just an assumption. Without his own financial records, I couldn't even begin to defend him. My point is, the paper maze he dived into exposed his employers and he probably kept a digital account of their scam with paper proof as insurance. I'll bet his entire analysis is sitting in the cloud somewhere. How to access that, well, I wouldn't know where to start."

"I would," said Beatrice. "And I should. They hired us to track down a man they said had stiffed the company. When Theo found him via some fitness application on the chap's phone, I gave the bank the address. I told them where to find him and they got there before me. No trial, no defence, just a quick execution and all personal effects removed. Oh my God!"

"What?"

"His flatmate. If they want a clean slate, Bikram Ghosh is a risk. I must call him immediately."

"Go ahead. Then I'll explain how this jigsaw fits together."

After three calls, five minutes apart, there was still no reply from Ghosh's number. Meanwhile, Marianne explained the logic between the payments and numbered accounts, with reference to the Cayman Islands and brand new companies with no seed capital.

"What are you going to do with this info, Beatrice? It's explosive stuff."

"If the paper is keen, not to mention willing to pay, I'll work with them. It means going back to Brussels, though." She shot a guilty look at the door.

"I was thinking about that. My plan is to start my own business and work as a freelance accountant. All I need for that is a computer and a quiet room to work in. Not so easy at my place 'cos it's directly opposite that new building site. What about while you're away, I work here, get some peace and keep an eye on Dad?"

"That is a wonderful idea! He'd feel much more comfortable than having a carer come in. Suits us all beautifully. And I'm very proud of you for striking out on your own."

"You did it."

"Yes, but it's not always easy, especially now I've got Theo."

Someone knocked on the door and Luke's head appeared. "Dinner's ready! Wash your hands and sit at the table."

Marianne raised her eyebrows at Beatrice. "Bossy little bugger, isn't he? Wonder where he gets that from?"

The two women did as they were bid.

Roasted cauliflower was one of the best recipes Gabriel had ever given them. Luke scoffed two portions, rather than pigging out on Matthew's Sunday spuds as usual. When Marianne announced her plan of using the cottage as her home office, everyone was delighted, especially Matthew. Tanya refused wine and opted for herbal tea, citing a dodgy stomach. Gabriel and Matthew became embroiled in a political discussion to which Marianne added her own views. Beatrice was just about to serve pudding – baked apples with frozen yoghurt – when her mobile rang. She took the call and paced into the garden for a moment of privacy, leaving Tanya in charge.

"Beatrice Stubbs. Who's calling?"

"Gael O'Connell, Ms Stubbs. You left me a message and I'm sorry it's taken me so long to respond. I had to be sure you were on the level. Always best to get a bit of background first. Your credentials are solid and I'd love to hear what you have to say. Am I disturbing you?"

"We're in the middle of Sunday lunch, but I have a few minutes. Thank you for calling and I completely understand your need to validate a potential source. You got my email regarding Franck et Schneider then."

"I did and it landed on the right desk. I've been on their trail for years so any information you can add, about the most recent incident in particular, would be a great help to the story. Is there any chance we could meet in person? There's a lot of detail I'd only want to share face to face."

A thrill buzzed through Beatrice's whole frame. "My assistant and I could be available for a short sojourn in Brussels, as we have further concrete information to share. My concern would be remuneration and expenses. Does your newspaper have a fund to pay freelancers, Ms O'Connell?"

She inhaled sharply. "I'd have to beat it out of them, but yeah, sure there's cash. How soon could we meet?"

Beatrice tapped her lips, thinking. "How about tomorrow lunchtime?"

"That's grand. You'll be coming on the Eurostar, right? I'll buy you lunch and we can talk terms. Let's say one o'clock at Eats Zuid. It's in the main terminal. See you tomorrow."

Chapter 8

Real.

Theo was indulging in very risky behaviour, namely comparing Catinca to his ex. But it helped. The shower rinsed him clean and he sloughed off more than dead skin.

The one word he would use to describe Catinca was real. Everything about her was authentic. Her sense of style, her appetites, her sudden flares of temper or joy, her unembarrassed attraction to him and her enthusiasm for all life had to offer. There was nothing affected about the woman and she had little patience with the affectations of others. She wanted Theo as he was. Not a bit more spiritual or esoteric, but the flawed individual she saw in front of her.

Last night had been so much better than he expected. Transitioning from friends to lovers could have been strange and uncomfortable, but for him, Catinca seemed tailor-made. He loved her company because she was like no one else. Part of him regretted refusing the offer of taking her home. Because he wanted to make love to her, like a supplicant, offering her everything he had. It was no more than she deserved.

At the same time, it was best to take things slowly. Better to talk, kiss, laugh and touch so that when it happened, it would be at the right time. "Take it slowly," he said aloud. But he changed the duvet cover, just in case.

He was leaving the house, wearing the aftershave she'd bought him, dressed in one of her shirts underneath his ski jacket, with a little present tucked in his inside pocket when his phone rang.

"Hello, Beatrice. What's up?"

"Plenty, since you ask, but first of all I want to know about last night. How did your date go? Are you going to see each other again, romantically speaking?"

Theo shook his head. No wonder Beatrice and Catinca got along so well. Both cut to the chase with minimal preamble. "As a matter of fact, I'm on my way to meet the lady in question right now. We're going skating."

At the other end of the line, there was silence for a moment.

"Beatrice? You still there?"

When her voice came, it cracked slightly. "Oh, that's so romantic! I almost wish I hadn't called now. Never mind, you enjoy your date and I will speak to you later. Give my love to Catinca."

"Oi! Don't do that. I will enjoy my date, I promise you, but not as much if I'm wondering what you were going to say. Talk to me. Have we got a case?"

Beatrice gave a whimsical sigh. "I'm not sure I ever told you this, but Matthew and I declared our feelings for one another in front of a body of water. It wasn't frozen or in the capital city or crowded with other pleasure seekers. Still, I have a feeling that lakes, rivers and even frozen ponds lend themselves to affairs of the heart. I wish you both all the luck in the world. That said, do you think we could go to Brussels in the morning? There's a train at 08.55 from St Pancras. Doable, do you think?"

If he calculated the journey from his apartment to the train station, the check-in time and Monday morning traffic, Theo would need to be up at six. Perhaps changing the duvet cover was premature. "I can do that. How long do you think we'll be away?"

"Not long. The plan is to hand over your research and Marianne's analysis to a journalist at the train station over lunch. There's every likelihood that'll be it and we can come home tomorrow afternoon. However, if there are developments and the news organisation is willing to pay, we may well stay over for a couple of days. I'm flying blind here, Theo, so can we scope the situation as an initial assessment?"

Light rain moistened his face. "Of course. Did Marianne find something? No, don't tell me over the phone. We can use the train journey to share our discoveries. I'll meet you at the ticket barrier at eight-thirty, OK?"

"That would be ideal. I'll let you go now and enjoy your second date. Apologise on my behalf for my bad timing in snatching you away, but you know what they say: absence makes the heart grow fonder. See you in the morning!"

He waited at the entrance until he spotted her coming across the Strand. Even bundled up in her silver puffer jacket and moon boots, she stood out, reflecting light and attracting attention. She saw him and waved, her smile as shiny as her clothes. This time, there was no awkwardness and he leant straight in to kiss her on the lips. She wrapped arms around his neck and looked into his eyes.

"I've been thinking about you all night," she said. Her huge brown eyes searched his and his insides turned into marshmallow.

"You may have crossed my mind once or twice too. Are you ready to go and make arses of ourselves on the ice?"

She grabbed his hand. "Hell, yeah!"

It was safe to say that neither of them excelled themselves on the rink, but that was hardly the point. They held hands, they picked each other up, they laughed, they side-eyed the show-offs and spent a lot of time in each other's arms. Theo had never been one of those people to snap every moment of his life and post it on social media, but at that moment he wished he could capture Catinca's expression, breath in a cloud, half obscuring her shining eyes. While he stood there staring, a small child cannoned into the back of his knees and sent him flying. While the kid skated on with a 'sorry!' over his shoulder, Theo attempted to right himself without getting his hands under other skaters' feet. His knee signalled it was more than a light bruise and he hobbled his way to the padded barrier, clinging on to relieve the pressure on his leg.

"Sodding little swine! Flattened you and carries on past as if nothing happened. You OK? You hit that ice hard." Her face wore a familiar expression of annoyance and indignation. It made him laugh.

"It's going to hurt tomorrow, that's for sure. Maybe I should cut my losses and take you for a hot chocolate. Or would you prefer to stay a little longer?"

"Nah, let's go. Getting too crowded anyway. I wanna hot drink, probably with a shot to warm me up. You gonna lean on me?"

"Between you and the barrier, I might be able to get out safely. Where do you want to go? Somewhere nearby would suit me." His knee throbbed and he cursed the kid's timing.

"There's a café just over there. Not sure if they serve shots of brandy but if not..." She opened her jacket and showed him a hip flask in the inside pocket. "Can't be too careful in this kind of weather."

The café did indeed serve brandy so they ordered a shot each along with a hot chocolate topped with marshmallows. The type of drink Theo regarded as pretentious under normal circumstances, but today that didn't seem to matter.

Catinca was telling him a story about Covent Garden. "And some of these street theatre guys are on unicycles six-foot high. If anybody falls from that height, they get hurt. I was walking past, on the way to Neal Street and I saw these kids, chucking coins at unicyclist's head. Two young boys, no older than ten, flinging 50p pieces they nicked from his busking suitcase, directly at his head. I was in a hurry but marched right over, caught them by the collar and smacked their heads together. Got a round of applause for that. Little shits."

"Goddess of the street performers. Beware her wrath! You're so much braver than me. If I'd seen kids chucking coins at a street unicyclist, I'd have walked on by, afraid of confrontation. I don't want to get involved. Still, I wish I'd seen that. You banging two ten-year-olds' heads together? I bet you weren't much taller than them."

Catinca scooped up a marshmallow and chewed it thoughtfully. "Size don't matter with the right attitude. I was raging and they knew it. What I did frightened them enough to do a runner, especially as crowd was clapping. Thing is, when something makes me angry, like bad treatment or shitty behaviour, I can't let it slide. I don't know that unicyclist but all bloke is trying to do is entertain people. Why they wanna hurt him? Gets right up my nostrils. Talking of nostrils, you got chocolate on your face." She wiped a finger across his foam moustache and pressed it to his lips.

He licked it and pretended the moan was for the chocolate.

"Anyway, you done much better than that in Finland. I know you don't want to talk about it so we won't. But I bullied story out of Beatrice and if you wasn't my superhero before, you are sodding Spiderman now."

Theo didn't want to talk about Finland or superheroes or anything other than the here and now. He stretched his feet under the table and caught her ankles between his. Her pupils darkened and that catlike smile spread over her face.

"Yesterday evening was perfect and today, despite my injury, was even better. I think it's your turn to ask me for a date. But before you do, I should tell you that I have to travel to Brussels early tomorrow morning. I might be back the same day or later in the week. When is your interview with the father of the bride?"

"Wednesday! Meeting him in posh hotel at two o'clock. If your Brussels trip goes well and my interview kicks ass, we should celebrate whenever you get home. Just tell Beatrice Stubbs not to keep you too long and I want you back in one sodding piece. I've been crazy about you for EVER and don't plan to lose you now."

Public demonstrations of affection normally nauseated Theo, but today he made an exception. He reached a hand across the table to cup Catinca's face and drew her lips to meet his.

When they broke apart, they gazed at each other like lovesick puppies.

She broke the moment, picking up her long spoon to stir her chocolate. "I know we agreed to take it slowly, but after Brussels, let's go slowly a bit faster, OK?"

Theo wondered why on earth he'd ever believed his dream woman was on a Spanish island when all the time, she'd been right in front of him.

Chapter 9

Adrian and Will were still asleep when Beatrice left their flat at a horribly early hour of the morning. She left them a note, thanking them for the use of Beatrice's Boudoir and wishing Will good luck with his first day as DI later that day. Then she called a cab.

On the ride across London to St Pancras station, Beatrice went over the details of the case again. Just to be sure she could explain to Theo how the top executives at Banque Franck et Schneider were lining their own pockets. It wasn't simply a case of fraudulent accounting by misrepresenting its assets and underplaying its expenses. This was far more complex. The company had several daughter companies to which it loaned money at favourable rates of interest. Some of those companies sold their debts to other banks and bought them back at a later date, investing the money they had made on the deal in tax havens. This enabled the smaller companies to evade tax and the parent company to exaggerate its profits.

Secondly, those subsidiaries often paid BFS top executives huge consultancy payments, which went into numbered personal accounts.

Thirdly, the employee pension system was invested into schemes which were deemed extremely risky, such as start-ups with no seed capital or shell companies which had no offices, employees or regulated activity.

On top of all that, the executives awarded themselves eye-watering bonuses based on the bank's inflated asset values, a large proportion of which had been neatly transferred to their own pockets.

The repercussions of this, according to Marianne, were enormous. Firstly, the CEO, CFO and chairman of the board must all be party to the financial shenanigans, as must the internal auditors. That was the only way the company could present innocent-looking books, and impressive growth in profits and shareholder value, while paying bribes for secrecy. Eventually, the house of cards would collapse, taking employees' jobs and pensions with it. Unless someone blew the whistle.

The accountancy jiggery-pokery was just about comprehensible to Beatrice, but the one thing she could not understand was how they got away with it. After the collapse of so many companies in the wake of the financial crash, one of the key EU recommendations was greater oversight and scrutiny by auditors and regulatory bodies. How many people did these bankers have to pay off to keep their nefarious behaviour quiet?

She tipped the cabbie and wished him a good day, then went to check in at the Eurostar. She was just coming up the steps when she saw Theo limping off the escalator from the Tube.

"Don't tell me that's an ice-skating injury!"

He looked sheepish. "Yeah, but not my fault. Some kid knocked me over."

"Oh dear. You're no Robin Cousins, are you?"

"Who?"

"Never mind. Are you sure you're up for this? I don't envisage any hot pursuits or parkour activity while we're in Belgium, but just getting around could be painful."

"I'll be all right. It's best to keep moving or I'll seize up. It's not broken or anything."

"If you're sure? Let's get ourselves some Business Premier

tickets and then breakfast is well overdue. You wouldn't believe how much I'm looking forward to the whole hog on the train."

"You know what? I would."

Half an hour later, they both devoured pastries, fruit, yoghurt and a full English with a cup of coffee as the train raced through the countryside.

"So injuries aside, how was your afternoon with the wonderful Ms Radu?"

Theo smiled as he buttered his toast. "As wonderful as you'd expect. She told me to pass on a message. You're not to keep me too long and she wants me back in one piece."

Beatrice laughed, delighted. "One sodding piece, I'll bet were her exact words. So it's official then? You are a couple? That is just marvellous! I couldn't be more thrilled!"

"Yeah, we're seeing each other and I'm pretty damn thrilled myself. Just kicking myself over why I waited so long. We wasted a lot of time while I was chasing fairy-tales."

"You're together now and that's all that matters. Best of all, my assistant is smiling again. Don't you want that sausage?"

"No, you can have it, I'm full. Tell me about today's meeting. The background of that investigative journo checks out, you know. I printed a couple more articles she's written about white-collar crime. She studied languages, like me. But unlike me, she knows her stuff and isn't afraid to go after the big boys."

"Good. Because need to tread very cautiously with this material. Marianne described it as 'explosive'. Personal jeopardy is not something I plan to factor into this project. Ideally, Ms O'Connell will pay us for the info and we can get home. Although it would be interesting to see how it pans out and whether she can take their dirty laundry to the cleaners. Another thing, I'm very concerned about Sonny's flatmate. I haven't been able to reach him at home or at work."

"Perhaps we should pay him a visit after the chat with the

journo. He's probably keeping his head down. If someone did get at Sonny Das, them going after his flatmate would raise suspicion."

"Depends how highly they value silence. Right, I think I've finished my breakfast. Shall we make a start on the meaning behind the paper trail?"

Eats Zuid was a noisy sort of diner just off the main concourse. It wasn't the kind of place one could make a reservation and Beatrice wondered how on earth they should locate the person they were supposed to meet. They stood in the doorway, trying to figure out how the place worked, when a short woman appeared at Beatrice's elbow.

"Hi, I'm Gael O'Connell. We're over here," she said, and led the way to a booth. Gael stood back to allow them in first with a quick smile. She wore casual trousers and a hoodie, no make-up or jewellery and her dark hair looked almost as unruly as Beatrice's own. Her eyes studied them both with interest.

"Good to meet you both and thanks for coming. How was the journey?"

Before they could answer, a waitress came by with some menus. Gael took one and passed the waitress a banknote. "Thanks for holding our spot, Francine. What's the special today?"

"We have two. *Boudin noir*, which won't interest you, or the superfood salad with quinoa, sprouting greens, edamame beans and white horseradish, dressed with hemp oil and sesame seeds. Or there's always your usual?"

O'Connell addressed Beatrice and Theo. "Every time I eat here, I swear I'll try something different. The simple truth is they do the best *moules et frites* I've ever eaten. Not to mention their grand selection of beers." She smiled at the waitress. "I'll have my usual. What about you two?"

"When in Brussels, one should go local. What's *boudin noir*?"

asked Beatrice.

"Blood sausage," said Francine.

"In that case, I'll have the same as Gael, but perhaps a white wine rather than beer. Theo?"

"The superfood salad sounds amazing. I'll try that with a sparkling water, please. Belgian beer and painkillers are not the best combination."

The waitress took their order and walked away, giving Theo an approving look. It could have been his choice of house special or the fact he looked strikingly good in his roll-neck sweater.

"You in pain, Theo? What is it, a hangover or something worse?" Gael's hazel eyes were warm and friendly.

"I fell over ice-skating and bashed my knee."

"You see, this is why I've always forsworn winter sports. You have to dress like a git, it costs the earth and then you'll only break something. Right, lads, I know this doesn't look like the best joint to have a discreet discussion, but that's exactly why it is. It's loud, crowded and I know some of the staff. And I wasn't kidding about the food. I spoke to my boss and she's agreed to pay your fees and expenses to a reasonable extent. I know, I know. 'Reasonable extent'? It all depends on what kind of story we have. I doubt you're ready to hand over whatever you found without knowing it's in safe hands. Will I start by telling you what I'm working on?"

"How can you be sure we're trustworthy, Ms O'Connell?" asked Theo.

"Your man gets right to the point all right." She grinned at Beatrice. "Call me Gael. I know you're trustworthy because I researched your background and your references. You two get around, don't you? To be honest, you should have done the same on me."

"We did." Theo smiled. "Your tenacious reporting on corporate fraud is impressive. Beatrice and I were saying on the train, it's a dangerous way to live. I'm guessing some very powerful people would love you to disappear."

"You got that right. Exactly why I spent several hours researching Beatrice Stubbs after you popped up offering me exclusive info. I'm impressed. Seriously."

Beatrice gave a modest shrug. "I don't want to blow my own teapot, but I have had some successes in the detection field. So if we're satisfied with one another's CVs, what next?"

"Here's the thing. I've been covering politics, business and media for longer than I care to remember. There's a loose collection of us across Europe rooting out corruption and exposing the swing doors between government and senior management of major businesses. Sometimes, we share our findings and shine a light on the worst abuses of power. On other occasions, my story-gathering focuses on one particular country. The lead you're offering me applies to what should be a local story. Except it's not. If the information we have is sufficient, this could crack open a network across the continent. My editor is more excited than I've ever seen her and chain-smoking herself into an early grave. I know they've buried their secrets and I spent years treasure hunting. Now a private detective agency brings me a map and if I'm not mistaken, there's an X marking the spot. Am I wrong?"

The waitress arrived with their food and drinks in three plastic trays. Beatrice took in the glass of wine, the bowl of *moules* and the twist of paper containing the *frites* with an approving nod. Gael picked up the bill and tucked it into her back pocket.

"You're not wrong, Gael. Thank you very much for lunch and we're willing to share what we know. I'm not sure whether we have a map or a single piece of the puzzle. Doesn't matter. If we can add something to your investigation and exonerate Sonny Das, that will suffice."

"Sonny Das?" Gael froze in the action of reaching for her beer. "Where does he fit in?"

As soon as Gael heard the story of how Beatrice had acquired the paperwork, she held up her hands in a gesture of patience and grabbed her mobile phone, pressing her thumbs in a flurry. Theo and Beatrice exchanged glances but continued eating in silence until she had finished. The *moules* in white wine sauce were utterly delicious, as were the fries.

Beatrice looked at Theo, who seemed to be enjoying his salad. "You should try one of these," she said, offering him her cone of *frites*. "The Belgians think they invented them. And judging by this lot, they may well be right."

Before Theo could reply, Gael O'Connell slapped her phone on the table. "We'll finish our food and get out of here. I booked us a place where we can talk and there's someone you need to meet. What do you think, Beatrice? *Pommes frites* to die for, am I right?"

Yet another taxi. Gael told the driver the address but did not join them. "Wait in the foyer and say you have an appointment with Hedda. H-E-D-D-A. She's our editor. Don't talk to anyone or do anything till I get there. Off you go." She slapped her palm on the roof and the car drove away.

Beatrice had faith in Theo's perception of people. "Well? Do we trust her?"

"I'd like to hear more. She's authentic and on fire with her mission. We just need to set boundaries. Her heart is in the right place but I wonder what's more important. Heart or gut. Something tells me the story comes first. If that's true, you and I need to be long gone when it breaks. The other thing ..."

She waited, watching him think.

Theo rotated his shoulders. "The other thing is we might just have sighted an iceberg. As it stands, we can reverse and extricate ourselves from danger. Or we can sail full speed at the thing until it sinks us. I gotta tell you, I'm not a big fan of cold water."

Beatrice nodded and looked through the window. Sleet spattered the glass, muddying the view of the buildings as low clouds obscured the view. Something about Gael O'Connell touched a chord. As Theo said, she was on fire and committed to her mission. Just like a certain DS Stubbs, many years ago. '*We can sail full speed at the thing until it sinks us*' sounded strangely familiar.

The editor met them as the taxi parked under the porch of a large office block. An extraordinary-looking older woman, she wore her hair in a huge beehive in various shades of silver. She put out a cigarette in the smokers' bin and came forward to greet them with a handshake.

"Hello, I'm Hedda! You must be Beatrice and Theo. Gael told me you were coming. Inside, quick, the weather is at its rudest. October, what else do we expect? Can I say how happy I am you've agreed to work with us on this story?"

"We haven't agreed anything yet," Beatrice replied, taking in the neutral grey lobby with no adornments other than some showy flowers on a low table. "To be honest, I'm not even sure who we're dealing with. My name is Beatrice Stubbs and this is Theo Wolfe. Gael sent us here and told us to ask for Hedda."

"That's me. Hedda Nordstrom, editor of *Euroline Times*. Hey, we're in the same boat. Gael told me not to talk to you and gave you instructions not to talk to me until she gets here. Want to get a coffee while we wait?"

"I'd love an espresso," said Theo. "We kinda rushed lunch."

"That's Gael all over. One hundred kilometres per hour and always in fifth gear. Talk of the devil." She pointed at the figure coming through the front doors, damp and bedraggled.

"The weather is shite!" Gael said, shaking herself.

"You should have come in the taxi with us," said Beatrice.

"No, no, I travel alone. Just in case. Have we a room, Hedda?" In response to her nod, she jerked her head towards the lifts. "Then why are we still standing here gabbing? Lead the way."

"How much do you know about our paper?" asked Hedda, her expression kind.

Beatrice looked to Theo for a reply. His research was impeccable.

"Quite a bit," he said. "You have a reputation for unbiased reporting with a left-wing slant. Gael is well-known as a thorn in the side of many politicians, business leaders and anyone who does not practise what they preach. Or practise what they try to enforce. You have a good relationship with many other European broadsheets and have scored some major success stories via those collaborations. Can't say I've seen many news outlets shine a light on the grey areas between government and business as you have done. We find your work admirable and that's why we brought you this information."

"Thank you. Compliments accepted." Hedda opened her briefcase and withdrew her files. "Before we go any further, I want to assure you we will pay all expenses and your daily fees. If we think it better for us to work in parallel, I'm prepared to negotiate a higher rate. First thing we need to do is sign an NDA for both our sakes. A non-disclosure agreement protects your identity as our source and will keep details of our contract solely between us. If this comes to court, as I sincerely hope it does, your names are not in the spotlight. The contract is standard but maybe you'd like a few minutes to read the small print. Take your time."

Beatrice and Theo pored over the legalese while Hedda and Gael went out onto the terrace so Hedda could smoke. As far as Beatrice could tell, it was the usual newspaper deal honouring anonymity for the informant in return for exclusive use of their data. She gave Theo the nod and they both signed all four documents.

When the women returned, Hedda and Gael added their own signatures. Hedda gave Beatrice, Gael and Theo a copy each then slipped her own into her briefcase.

"Thank you. As I understand it, you came into possession of some incriminating material regarding Banque Franck et Schneider and contacted Gael. This is vitally important to a major exposé we are working. I must warn you, this is a wide-ranging operation involving some powerful and unpleasant people. When we are ready to run this story, it will send shockwaves across the continent. We've been working a lead so secret, only Gael and I know the names of the people involved. Now she tells me your information is connected to Sonny Das. Would you like to start from the beginning?"

Chapter 10

It was immensely gratifying to hear that three out of seven key clients were willing to continue using Marianne as a freelance accountant. That meant she had work to do from first thing on Tuesday morning. She called into her ex-office to retrieve the relevant files and inform her previous bosses of her plans. They understood and wished her luck. Josephine even helped her carry some of the paperwork to the car and apologised one more time for the unfortunate set of circumstances. Marianne gave her a sad yet gracious response. No matter how badly things had ended for the company, they parted on good terms.

She spent a couple of hours rearranging the spare room in her father's cottage to create the semblance of an office. He had offered her his study, but she knew that was his man cave, the place he liked to retreat to when he wanted to be alone. Not only that, but it was also Beatrice's workplace when she was at home. The spare room upstairs was at the front of the house, overlooking the road. Very little traffic passed the cottage and if Matthew was out back in the garden, mowing the lawn, making a bonfire or throwing a ball for Huggy Bear, Marianne would not be distracted.

At quarter past twelve, she descended to the kitchen in order to prepare lunch, which was part of their arrangement. Everything was quiet and the study door closed. As usual,

Dumpling slept on Matthew's chair in the kitchen, but Huggy Bear's basket was empty. Marianne chopped onions, peeled potatoes, made stock and washed leeks to create a warming vichyssoise. She was slicing a loaf of wholemeal bread when she heard the front door open and the sounds of her father unleashing the Border Terrier.

"I'm in here, Dad, making some soup. Are you hungry?"

"Ravenous. We went all the way through the forest, through the village and back along the lane. The very definition of intrepid." He handed Huggy Bear a chew. "Oh, I say, that smells good."

They ate at the kitchen table, warmed by the Aga, chatting about Beatrice's vague plans, their various intentions for the rest of the day and potential clients for Marianne.

"I'm going to build myself a very simple website and order some business cards. Then I need to hit the phones. It's a bad time of the year to try drum up business, but at least I can start putting out feelers. What about you?"

"First things first, I'm going to have another bowl of soup. It's awfully hearty and just what I needed after our morning walk. After that, a little rest will be necessary. When I can put it off no longer, I have some jobs to tackle in the garden. Pruning, raking up leaves and protecting the pots from frost. A gardener's work is never done. Thank you for lunch. You toddle off and I'll see to the washing-up."

Marianne patted him on the shoulder and returned upstairs. The creation of a website was not as straightforward as she'd thought. With much swearing and frowning at the screen, she succeeded in establishing a home page. She decided to leave client testimonials and her own credentials until the following day, as she was growing tired of looking at the screen. She picked up the phone and began on her list of prospective customers. It was a depressing task. Mostly polite 'no thank yous', one 'maybe next year' and two-and-a-half possibilities. She made a note of the meetings she had arranged in her calendar and tutted. How she was supposed to work with that dog barking all the time, she had no idea. She went through to the main bedroom and opened the window. Huggy Bear stood at the end of the garden, barking at the stream. Of her father, there was no sign.

"Dad! Will you shut your dog up! I'm trying to make important calls in here. Dad! Dad?" Huggy Bear let out a fresh volley of barks and scampered up and down the bank.

Marianne's breath caught. She ran down the stairs and out through the conservatory. The dog was still barking. When she got to the point where the terrier stood, she understood why. Matthew was lying on his back in the stream, vainly trying to pull himself upright one-handed.

"Oh my God! Dad, are you all right?" Marianne scrambled down the slope and tripped into the stream. It was icy cold but not deeper than her ankles. Positioning herself behind him, she attempted to push him upwards. That got him into a sitting position but no further. She came around the front and reached for his hands. He pulled away.

"No! No, not like that. Hurt my ... my watch, you see."

The cold water was turning Marianne's feet numb. "We have to get you out. Can you crawl? Dad, can you get on your hands and knees?"

Matthew did not reply but feebly tried to turn. His face was white and his eyes wide with shock. His lips had turned a worrying shade of pale blue.

She had to get him out the water. She splashed behind him again and stuck her forearms under his armpits. With a huge effort she managed to get his bottom onto the shelf beside the bank. His legs still dangled into the water so she got back in and hauled his ankles out. The movement rolled him from a sitting position onto his side. Tears of frustration spilled from Marianne's eyes. There was no way she could heave her father up the slippery slope to the garden. She simply wasn't strong enough.

In a panic, she ran past Huggy Bear, into the house and upstairs for her mobile. She grabbed a blanket off the spare bed and rushed downstairs again, dialling Gabriel's number. When she returned to his side, her father was now shivering so much his teeth chattered.

Finally Gabriel answered, his slow voice instantly soothing. "All right, Marianne?"

"Gabe, thank God! I need your help. Dad has fallen in the stream. I got him out of the water but I can't get him up to the garden on my own. Where are you? Can you come and help me?" Her voice sounded wobbly and breathless.

"That's not good. I'm just on my way to Appleford Woods. I'll turn around now and be with you in ten. Keep him warm. Use your own body heat. I'm on my way."

Shaking with fright and cold, Marianne positioned herself behind her father, spooning her body around his. All the while, she tried to reassure him. "It's all right, Dad, Gabriel is on his way. He's going to get you out of here and indoors for a nice cup of tea. He'll be here any minute and you're going to be fine. We just have to keep you warm until he arrives. You'll be all right, everything is OK, don't worry."

As his body trembled uncontrollably, Huggy Bear continued her alarm call from her vantage point on the lawn and with classic timing, it started to rain. To Marianne, it seemed hours passed before she heard the crunch of Gabriel's Land Rover on the driveway.

In a second, he was by her side, pulling her to her feet. He bent down and scooped an arm underneath Matthew's knees and another behind his shoulders, then powered up the bank across the garden and into the conservatory.

"Fetch the heat blanket from my Land Rover and then put the kettle on. We need hot-water bottles and see if we can get him to drink something. I'm going to take off his wet clothes and get him dry."

Marianne was retrieving the blanket from the Land Rover when Tanya's car pulled up beside her.

"Gabe called me. Is Dad OK? What happened? Where is he now?"

"In the conservatory. I don't know what happened and I'm not sure how he is."

The sisters hurried indoors to find their father lying under a pile of towels on one of the conservatory recliners. Gabriel took the blanket and tucked it carefully around Matthew's body. "What about those hot-water bottles, Marianne? While you're in the kitchen, make some Bovril. Tanya, see if you can find a bobble hat or something we can use for his head. It looks like he sprained his wrist, but I can't find any other injuries. When we've got him warmed up, we might need to take him to the surgery for a check-up."

Two hours later, the three of them sat at the kitchen table. Tanya made tea and Marianne switched on the lights as dusk fell across the garden. She gave in to the temptation to check on her father for the hundredth time. He was sleeping, his skin pink and his breathing steady. On the rattan flooring by his side lay Huggy Bear, her head on her paws.

Marianne stroked her. "You're a good dog, you are. When I do the shopping tomorrow, I'm buying you the poshest dog food there is. Good girl, Huggy Bear, good girl."

The terrier's tail wagged twice and Marianne returned to the kitchen.

"... because even if it is only a sprain, he's going to need help." Gabriel looked up as Marianne entered the room. "We're just talking about how best to manage the situation."

"Gabe thinks we should have a carer," said Tanya, cradling her mug of tea.

"Not just for situations like this, but everyday assistance.

Look, I took off all your Dad's clothes and dried his whole body. How do you think he'd feel if one of his daughters had done that? My opinion, for what it's worth, is that he needs some daily support. Like a bloke who's capable of lifting someone Matthew's size. If he falls when Beatrice is here on her own, she'll never be able to cope."

"Talking of Beatrice, we should tell her what happened," said Marianne, sitting at the table beside her sister. "I don't want to worry her, but she ought to know."

Gabriel nodded. "I agree. But rather than present her with a problem, we could suggest some solutions. Just so she doesn't feel she has to handle this alone."

"Right. Here's what I think." Tanya glanced at her watch. "I need to collect Luke from the Harvest Festival rehearsal, then I'll bring him here. See how Dad feels when he wakes up and if he's up to it, we can have dinner as a family. Marianne, do you want to research support services, how much they cost, what they do, etc? Beatrice usually calls around eight, so we should have a plan what to say."

Marianne had an idea which instantly became a conviction. "The best person to tell her is Gabe. He's calm and reassuring, plus he puts it more neutrally than you and me. She will listen to him and not feel we're ganging up on her as his daughters."

Tanya agreed. "That's a good point. Can you handle that, my lover?"

Gabriel drained his tea and stood up. "We'll see. I'm going to check on our patient and if I have the smallest doubt, I'll drive him to the doctor's. You head off and explain what happened to Luke. He's got to be very gentle and quiet around his grandfather for a while."

Chapter 11

Whose advice to take? Know your priorities, James had always said, whereas Will emphasised the importance of being present. On the other hand, Gabriel sounded convinced there was no need for her to hurry home. Matthew's son-in-law and two daughters had the situation covered until they could interview and employ a professional carer.

Nevertheless, Beatrice agonised late into the night about catching the first train to London. Even if she could do nothing more than sympathise, Matthew would be reassured by her presence. She fell asleep having made the decision to return to her cottage in Devon. First thing in the morning, she would apologise to Theo and the newspaper people but insist on their withdrawal from the case. All the unanswered questions and loose ends frustrated her but there was nothing to be done. She threw back the duvet and rummaged about in the hotel wardrobe for an extra blanket. Not that the budget hotel was cold. It was just when she was warm and cosy, sleep became irresistible.

Due to her restless night, she woke late. Her immediate instinct was to reach for her phone. She noted with a start it was already twenty past nine and she'd received several messages. The first was from Theo.

Missed you at breakfast but I guess you needed a lie in. Leaving for Bruges now. Depending on how it goes, I'll see you for lunch or failing that, dinner. Have a good day.

Beatrice released an impatient curse aimed more at herself than her assistant. Then she saw the second message was from Marianne.

Morning, Beatrice! Good news from Brampford Speke. Dad slept well and apart from his wrist, he's bright-eyed and bushy-tailed this morning. We took HB for a walk together and he'd like to talk to you because he doesn't want you to panic. Could you call when convenient? Mx.

There were several other messages but Beatrice's priority was Matthew Bailey. She hit speed dial and waited for the ring tone. He answered almost immediately.

"Matthew, it's me."

"Hello, Old Thing! Sorry I missed our chat last night. As you will have heard, I went into battle with the stream and the stream won. I hope hearing of my mishaps second hand did not worry you unduly. The only damage is a mild sprain to my wrist. Although my gardening trousers may never be the same again."

Her heart swelled to hear the positive note in his voice. "What on earth possessed you to go clambering about by the stream? Never mind, you can tell me when I get home. All I can say is, thank God for your daughters and Gabriel. I dread to think …" She didn't finish that thought.

"Absolute bricks, the lot of them. Gabriel made us all stew, Tanya set up an interview with some sort of home help and Marianne stayed over to keep an eye on me. Even Luke volunteered to take Huggy Bear out for her evening walk. So you see there's really no need to worry."

"They are all wonderful and I'm incredibly grateful. That said, I'm dropping this case and travelling home today. It's not fair to leave all this to your girls."

"I am having none of that! The only reason I agreed to give this home-care malarkey a shot is to give you the freedom to work. I don't want you to give up your agency to follow me around making sure I don't fall over. That would be frustrating for both of us and leave Theo high and dry. You stay in Belgium and finish your case. We can hold the fort here; that much I promise you. Listen to me, Old Thing, do not drop everything and hurry back on my account because it is not necessary. There will come a time when I need to lean on you. I understand and accept that, but the time is not now. Do I make myself understood?"

Beatrice closed her eyes and swallowed. "Yes. Message received, loud and clear. In any case Theo has gone to Bruges, so I can't talk to him till later today. Your circumstances notwithstanding, Team Stubbs has done its duty and handed over the information to the right people. I can't see any good reason for us to stay on after tomorrow. Whether you like it or not, I'll probably be home on Wednesday evening. How's your wrist?"

"Bloody painful. I'm doing everything one-handed which means it will be a good stretch before I mow the lawn again."

"Good job it's October then. I overslept horribly so need to crack on. I'll call you again later this evening and with any luck, see you in person tomorrow afternoon. Matthew, you're very precious to me. Please take care."

For a moment, he didn't respond. "I shall do my very best. So long as you promise to do the same. Dear Lord, our future is shaping up to be quite the adventure. Have a wonderful day."

She ended the call and stared at the handset for two full minutes.

Repeated calls and emails had produced no results. Bikram Ghosh was not responding. While Theo was checking out the crime scene in Bruges and Gael was investigating the paper trail unearthed by Sonny Das, Beatrice's task was to find out what happened to Ghosh. Her first port of call was his apartment. No one answered the door and Beatrice examined the other names beside the building's buzzers. Bottom left read Dries Smet (Concierge). She pressed the button and waited.

The door opened and a tall man in a three-piece suit appraised her.

"Good morning. My name is Beatrice Stubbs. I'm a private investigator." She offered her card. "Do you speak English?"

"Dries Smet. I speak English." He took the card and read it carefully. "You were here before. I remember you."

"Yes. I've been here twice before. I'm looking for a man who lives here, Bikram Ghosh. He's not answering the door and I'm a little worried for his welfare."

"He doesn't live here. Not anymore. He left at the weekend. Very sudden. His rent is paid until the end of the year. He said it was a family emergency and he was returning to Bangalore. He took his belongings and didn't leave a forwarding address. Why does a private detective need to talk to one of my tenants?"

The man's formal manners and stiff dress had given Beatrice the first impression of an impatient clerk. Now, she saw the worn cuffs of his jacket and the glimpses of scalp through his thin hair and realised how he clung on to what remained of his power.

"Mr Smet, it's a long story and I would appreciate any insights you can offer. I don't wish to intrude or take up too much of your time, but may I buy you a coffee from the place over the road?"

His curiosity ignited a light in those dull grey eyes and he gave her a slow nod. He locked his apartment and followed her to the highly coloured café, which incongruously played Brazilian beach music in the chill of a European October.

Over a couple of milky coffees with an unpronounceable name, Beatrice gave Smet the sanitised version or in other words, everything he already knew. His grey eyes sharpened when she explained her concern for his tenant.

"Why? His friend committed suicide. Why would he do the same? They were both clean-living, hard-working young men, not members of a cult or something like that. Why is a private detective following up a case of suicide? I don't know the details, but Das stole a lot of money from the bank, ran away and killed himself. Do you think he and Ghosh were part of a team?"

Beatrice pushed her coffee away. "No, not at all. I know for a fact Bikram Ghosh wanted nothing to do with Sonny Das's endeavours. I have no agenda here, Mr Smet, but I liked Bikram Ghosh and just wanted to reassure myself that he's fine. My concern was more for his mental health. Living in a strange country, working long hours and losing a friend can upset the balance. Now I know he's returned to India, it seems I had nothing to worry about. Did you know them at all?" she asked, as if making casual small talk.

He tugged down the corners of his mouth. "They paid their rent, they kept quiet, they worked long hours. I could use more tenants like those."

The concierge was unlikely to give her anything of use and even less likely to allow her into their apartment. She cut her losses, paid the bill, thanked the man and headed out into the cold and windy streets of Brussels.

Banque Frank et Schneider sat on a junction of two major dual carriageways. It was not an attractive building. Large grey slabs were enlivened by slits in every other panel, reminding Beatrice of mediaeval castles or the faces of scarred warriors. Yet the only battle gear people wore on these streets was a financier's suit. She hopped off the tram and approached the main entrance, focusing on her performance.

After leaving the coffee shop and Mr Smet, Beatrice had stopped into a teen fashion store. Not the usual place she might frequent but she had seen some faux deerstalker hats in the window. One of those could serve two purposes: keeping her head and ears warm, plus hiding her distinctive hair. She waited until ten past the hour and walked into the foyer with a sense of purpose, returning the receptionist's plastic smile with one of her own. The reception area was not somewhere you would want to hang around. Tiled floors and a low ceiling created an unpleasant metallic echo as visitors' heels crossed from the entrance to the front desk. Either side of the doors stood unsmiling security guards, and cameras whirred in a not-so-subtle manner above their heads.

"Good morning. I have an appointment with Mr Bikram Ghosh at eleven am. I'm sorry I'm late but I'm afraid I got a little lost. Could you let Mr Ghosh know that I'm here? I do apologise for the delay."

The young man took her name and checked his screen. His eyes flicked from one place to another, a frown of confusion furrowing his forehead. "I'm very sorry, Ms Stubbs, but you are not on our visitor list. Nor do we have anyone by the name of Bikram Ghosh in our personnel. Are you quite sure this is the right bank?"

"Most definitely. Here's his card."

"You're right. This is the correct address on the card, but he doesn't seem to be one of our employees. Could you wait while I call Human Resources? I'll do my best to find out where the misunderstanding occurred."

"That's very kind of you."

He tapped a few keys and spoke into his headset. His French was fast and colloquial, but Beatrice caught a few words, including her own name. He lifted his face with an apologetic smile.

"Now it makes sense. I'm afraid Mr Ghosh left our organisation on Friday and returned to India for personal reasons. Perhaps he forgot to cancel his appointments. I'm terribly sorry. Would you like to speak to his replacement?"

Beatrice released a deep sigh. "What a shame. He was a very nice young man. Ah well, our loss, India's gain. Thank you for your help and have a nice day."

How incredibly efficient. Ghosh had left the bank on Friday and within two working days he was deleted from the personnel database. Interesting.

Chapter 12

Catinca would love it here, thought Theo as he limped along the banks of the canal. Maybe they should come here in the next couple of months. They'd hold hands in the cobbled streets, drink *Glühwein* and explore Christmas markets. Half of him hoped they would find nothing of use today and could leave the case with Gael and her editor. Then he could return to London and wish Catinca good luck for her interview tomorrow in person. He missed her, which was crazy after two dates. But he had that light-headed rush of excitement every time he thought of her smile, her laughter and her arm around his waist.

He winced as his foot trod awkwardly on a cobble and wrenched his knee. After visiting the B&B, he'd have a rest in a café somewhere. Hostel Herribert was a depressing sort of joint, not the kind of place you'd voluntarily choose to stay. If Sonny Das had absconded with a chunk of the bank's cash, couldn't he have found somewhere a little further afield? Why Bruges, Sonny? For someone doing a runner, you didn't get far.

He opened the hostel doorway and noticed the fetid smell immediately. Like rotten oranges with an artificial note, as if someone had tried to disguise it with a cheap air-freshener. No one supervised the reception desk or occupied the office behind. Theo called out. "Hello?"

A door opened at the end of a corridor and a man's head

poked out. His hair was thin and his expression suspicious.

"*Bonjour. Goedemorgen,*" said Theo.

The man answered in English. "No rooms. Fully booked. Sorry."

The sign outside said Vacancies but Theo decided against challenging the old geezer. Instead, he approached the bloke with a smile. "That's OK, I'm not looking for a room. I wanted to ask you some questions. My name is Theo Wolfe and I'm a private investigator." He reached inside his coat for his card.

The guy looked at it briefly but made no move to take it. "What do you want?" His voice was loud. Theo suspected the guy's hearing was not the best.

He raised his voice. "It's about the death of Sonny Das last Friday. It won't take long but I hurt my leg. Could we sit down somewhere?"

"Too busy. Sorry. Nothing to say. I spoke to the police. Sorry. You must go now." He emerged from behind the door, waving his hands as if to shoo Theo out into the street.

"Just a moment. My partner, PI Stubbs, was the one who found the body."

"Your partner?" His eyes grew fearful and his mouth pinched. "She did not have permission to come in. She should not ... I want that you leave now. Go, you are not welcome. Goodbye."

Theo suppressed his anger at the man's rudeness and turned to leave. As he did so, he saw an old woman watching him from a room opposite the office. She was bundled up in a blanket, sitting on an upright chair with a view of the street outside. She gave him a nod of greeting, but Theo had no time to respond as the miserable old git was all but shoving him out the door.

He opened the front door and went outside, turning to say "Thanks for your time," but the door slammed in his face and the bolts shot home.

"Nice, friendly sort of bloke," said Theo, under his breath. He looked sideways to the window, to where the old lady still watching him. She lifted a hand from beneath her blankets and gave him a little wave. Theo returned the gesture then turned to walk the way he had come. A bar stood on the corner of the street. He considered dropping in for some lunch, but decided to cut his losses and head for Brussels. Depending on how Beatrice got on, maybe they could get a train to London this afternoon. As he walked past the café, he saw there was a counter running the length of the window, where customers were drinking coffee and people-watching.

He'd gone ten paces past before he stopped. People-watching. That's what the old lady did, and judging by her blanket, she watched all day. Of all the people to ask about last Friday's events, she would be ideal. But how the hell was he supposed to talk to her while that inflexible git refused to let him in? Theo entered the café. He ordered a beer and a sandwich then found himself a stool by the window. The chances of the old guy popping out for an hour to give Theo time for a nice cosy chat were negligible. He couldn't sneak into the building with the door bolted so his options were to mime through the window or find some ruse to get the man out of the house. He gazed around the room for inspiration.

His eyes fell on the fire extinguisher. He pulled out his phone and searched for the information he needed while he ate and rested his leg. Then he went outside and found a quiet place to make his call. He could speak both Dutch and French with relative ease, but guessed the landlord of Hostel Herribert was a Flemish speaker. So French it was.

It took so long for the guy to answer, Theo almost gave up. But then a voice came on the line. "Vleek?"

Theo adopted his most crisp and officious tone, checking Monsieur Vleek was the owner of Hostel Herribert. On receiving confirmation, Theo announced himself as the fire officer responsible for guest houses and hostels in the city of

Bruges. Hostel Herribert was overdue a check of smoke alarms and fire safety compliance, which must be done by the end of the year. As the department had just received a cancellation due to bankruptcy, he could fit in an inspection tomorrow morning. Would eight am be convenient?

Vleek blustered and attempted to put Theo off, but it was not going to wash. Surely there was no need to delay if everything was working perfectly, all alarms had batteries, fire doors were clearly marked and extinguishers had been tested by the manufacturer in the last twelve months? Seeing as the fire officer was particularly busy at this time of year, it might be wise to grab the opportunity or risk losing the hostel's safety certificate. And eight o'clock tomorrow was agreed.

Theo returned to the café to wait as standing around in the cold did his leg no favours. It was a risk because if Vleek came out of the hostel and turned in the other direction or took his car to get supplies, Theo wouldn't be able to see him. But the risk was calculated. Most of the shops were this side of the quarter and in Bruges, it was easier to walk than drive.

It didn't take long. Nursing his cup of fennel tea, Theo tuned out the café sounds and focused on the street outside. He studied every face while keeping his own in shadow. Around forty-five minutes after the call, Vleek passed by on the opposite side of the street in a tatty coat. Theo moved fast. Even if the landlord had locked the door, he might be able to persuade Window Lady to open it, assuming she was mobile.

The door was open, to his relief. Theo slipped inside, silent as a slightly lame cat. The woman in the sitting room appeared to be waiting for him. She faced in his direction, an expectant smile on her face. He bowed in her direction and opened his mouth to speak, but she got there first, speaking fluent English with a strong French accent.

"You understood me, well done. Come in and sit down. We must be quick. That idiot won't be gone long. You want to know about the dead man, yes?"

"Yes, please," said Theo, sitting on the sofa and stretching out his leg.

"What did you do to your knee?" she asked.

"I was ice-skating and a kid cannoned into me."

"Serves you right. You're too old for that sort of foolishness. What do you want to know about our unfortunate guest?"

Theo took a moment to catch up. "What happened on Friday, or at least what you saw. Just so you know, I'm not police."

"That much is obvious. I've never seen a good-looking *flic* in my life. You're a private detective, no? The lady who was here on Friday, I heard you say she was your partner. Business or pleasure?"

This conversation was not going the way it should. "She's my boss. Her name is Beatrice Stubbs. She found Sonny Das, the man upstairs who killed himself."

"He didn't kill himself. My name is Marguerite Vleek. And you?"

"Theo Wolfe. Why do you say that? The police believe it was suicide."

"But you don't and neither does your partner, otherwise you wouldn't be here. That idiot, also known as my son, thinks I'm senile. My hands shake, you see." She demonstrated, holding a wobbly right hand in front of her. "Nerve damage. But there's nothing wrong up here." She placed a finger on her temple. "Whereas he, on the other hand, doesn't have the brains he was born with. He has a lady friend he sees in the afternoons. I'm quite convinced the arrangement must be financial because who would voluntarily spend time with such an imbecile? Whether he pays her or not, I cannot say. One thing I do know is that he leaves here the minute he has finished his lunch and returns around three-thirty. He persists in the myth that I need an afternoon nap. So he closes the curtains, leaves the house with indecent haste and closes the parlour door behind him in case I am disturbed. I'm rarely disturbed. Our tenants spend as much time out of the building as they possibly can and who would blame them. Therefore, most afternoons, I sit in semi-darkness alone until the idiot returns."

Under different circumstances, Theo would have engaged the woman in conversation and tried to find out more about her lonely existence. Only the threat of Vleek's imminent return focused his mind. "Not last Friday."

Her eyes fixed on his, with surprising brightness. "Not last Friday. You know, of all the people who have been in and out of this house in the last five days, you and your partner have been the only ones to speak to me. *Tempus fugit.* I have something to tell you."

"Do I have your permission to record this conversation?" Theo scrabbled for his phone.

"With the greatest of pleasure. Last Friday, we had open sandwiches for lunch before he rushed out the door. I drew the curtains and opened the parlour door, just a crack. Watching the people pass by makes me feel a part of things, you see. At just after two o'clock, an expensive car stopped outside the house. A man got out of the passenger side and came up the steps. I listened and waited for the bell to ring but nothing happened. Our visitor did not even knock. Then I heard the front door open. Whoever it was closed the door and stopped for several minutes. Eventually, he started up the stairs. This is an old house and I know every creak of every floorboard. He was stealthy, treading on the edge of every step, hence making very little noise. I could hear him as far as the second floor until he began his ascent to the attic. From there, I heard nothing at all. Nothing.

"Even in the half-light, I can see the clock. A full fifteen minutes passed before I heard him descend and leave by the front door. The same vehicle appeared to pick him up. It must have been waiting down the street. Ten minutes after that, the idiot returned. He raced upstairs, cursing all the time until he ran out of breath. He spent five or six minutes up there and came downstairs carrying a suitcase. A shiny suitcase exactly like the one Mr Das had in his possession when he checked in. Why don't you pour me a glass of water?"

Theo placed his phone on the table while he filled a tumbler and handed it to Marguerite.

"You're very kind. He took the case down to the cellar, still mumbling and swearing, and then came in here to check on me. Naturally, I was fast asleep, mouth open and snoring." She gave him a wink.

Theo couldn't help but admire the woman's attitude. Her son was around seventy years old so she had to be knocking ninety, but she still enjoyed a flirt.

"When he was satisfied I was in dreamland, he took a bottle from our drinks cabinet. God knows what it was. Everything in there is over two decades old. He went into the kitchen, made a call and had a heated conversation. Unfortunately, he closed the door so all I could hear was the timbre of his voice. He was angry and upset but about what, I cannot say. While he was arguing with whoever it was on the other end of the line, your partner arrived. He didn't hear her. He misses a lot these days but is too vain to get a hearing aid. She asked me where the owner was and I pointed her in the direction of the idiot. His voice continued from the kitchen without interruption. Shortly after that, I heard her footsteps creep upstairs. When she got to the attic, there was enough creaking and movement to alert even the stupidest of men. He chased up three floors and I heard her shouting. She talked to him as if he were an idiot. Observant lady."

Theo laughed, despite himself. "Can you describe the man you saw getting out of the car?"

She cocked her head, widened her eyes and motioned him away with a trembling hand. Theo finally understood. After standing outside, kicked out by her son, he'd seen her beckon him to return. His own presumptions saw a little old lady giving him a wave. What had he done? Given her a patronising wave back. Who was the idiot?

He crept further into the sitting room and ducked behind one of the breakfast tables. The clatter of the front door reached Theo's ears, along with Vleek's mutterings as he took off his outdoor gear. The landlord stomped up the stairs and Marguerite indicated Theo should go. He didn't need telling twice. He pulled one of his business cards from his inside pocket and slipped it into her hand. With one last glance up the stairs to check the coast was clear, he eased his way out the front door. Under the porch so that he could not be seen from an upstairs window, he looked at Marguerite, visible through the curtains and bathed in afternoon sunshine.

He mouthed the words 'thank you' and blew her a kiss. She cupped her hands in front of her face and opened them as if she was releasing a cloud of yellow butterflies.

Once he arrived in Brussels, he caught a cab, bursting to share his news with Beatrice. But first there was an important call he needed to make.

"Good evening, London. This is Brussels calling to award you *douze points*!"

"Theo! I was hoping it was you! *Douze points* for what?"

"For your performance tomorrow. I know you're going to win the guy over and get the commission of a lifetime. I'm just calling to wish you luck."

"Aww, you. When you coming home? If interview goes well, I wanna celebrate."

"Not sure yet. I found out something today which might accelerate the investigation. I'm on my way to tell Beatrice and the news people right now. Are you all prepared for your meeting?"

She let out a low moan. "I dunno. I think so. Thing is not to get stressed, innit? It's just weird watching the guy on telly and knowing we're gonna be face to face tomorrow afternoon. Maybe I'll just turn telly off. Not helping. How's Brussels?"

"I was in Bruges today. It's one of the most beautiful cities I've ever seen. Maybe we should spend a weekend there together. I kept imagining you there today. You'd love it."

"Sodding hell, two dates and he's already planning a mini-break! Hell, yeah! Romantic weekends in European cities with dream man? Sign me up! Theo?"

The taxi pulled up in front of the newspaper building. "Yes?"

Her voice was soft. "Come home soon. Because I keep thinking I dreamed all that and it's not real. It is real, right?"

Theo thrust some Euros at the driver and got out into the cold. "It's real. I promise you. I'll be home as fast as I can. Every minute I'm away from you feels like a waste and I've thrown away enough time." A movement above his head caught his attention and he saw Beatrice, hands on hips, staring from the boardroom windows. She seemed to be wearing a trapper's hat. "I have to go. Good luck tomorrow, call me when it's done and I'll be thinking of you all day. As if I wasn't all day today."

Her laugh was part relief, he could tell. "OK, good luck to you too and remind that Stubbs woman to take care of you. Talk to you tomorrow."

There was a hesitation, as if she had something more to say.

"I can't wait, Catinca. It's all I think about. Goodnight."

"Goodnight," she whispered.

For a wild second, he looked at the taxi's disappearing headlights and planned an insane dash across Europe to be with her. Then he remembered her interview and his own responsibilities. Not that he could forget, with the shadow of Beatrice Stubbs blocking out the light.

Chapter 13

Remember it's pronounced Trozley. Trozz-lee. But don't forget, posh name and all, they're no better than I am. They can't intimidate me. He's got power, cash and a title, so what? It's all inherited. She's pretty and famous because her mum was Russian supermodel. People like them cruise on past glories but I earned what I got. Catinca Radu is self-made woman. If either of them tries pulling snob status with me, they can stuff it where the sun don't shine.

Her confidence-building mantra was going off course. In her mind, she was starting a fight before she'd even met the Trottiscliffe family. She realised she was frowning at her fellow passengers on the District line and bowed her head to stare at the portfolio in her lap.

Lord Tobias Trottiscliffe. His jovial persona and constant presence on current affairs programmes made him one of the most recognised faces in Britain. Balding, bearded and with a distinctive laugh, he was guaranteed good value as a pundit, posing as an old-school unreconstructed male, expressing outrageous sentiments softened by a booming chuckle. The media, and therefore everyone else, referred to him as 'Tobe', as if he were a close friend.

His daughters were fortunate enough to inherit their

mother's looks. Each of the three was slender, pale and wore a perpetual pout. Agnessa – pronounced Ag-NESS-a – was the youngest and prettiest of the lot. Also the last to get wed.

Older sister Alexandra's wedding to a billionaire Russian businessman made the front page of every gossip magazine two years ago. 'LEXY AND LEV IN LOVE!' The middle one, Anoushka, seemed the only one worth her salt. She didn't appear on the party circuit, studied for a degree in international relations and worked for an NGO. No pictures of her wedding surfaced after she married an American documentary filmmaker in a private ceremony. Anoushka didn't use a silly diminutive, took her husband's name and relocated to Seattle.

Now that the family favourite was about to earn herself a title by marrying Baron Kinnloss, everyone was in uproar. At the society wedding of the year, Catinca had the chance to design the centrepiece of the whole event. If she got this gig ... *when* she got this gig, her career was sorted. All she had to do was keep a cool head, show the bride-to-be these gorgeous designs and get Daddy's agreement. Because if Nessie didn't like any of the perfectly flattering and magical dresses Catinca proposed, she was a stupid cow who didn't deserve an original Radu.

She was doing it again. She opened her eyes and practised a smile. Her fellow commuters looked away. Random friendliness on the Tube was even scarier than hostility.

The meeting was arranged for two o'clock and Catinca was early. She got out at Green Park and walked up Stratton Street, heading for Berkeley Square. In a shop window, she assessed her appearance. Sleek and sophisticated was her look *du jour*. Hair pulled back into a French roll, high-collared black jacket, cigarette pants and black riding coat keeping her warm. Her fingers grew cold clutching her portfolio and she stopped under a green awning to put on her gloves. They were faux leather with gold studs and made her feel invincible. Invincible was exactly what she needed. She looked at her phone. 13.49. Time to announce herself at Jeremy's.

The door geezer did one of those nostril flares when she came through the door, but didn't argue after she gave him some attitude. Her name was on the guest list so he had no choice but to show her to the lift. He stepped in beside her and pressed a code, making sure to shield the keypad with his body. She affected disinterest. They rode in silence to the fourth floor and he escorted her along a passageway with numbered doors either side. More like a hotel than a restaurant.

He slowed and gestured to Room 467. "Here you are, madam."

Catinca lowered her brows. "The meeting's in the restaurant."

"There seems to be a misunderstanding. Lord Trottiscliffe prefers to conduct his meetings in private rooms. Many members do." He rang the bell and once it opened, announced her arrival.

The door swung open all the way and a cross-looking young woman scowled at her. "The dress designer, are you? Come in and wait here till the Trottiscliffes are ready." She didn't even acknowledge the club employee and shut the door in his face. A twinge of annoyance pricked Catinca. The poor guy was only doing his job.

They made her wait thirty-five minutes. She worked herself up into a state of extreme indignation and several times picked up her things and prepared to leave. It was the arrogance that drove her crazy. The third time she got to her feet and picked up her precious portfolio, she had made up her mind. How dare they waste her time in such a way? It was great publicity, good money and a great stepping-stone into high society, but Catinca Radu would not be treated like a tradeswoman. That was when the door to the inner room opened and the cross woman jerked her head to indicate Catinca should enter. She pulled her lips upwards for a second and her face snapped into its previous expression of contempt.

"Go in, they're waiting," she hissed, as if Catinca was the one delaying proceedings.

"I'm ready," Catinca replied and waited for the woman to introduce her.

Instead, the woman slipped on a coat and looped a bag over her forearm. She frowned at Catinca. "Why are you hanging about here? Get in there and do your stuff. Busy people won't wait forever." With that, she left the suite with a flourish.

Horrible cow. Catinca rapped a fingernail on the open door and entered the room. Autumnal sun added a hint of natural light to the dining area and salon, each illuminated by wall sconces. The bride-to-be was on her phone, standing by the floor-to-ceiling windows. She gave Catinca a critical look but did not interrupt her call.

"What? No, of course he doesn't. Never mind any of that. Tell him we'll go elsewhere unless he plays ball. Look, darling, I have to go. Dress designer!" she whispered, loudly enough to be heard across the entire floor.

While she said her goodbyes, Catinca waited beside the entrance. A door opened and Lord Tobias Trottiscliffe emerged, a smile splitting his face.

"The lady we've all been waiting for. Do come in, my dear! My daughter is more excited about this dress than she is about her husband-to-be. Can I get you a drink? There's a bottle of Bolly somewhere. Grete, bring our guest a drink, will you? Where do you want us? The coffee table is a good place to display your ideas." His gaze lingered over her outfit, only reacting with a laugh when he saw her trainers. "No question you understand fashion. Nessie, put that damn thing down and come over here. If I'm putting fifteen grand into a frock, you could at least pay attention. Where's the Bollinger, Grete?"

Agnessa fluttered across the room. "Ms Radu! Squeak! You were my first choice. I cannot believe you will design my dress.

I drank nothing at lunch but I already feel dizzy, yeah? I'm so excited."

"Pleasure to meet you, Ms Trottiscliffe. It's an honour to have the opportunity of designing your wedding gown."

"Grete! Bring the bloody Bolly!" Trottiscliffe yelled, wafting a hand at the sofa. "Please have a seat, young lady."

Agnessa tapped him on the shoulder in a light reprimand. "Babar, you sent Grete home. I'll fix our guest a drink."

"You damn well won't. You girls sit, look at the pictures and I'll pour us all some bubbles."

Catinca settled herself on the sofa beside the coffee table. She moved several vases of flowers in order to place her portfolio. She unzipped the case but before opening it to reveal her designs, she made her speech. It came out smoothly and so it sodding should, considering the number of times she rehearsed it. She explained how she had interpreted Agnessa's brief and talked about her interpretations; the fabrics, the magic and the story of each one's relationship to the bride.

"Three different angles, depending on which aspect of personality you want to show. Number one is inspired by Saint Agnes. Patron saint of virgins, lambs and chastity. Fabric is mixture of chiffon and silk. Simple sheath to shape body and chiffon oversized shawl to frame face. Longer at the back to create little train, like pool of white as you walk. Watered silk reflects light so rainbows can bounce off you. Idea is you look like blush rosebud in white glass vase."

The girl sat rapt throughout and gasped when she saw the design. "That's me! Oh my God, that is so me, yeah? Babar, look at this! My dream dress! Squeak!"

Trottiscliffe placed two glasses of champagne in front of them. Catinca immediately relocated them to a side table where they could do no damage to her precious work.

"Oh yes, that looks very nice. Let your natural beauty shine through, Nessie, my girl. We should see the other ideas though, since she's come all this way. Chin-chin, ladies." He sat on the opposite sofa and raised his glass.

Although Agnessa took a slug, Catinca merely wet her lips. Midday on Wednesday afternoon while trying to land the most important job of your life was no time to start drinking.

"Wait till you see number two. You marrying baron and becoming baroness. Not just any baroness but the modern version. This dress is all about tailoring and structure. Fabric is satin. You have collar, like fantasy queen, long cape, corseted bodice with bare arms while skirt is panels of satin and net. This dress says power and beauty with contemporary hints. Imagine this with an up-do sprinkled with red rosebuds and Louboutin heels. You'd knock it out of the park."

The bride to be remained silent and Catinca peered sideways to make sure the woman was still awake. She was awake, eyes wide and her hands pressed together across her nose.

"That is *the* dress. Oh my God, you're right, I would knock it out of the park. This is going to make Lexy's gown look like a nightie. It's a statement nobody could mistake. A dress that says I have arrived. I love it, I love it and I want it. You said I could have my dream wedding dress because I'm the last of your daughters to get married, yeah? This is the dress I want."

Trottiscliffe tilted his head this way and that before flopping backwards on the sofa. "Your choice, my little pearl, but to me that's borderline Disney villainess. Let's have a look at number three. Top up, girls?"

They both shook their heads and Catinca prepared to introduce her lethal weapon. "I studied your style and I know you love the dramatic. I never met you before but this design represents what I know of your personality. Everyone is gonna be talking about your dress because you're a celebrity. So what if the reveal of bride and dress happens at the same time? The thinking here is you are a sculpture under wraps. You walk up the aisle, under cover of a gauzy, sparkling cloak, and then when you stand beside the groom, the unveiling happens. Your bridesmaids take off the mysterious wrapping to show you in this dress. Fabric is lace, net and cotton. Embroidered lace bodice off the shoulder with full length sleeves. Dramatic V-cut to base of spine, showing beautifully toned back to congregation. Guaranteed gasps. Skirt ruched and semi-transparent, so shape of legs is partly visible in photos. Now you see it, now you don't. This dress says one thing loud and clear: I'd look even better naked. Not slutty or cheap but just shows enough of the fabulous body underneath. Ms Trottiscliffe, you are one of the few people who could carry this off. Every man in the room will envy your husband and every woman in room will wish she was you. It's classy, elegant, shocking and decorous all at same time. I tell you one thing, when the bridesmaids take off the veil, your husband will be the happiest man on earth."

"Not bad. Not bad at all. I'll say this for you, Ms Radu, you can sell a frock. What do you say, Ness?"

Agnessa was actually crying. She stared across the table at her father, nodding and sniffing. "I have fallen completely in love with this dress. She's right, it sums up my personality. I knew I'd done the right thing by choosing a new designer rather than any of the established old farts. All your designs are absolute bliss, but this one is for me. Can I take some photographs so I can plan the rest of my bridal outfit?"

Catinca's slammed her portfolio shut. "Sorry, no. No one sees these designs until contract is agreed. Then we select final fabrics. After that, tailoring measurements, underwear and accessory discussions, hair and make-up consultation and first fitting. Only when I have payment can you share my ideas. Otherwise is unprofessional."

To her credit, Agnessa looked abashed. She dabbed at her nose with a tissue and blinked away her tears. "Of course not. My bad. I got overexcited. As soon as my father has paid you, let's have a second meeting to discuss materials and how we put together the rest of the outfit. Perhaps we can commission you to make my going-away outfit as well. You're obviously prodigiously talented."

"Less of the we," said Trottiscliffe. "If you want any more of this girl's overpriced frippery, get your husband to pay for it. Or pay for it yourself, woman! God knows you can afford it. Right, have you decided on the third design, the one with the veil, or do you want more time to think about it? I know how you girls flip-flop between decisions. All I'm prepared to do today is engage this young lady to make your dress. Which one you opt for is up to you. Come along, Nessie, I need to get off to the Lords. Do you want this designer or not?"

From Agnessa's handbag, a mobile phone's ringtone drew her attention. The woman snatched it up and declined the call. "My car is outside, I have to go. Yes, Babar, yes please. This is the designer I want and this is the dress I am going to wear to say my vows. Ms Radu, thank you for being the best I've ever encountered. I look forward to working with you and let's talk very soon." She grabbed a poncho and her handbag, kissed her father and ran out the door, already on her phone.

The whole encounter left Catinca deflated. She started packing away her display.

Trottiscliffe was leaning back on the sofa, watching her with a benevolent smile on his flabby face. "We should toast your success, Miss ... Radu, is it? What's your first name?"

She couldn't see a way of avoiding the question. "Catinca. But design name is Radu."

"Now then, Catinca, this is quite a significant commission for someone trying to make a name for herself in the fashion industry. Congratulations and well done on a perfectly prepared pitch." He held out his glass and Catinca reciprocated the gesture, once again taking the smallest sip of champagne.

"Thank you. I'm very pleased your daughter liked my suggestions. She told me to give my quotation to you. I have it all prepared, per design, with provisional materials, consultation and labour included." She retrieved the envelope from inside her portfolio and handed it to the man opposite.

He ignored it completely, continuing to stare at her. She placed the envelope on the table in front of him, zipped up her case and looped her handbag over her shoulder.

"Oh, but you can't leave yet. Much more to discuss. We have a deal to negotiate, do we not?" He indicated her envelope. "That is merely your opening offer. My daughter may be smitten by your ideas, but she has no head for business. That's where I come in. Let's talk and see if we can't find some middle ground. We may need another bottle of Bolly."

Catinca got to her feet. "Unfortunately, I have another meeting. Thank you for the drink but I must leave now. I will be in touch with your daughter."

For a big man, he was light on his feet. He moved off the sofa and came to stand in front of her, holding out his hand. "May I?" he asked. Without waiting for an answer, he took the portfolio out of her grip, taking it across to the dining table where he unzipped the case.

Catinca clenched her fingers and toes, suppressing the urge to scream. No one, but no one, ever touched her work. He seemed to sense her hostility and stopped short of opening the flap.

"Come, sit down, explain your designs to me again. I found your passion incredibly inspiring. You, in my opinion, have an extraordinary future."

"Very kind of you to say and I appreciate the chance to show my designs to bride. But this appointment went on much longer than planned and I am expected somewhere else. I'm sorry, but I need to take my portfolio with me."

He didn't acknowledge her statement but crouched down in front of a wine fridge, humming to himself. "What to do, what to do? There's a Laurent Perrier in here. Rosé! You girls love your pinks, don't you? Yes, let's have a bottle of that. I understand your shop is somewhere in the Liverpool Street area. Good choice. Heavy footfall. My girls tell me you're doing rather well. Have you designed any wedding dresses before? One wouldn't want any sort of wardrobe malfunction like the Melville fiasco, would one?"

A low pulse of anxiety throbbed in Catinca's veins. She knew nothing about anyone called Melville and wanted to get out of this room, far away from this man. If there were any negotiation to be done, it should be done in an office with witnesses. "I won't have any more champagne, thank you. As I said, I have another meeting and I really must leave now." She made to zip up her portfolio case but he stayed her hand, looking deeply into her eyes with a sardonic smile.

"I doubt you have any other meetings for the rest of the week as significant as this one. If you get this commission, you will have sealed the deal of the decade. Then, when your name is on everyone's lips as the designer of the moment, you will advance your reputation. We have many contacts and can open plenty of doors someone with vision, imagination and flexibility. Sit down, Catinca, it's important that we understand each other. My way of doing business is based on a good working relationship. I only do business with friends."

She sat in the chair he withdrew, and froze as he placed a hand on the back of her neck. "I have to say, very few women could pull off an outfit like that with teenager's trainers. Here's to you and your sense of style. Cheers!"

Catinca twisted around in her chair to face the man and dislodge his hand. "Thank you for compliment, but I should say I don't drink alcohol and I don't call people by first names unless invited. I'm professional designer and I don't haggle. Your daughter wants my design. Price is price. You don't want, fine with me. I have to leave now." She moved to the other side of the table and began zipping up her case. Tears flooded her eyes as she realised the golden ticket had just fluttered out of reach. No matter how much Nessie wanted that dress, she wasn't the one picking up the bill. And Catinca had no intention of negotiating with the man who was.

Her eyesight flooded and her head hot, she failed to see that Trottiscliffe had sidled around the table to stand behind her. He wrapped his arms around her waist and caught her wrists, and then he planted a wet kiss on the side of her neck. She tried to pull away but his arms tightened around her like a straitjacket. "Let me go! I don't want this! Leave me alone!"

He breathed into her ear. "Wild gypsy girl with flashing eyes and supple mouth. We're going to have so much fun." His erection pressed against her and she tried once again to yank her arms free. That was when he slipped a hand between her legs and licked her shoulder. She threw back her head, her skull making contact with the bridge of his nose.

When he cried out in pain and released her arms, she pressed home her advantage. With her right arm, she elbowed him in his substantial gut, knocking the contents of her portfolio all over the carpet. She used her left fist to punch him in the groin. She missed hitting his junk but the blow showed she meant business. He stumbled backwards against the wine fridge, causing a clattering of expensive bottles. Catinca sprang away, crouching like a cat, ready to fight tooth and nail. Trottiscliffe swore and held his nose, rummaging in the fridge for some ice.

"You're going to regret that, you silly bitch!"

Catinca grabbed her handbag and fled, leaving her precious designs behind, racing from that room as if devils were at her heels.

The shop was a bad idea. That was her HQ and the first place anyone would look for her. She didn't want to go home either, just to pace and worry and agonise over what had happened. She couldn't go to Dionysus to see her friends as they would all be eager to hear about her brilliant high society commission. She walked to Green Park and sat down on a bench until her breathing returned to something like normal. Then she made three decisions. First, she would call Jeremy's and enquire about a mislaid portfolio case. Second, she would call Agnessa and offer to make her wedding dress on one condition: Catinca had nothing further to do with the father of the bride. Third, she would ask Will how to file a complaint about sexual harassment.

Her mind calmer, she made her way to Victoria, got on a Circle line Tube and rode around for hours, sure that was one place she would never encounter a Trottiscliffe.

Chapter 14

It was impossible to concentrate until she heard his key in the lock. His voice floated up the stairs as he talked to the dog, and Marianne released a sigh. Now Dad was home and safe, she could return her attention to the third quarter's profit and loss accounts of the garden centre. She achieved more in twenty minutes than she had in the previous hour and a half. She stopped work at quarter to six and went downstairs to begin dinner. There would be five of them today before the interview with the first potential care-worker. Even though she wouldn't have admitted it, Marianne was nervous. It seemed a huge responsibility to choose the right person for her father's support. If only Beatrice was here.

Huggy Bear greeted her with a wag of her tail as she entered the kitchen and even Dumpling opened his yellow eyes, but there was no sign of her father. She checked the conservatory, cast a worried glance into the garden and then heard the sounds of Radio 4 coming from his study. She tapped on the door and stuck her head in.

"I'm going to start cooking. Any special requests?"

Matthew put down his book and pulled down his glasses, peering at his oldest daughter as if he'd never seen her before in his life. "Requests?"

"Tanya and Gabriel are having dinner with us before the

interview. Obviously, Luke will be with them so I thought spag bol as a classic crowd-pleaser. What do you think?"

"Indeed, an Italian dish would be warming and familiar. If I had a say in the matter, I would plump for *panzanella*. In fact, I shall come and supervise. Do we have any cauliflower?"

"Dad, no child in the world likes cauliflower."

Luke ate everything on his plate and asked for seconds. Marianne could see why. Matthew had directed her to create a winter salad of steamed cauliflower florets, chunks of bread fried in olive oil, mixed up with chopped radishes, peppers, tomatoes and a puttanesca dressing. It was too delicious to call itself a salad.

Gabriel checked his watch. "That was a beautiful meal, thanks, Marianne. I need to steal that recipe. OK, the support guy from the care agency is due in fifteen minutes. How about Luke and I clear up in here and you three prepare the dining room? I'll join you as soon as I've started Luke on his homework."

"My homework will take me ten minutes, tops. When I finish, can I come and listen?"

Gabriel met Tanya's eyes. It was sweet, thought Marianne, how he always deferred to her when handling Luke. But it was not Tanya who answered the boy's question.

"Under normal circumstances, Small Fry, I would welcome your input. Today is different. We need to speak to this man and assess whether he's compatible with our household. Your contribution could be on the side of keeping the animals entertained. Another duty you could perform would be to answer the telephone. Beatrice usually rings around eight and if we are still discussing the practicalities, I would be grateful if you'd pass on the message that all is well. How does that sound to you?"

Luke shrugged and stole a piece of bread from Tanya's

leftovers. "All right, I suppose. Can I tell her ...?"

"Just tell her about Granddad," Tanya interrupted. "Tell her stuff about school, the animals and that sort of thing. Get a shift on, the man will be here any minute and we're still grazing. Shut the kitchen door and keep the creatures in here with you. Dad, you ready?"

They had only just set up the dining room when the doorbell rang. Marianne answered and saw a tall serious blond with a dark beard on the doorstep. He wore the white uniform of an orderly and an outdoor jacket.

"Good evening. Thank you for being so punctual. My name is Marianne Bailey, the professor's daughter. You must be Axel Zand."

"Good evening, Marianne Bailey, the professor's daughter. Can I meet the client? I have to be in Appleford by eight."

Marianne led him to the dining room, more than a little irritated by his brusque manner. Patience was exactly what her father needed. Not busy people who could only spare the minimum if civilities.

"May I introduce you to Professor Bailey, my father? Dad, this is Axel Zand, from the agency."

The tall man bowed towards Matthew. Tanya stood up and Gabriel entered the room.

"And this is my sister ..."

"We'd like a few moments alone, if you don't mind. We'll call you when we're ready to talk. Thank you."

"Of course. No problem," said Tanya before Marianne could formulate a response. "Help yourself to water. We'll wait in the kitchen." She led the way out of the room as Axel pulled out a chair and watched them leave.

Once the door had closed, Marianne wrinkled her nose. "He's got quite an arrogant attitude."

"Give him a chance," said Gabriel. "It's a good sign he wants to connect with Matthew first. Into the kitchen and say nothing in front of Luke."

They sat there for twenty-five minutes. Gabriel guided Luke through his homework, Marianne helped herself to another glass of wine and Tanya drank a pot of peppermint tea. Eventually the kitchen door opened and Axel Zand stood on the threshold. Huggy Bear leaped out of her bed and rushed towards him, leaping up on her hind paws. He crouched to stroke her and said some words in a foreign language.

Then he looked up and addressed them. "You have a dog. That's a good sign. My name is Axel Zand. I'm from Uppsala in Sweden and I have worked as a carer in the UK for over five years. You can view all my qualifications and experience and references online. I will take this job. Matthew and I understand each other. That is only part of the situation. Just like with dogs, sometimes the problem is not the animal but its owners. If you employ me, I don't just work with Matthew. I will need to work with you as well."

"Dogs? Owners?" Marianne snorted. "I'm sorry but..."

He fixed her with a cold stare. "You're his oldest daughter, is that correct?"

"Yes, I am. My name is Marianne and this is my sister Tanya and her husband Gabriel. In the absence of Beatrice, my father's partner, we are responsible for his care."

He got to his feet and Huggy Bear returned to her basket. "Beatrice, yes. I will need to have a conversation with her. The situation is this: your father will need a regular routine, set by me and followed by all of you. We must work together to manage his condition. My next job is due now and I am leaving. Tomorrow, I will send you a proposal about how we can cooperate to ensure Matthew is properly cared for and has sufficient freedom to make him happy. Look over my terms to decide if they are realistic. If you agree, sign and return the document. I am prepared to start on Monday. Have a nice evening, goodbye."

Marianne, Tanya and Luke stared wide-eyed as the tall Swede left the kitchen. The only one to remember his manners was Gabriel, who jumped out of his seat to escort the visitor back to his car. Marianne drew in a breath to express her disapproval but Tanya shot her daggers, with a pointed glance at Luke. Huggy Bear jumped out of the bed with a yelp of excitement and ran across the tiles towards Matthew.

That dog, thought Marianne, *has a real thing for men.* She looked at her father's face as he smiled at them all.

"Well, I don't know how you did it, but you found the perfect chap. Had I designed my ideal helper, I'd have fallen short. He is no nonsense, very practical and assures me he understands this bloody evil progression. I have to say, I feel in enormously capable hands. Can we keep him, Mum? Can we, can we, please?"

Tanya burst into laughter, which Marianne thought in very bad taste. "Glad to see you still have your sense of humour. If you like him, Dad, let's give the fella a trial run. He's sending a proposal tomorrow, so Marianne and I will scrutinise it and send a copy to Beatrice. Do you want a cup of tea?"

Matthew ruffled Luke's hair. "Had enough tea for one day. Just wondering what's for dinner. I'm starving."

This time, Tanya didn't laugh. "I suppose *panzanella* could be considered a starter. How about a slice of quiche?"

"He's a very decent bloke," said Gabriel, as he came in from the hall. "I have a good feeling about him. What did you think, Matthew?"

There was no reply. Matthew was looking over Luke's shoulder. "That looks splendid! I'm very impressed. Although you might want to look at the gender agreement on question number six. It's ducks in the plural, you see?" His eyes focused on Gabriel. "Marvellous! A slice of quiche is exactly what the doctor ordered. Marianne, be a sweetheart and fetch a bottle of wine from the cellar. Alsace, ideally. Lord, is that the phone?

Beatrice, dear heart, I'm on my way."

Chapter 15

Cooped up in the boardroom all morning with Gael and Theo, Beatrice grew fidgety and impatient. While it was essential they prepared their case meticulously before approaching the police, the details were beginning to give Beatrice a headache. Theo and Gael showed no signs of flagging and a complete unawareness of how stale the air in the room had become. Not only that, her stomach was rumbling and no one had mentioned anything about lunch.

At one pm, the editor arrived. "Hard at work, I see. I appreciate the effort you're putting into this story, but it's time for a break. This place smells of coffee breath. Why don't we open the windows for an hour and go get some food? You could all do with a walk and some lunch, I'm sure."

"What an excellent idea!" said Beatrice, practically leaping out of her chair.

Gael looked at the paperwork spread all over the table. "I don't want to leave this lot lying around. Maybe we should get a sandwich and eat al desko while we update you."

Hedda shook her head. "I want something more than a sandwich. We'll lock the door and everything will be as you left it when we return. The canteen is doing ratatouille with polenta. Let's go. The change of scene will do you good." She walked around the room opening windows.

Theo got up, stretched and yawned. "Yeah, I need to stretch my legs. Anyway, I think we got this thing nailed."

Hedda looked at Gael, her eyes bright. "Have you?"

"Thanks to these two." Gael pointed her index fingers like pistols at Beatrice and Theo. "I think we have."

The newspaper canteen was a lively sort of place with pine walls and long refectory style tables. Large windows to the south and west allowed autumn light to spill across the space. They queued to choose their food, Heather put the bill on her tab and they retreated to a small table near the kitchen to secure themselves some privacy.

With a plate of ratatouille, two slices of polenta and a bread roll on her tray, Beatrice started to feel better. She left the talking to Gael as her attention was mostly occupied by her meal.

"Right, so. Here's the deal. Beatrice and Theo gave me a story in itself. What we found out since makes this way more than a newspaper splash. It's huge and needs to be investigated by the law. What we've been doing all morning is preparing a watertight case to hand over to federal investigators. Don't look like that, Hedda, we'll still get the credit for breaking the story but it might take a lot longer. We might want to involve other papers as this is not exclusive to Benelux."

Hedda spooned up some more aubergine and said, "Go on."

"Sonny Das made the connections between the parent company, Banque Franck et Schneider, and its subsidiaries. He traced all the links, cross-checked with amounts and amassed sufficient evidence to prove the bank's board and executive officers were lining their own pockets. It's a complicated trail to follow and few people would have the expertise, persistence or time to join the dots. Das had all three in spades. Due to a health situation, he confided in his flatmate, Bikram Ghosh. Thanks to Beatrice, we know that guy has disappeared, apparently gone back to India. Oddly enough on Friday, a few hours after Beatrice told him what happened to Das."

"Yesterday," added Beatrice, "both his landlord and employer informed me Ghosh made a sudden return to Bangalore due to a family emergency. We've been checking the veracity of that statement but so far found nothing. Another reason why we need to get law enforcement involved. They'll be able to check if he did indeed get a flight out of Brussels on Friday."

Gael drank the rest of her water. "On top of large-scale industrial fraud, we have a missing person and a suspected murder. Theo found a witness in Bruges who saw someone enter and leave the hostel shortly before Beatrice found Sonny Das hanging from a beam. This is far bigger than a news story. This afternoon, you need to call the third policeman."

"Who's the third policeman?" asked Theo.

"Hedda is a personal friend of a senior detective on the Brussels force. Very handy fella to know, except he's killed more than one of my stories before. Not this time, though. Not this time, right, Hedda?"

They continued eating in silence while Hedda considered Gael's words. Finally she addressed them all. "Are you definitely ready? Do we have everything we need before involving the police? Are you two prepared to stay on till the weekend? Because when this kicks off, it's going to be twenty-four-seven."

Beatrice met Theo's eyes and he gave her a resigned shrug. "Speaking for the Stubbs agency, yes. We are prepared to speak to the police, give statements and hand over everything we have acquired."

Everyone looked at Gael, who was prodding a piece of polenta as if to be sure it was dead.

"Gael?" asked Hedda. "Are you ready?"

"Yeah, ready as I'll ever be. My gut tells me we need to move as fast as a rat up a drainpipe. If anyone makes the connection between Beatrice finding the body, Theo attending the hostel where Das died, me certifying these financial transactions, plus enquiries regarding the whereabouts of Bikram Ghosh, they're going to shut us down. We've got all the information necessary to open an investigation with Europol. We should act this afternoon."

Hedda put down her knife and fork and patted the fingers of her right hand against the palm of her left, applauding each of them in turn. "We won't need Europol. We'll do the local guys a favour and keep them sweet. Fantastic work! Damn shame we can't make our front-page splash next week, but our time will come. This afternoon is too soon because I need to make some calls. I'd say we move tomorrow morning. You prepare everything today, then why don't we meet somewhere out of the office to work out a game plan? How about my place? No eavesdroppers there, I guarantee it. We can have dinner together and a celebratory glass of wine."

Beatrice mopped up the last of the tomato sauce with her squishy roll. "That's very kind of you. But I wouldn't want you to go to any trouble, cooking for all of us."

"Cooking?" Hedda laughed. "I'd never subject you to my cooking. Fate worse than death. Even Gael's a better cook than I am and she's awful. We're going to have takeaway pizza and live to see another day. I'm off to call my contacts. Is seven-thirty a good time?"

"Seven-thirty for dinner? I don't normally leave here till seven at the latest!" Gael opened her palms.

"No one expects you to dress for dinner, Gael. Leave at seven, call a cab and charge it to the company. Just come as you are. Here's my home address." She distributed cards to each of them. "Have a good afternoon, everyone. You've done a terrific job." She flashed a warm smile and strode away.

By half past four, the team was ready. An ache for solitude buzzed like a wasp in Beatrice's head. She and Theo packed away their papers and prepared to leave.

Gael shut her laptop with a wide grin of satisfaction.

"Luckiest day of my career the day I got your email. This story is going to make me, I swear. All these years, I've been chasing those sharks and now we caught the lot in one tight net. I'd hug you both if I wasn't so rank. As it is, I just want to say, you're a terrific team and I'll recommend you to anyone who'll listen."

"You're not so bad yourself," said Theo. "It's been a weird sort of case, kind of mopping up after the event, but I doubt corruption on this scale would have seen the light of day without someone like you. Congratulations, and I can't wait to read the exposé when it breaks."

Beatrice was bouncing on the balls of her feet with impatience. Surely they could do all the back-slapping later over pizza and Valpolicella? "It's been a pleasure, Gael. As Theo says, your tenacity does you credit. Now, shall we have a rest before our celebratory meal with Hedda?"

She and Theo took a taxi to the budget hotel. Neither spoke on the journey, relaxing into comfortable silence. In the hotel lobby, Beatrice mentioned she might have a nap for a couple of hours and Theo's face creased into a grateful smile.

"That works for me. I'm itching to call Catinca and find out how her interview went. Meet you here at seven?"

"Of course! I'd quite forgotten about that. Do give her my love and congratulations. I know she will have aced it. Oh, listen to me! Aced it, indeed."

She unlocked her room, checked her messages and decided to have a lie down on the bed. There was no point in calling Matthew yet and no need to shower and dress for dinner for another hour. Something was bothering her and she needed to focus her mind on what it might be. Deep in her subconscious, an alarm was ringing. She closed her eyes and listened. A phrase floated to the forefront of her mind. 'They're going to shut us down.' That was ridiculous. This was Europe, Brussels, the heart of democracy, not some dodgy failed state where journalists and private investigators went missing. Her headache threatened a return and she got up to open the window. All day in a closed room or taxi or elevator was not a healthy way to live one's life. She got back onto the bed and closed her eyes.

The windows. On returning to the boardroom, the air was icy because Hedda left all the windows open before leaving for lunch. Many of the papers they had assembled into piles had blown around the room, presumably due to gusts of wind. It had taken them several minutes to collect and reorganise all the documentation. But what if it was not the wind?

The boardroom was on the first floor, so Beatrice assumed the only access would be through the door Gael had locked when they left the room. Yet outside, there was a roof garden, naturally neglected in autumn as smokers tended to stand underneath the front portico. If someone wanted to access the boardroom while its occupants were stuffing themselves with ratatouille in the canteen, all they needed to do was climb through a window. Their undercover investigation was nowhere near as secure as they hoped. Beatrice rose again and closed the window, her skin in goosebumps for more reasons than the cold.

Chapter 16

Catinca's mobile went straight to voicemail. Maybe she was in a meeting and didn't want to be disturbed. It was only four o'clock in Britain and she was probably still at work. He sent a message instead, asking her to call when she could. He added three kisses.

He stared out of the window for a few minutes, hoping she'd reply. No response. His body, stiff and creaky after hours in a chair, cried out for some exercise. He put on his jogging gear, laced up his trainers and headed out into the chilly afternoon. He had no clue where to run, but followed the brown tourist attraction signs toward the Grand Place. Theo was curious. Since they arrived, he'd seen almost nothing of the city and its landmarks.

Dusk had fallen and streetlamps shed pools of light on the traffic along Boulevard Adolphe Max. Running next to vehicles made Theo feel dirty, so he took a left onto Rue Neuve. It became obvious that running along a crowded pedestrian avenue, slaloming between shoppers and street vendors was not going to work. He slowed to a fast walk, taking in the busy ambience of a city adapting to darker October nights. Groups of people circled markets stalls selling spiced wine and waffles, amid other things Theo hadn't seen. He lurked behind a family buying portion of *caricoles*, which looked like the least appetizing thing anyone would want to put into his mouth. In French, he asked the oldest man in the group what it was.

"Sea snails. Delicious! Try one?"

Theo took a cocktail stick from the stall and hooked one of the grey lumps from the man's bowl. It was salty, sweet and chewy. Not something he'd request for his next birthday dinner, but tasty enough on a cold night.

"*Pas mal. Merci, M'sieur. Bonne soirée*!"

The family returned his wishes and he powered onwards to the Grand Place. On entering the enormous square, he stopped to stare. Like the rink where he'd been skating with Catinca, this was a square, bordered on all side by impressive contemporary buildings. Unlike the rink at Somerset House, this was the length of several football fields. These venerable buildings were mediaeval and held all the hauteur of civic pomp. Cafés and restaurants catered for the endless streams of tourists and wherever he looked, cameras snapped panoramic views, family groups and decorative detail. He wandered aimlessly, absorbing one sight after another, admiring the architecture and wishing once again Catinca was by his side.

He reached for his phone and remembered he'd left it in his room to charge. She might have called him by now. He set off at a loping run on various parallel streets to the main drag and after a quick detour to buy a bottle of wine, he found himself at base camp in under fifteen minutes. Not exactly a marathon, but he'd done something other than stare at a screen. He ran up the stairs rather than taking the lift, entered his room and snatched up his phone. No messages.

He tried her again. Voicemail. He didn't leave a message. He found her home number and called that. No reply. Not even an answer phone. As a last resort, he looked up the number of the shop. Once again, a recorded message asking him to leave a message. The only difference, this was her voice, not some mechanical robot. He listened with a smile, fumbled a message and tried again.

You out celebrating already? You're on my mind and I'm curious to hear the news, but you can tell me in person tomorrow. Beatrice and I are done. It's now up to the newspaper. I'll be in London by tomorrow evening. Do you have plans?

Two minutes passed with no reply. He sighed and got into the shower.

After packing for an overnight stay and spending three days in a budget hotel, Theo had run out of clothes. The shirt he'd hung out of the window that morning smelt reasonably fresh and he always carried a surplus of underwear. By seven o'clock, he was dressed, shaved and scented with Catinca's gift of aftershave. Beatrice was already waiting in the lobby with a glass in her hand.

"Sorry to keep you," he said.

"It's only just seven." She glanced at the bag in his hand. "Is that a bottle of wine?"

"Yep. Is that gin?"

"Yes, it is but it's too late to order one for you. We have to go. Listen, I've had a thought. I'll tell you all about it outside while we wait for the taxi. Thank you for thinking of the wine."

They went out into the night to find the cab was already there. Once they'd been driving for several minutes, he looked at his boss. "You had a thought?"

Beatrice flicked a glance at the driver. "Yes. I was thinking about you and Catinca. Why don't you go away for a couple of days over to make the most of this Indian summer? You're due some time off. The pair of you could do a train trip to Paris, for example. Very romantic."

"I was thinking of Bruges. Not as weighted with expectation as Paris and it's a crazy cute city. She'd love it."

"Oh, yes! She would. How did her interview go?"

"I couldn't reach her. She's probably in Dionysus, knocking back the bubbles." A sense of unease shadowed him and he changed the subject. "Have you spoken to Matthew?"

"No, I'll call him after they've interviewed that carer. Shall we take the morning train tomorrow?"

"Yeah, I can't wait to get home," he sighed.

Beatrice gave him an indulgent smile. "Young love knows no patience."

He snorted. "We're not that young."

"Young enough. Look lively, we're here."

Hedda's apartment was on the ninth floor of a tall block and from her living-room, she had the most spectacular views over Brussels. Theo noted the room was very clearly designed for one person. A reclining chair in front of a wide-screen TV, female shoes and coats in the hallway and no sign of a male presence. Hedda buzzed them in and called from the kitchen.

"Come on in! I'm just making us an aperitif. Do you like gin?"

They answered as a chorus. "Yes, please."

Beatrice enthused about the views while Theo inspected Hedda's bookshelves. You could tell a lot about a person by what they read. The shelves were filled with non-fiction: autobiographies, true crime, political analyses, train journeys across India and reference books. What else did he expect from a journalist?

"It soothes me," said Hedda, coming out of the kitchen. "Being up here, watching over the city, observing all of the activity but keeping out of it. After a full day at the paper, it's exactly what I need. Here you go. Cheers!"

They drank and Theo noticed there were only three glasses. "Hey, this is a nice gin. Smells of apples. The colour is classy too."

"Isn't it? Buss No. 509. They do other fruit flavours but this apple one always reminds me of the last days of summer."

"Very tasty," Beatrice agreed. "No news of Gael yet?"

Hedda gestured to the sofa. "She's always running late, but her excuses are so incredibly creative, I can forgive her. A neighbour's hamster escaped, the bus driver had a heart attack, she saw a man being mugged and chased his attackers until she got lost. The list goes on. The fact is, she's a workaholic and doesn't know when to stop."

"She's certainly passionate about her job," said Theo.

"Too right. Anyway, we can go ahead and order the pizza because she always has the same thing. It's not the first time we've worked late into the night over a Hawaiian. What would you like?" She handed Beatrice a delivery menu.

Theo got up and retrieved the wine from where he'd left it in the hall. "We brought some wine. Can't eat pizza without red wine."

"Thank you! Good choice. Sicilian wine and pizza is a match made in heaven. Have you decided, Beatrice?"

"Quattro Stagione for me. The ideal pizza for the person who can't make up her mind." She offered the menu to Theo.

"Napoli and if they do garlic bread, I'd like a portion of that."

Hedda went into the hallway to call the pizzeria and Theo tried again. "Do you want to talk about your thought now?"

Beatrice gave a brisk shake of her head. "Definitely not. Let's save that till we're back at the hotel. I can't get over this view. You can see the entire city. From my flat in London, all you could see was the other side of Boot Street."

"You've made up for that in Devon. I don't think I'd ever be stressed again if I woke up to your garden every day."

"Twenty minutes," said Hedda, returning to the room. "I'd better ring Gael. Her place is half an hour's bus ride away, so if she hasn't left yet, she'll be eating her pizza cold. Theo, why don't you freshen our drinks and you can check out the gin bottle at the same time. Tonic and ice are in the fridge."

Her tone was friendly and Theo dismissed the temptation to say 'Yes, madam, right away, madam'. A newspaper editor must spend a lot of time telling people what to do and she meant nothing by it. Better to save his energies for when they achieved something.

In the kitchen, he examined the lovely-looking bottle and memorised the name, then added a little splash to each glass. He found the tonic in the fridge door, observing that Hedda kept very little in the way of food, but plenty in the way of booze. He added ice and returned to his spot on the sofa.

"Ladies, your gin. Is Gael en route?"

Hedda shrugged. "No answer. That's not unusual. If she's still home, she'll be flying out the door any second. If she's on her way, she'll ignore my nagging. How did you decide she was the one, Beatrice? I mean the one you could trust with what you unearthed."

They chatted about the origins of the case and Theo's discovery of Gael's previous investigative exposés. Hedda was alert and sharp, her face showing real interest in what they had to say. She asked a lot of questions. Theo was surprised to see how closely Beatrice played her cards to her chest. He would have expected her to be open about all they knew, since they were no longer working the case. The more information Hedda had, the better case they could present to the police. Perhaps it was out of loyalty to Gael she wasn't saying much. Theo knew better than to diverge from the party line so answered a direct question vaguely and changed the subject.

"Something I'm curious about is how European papers like yours are covering the Brexit situation. How can a paper based here maintain any kind of neutrality?"

A spark flashed in Hedda's eyes and he saw he'd hit upon the right topic to distract her. She was in the middle of giving them both some context when her mobile beeped.

"OK, let's see what outlandish story she's concocted this time." She read the screen and Theo noted her eyes darken. "That wasn't Gael, but one of my team reporting a dead end. Oh, well. Some stories just aren't worth chasing. Where was I? Oh, yes, the referendum."

By the time the delivery driver turned up, there was still no news from Gael. Beatrice suggested putting her pizza on a low heat in the oven until she arrived. The minute Hedda went into the kitchen; Beatrice shook her head at Theo. He gave her a puzzled look but there was no time for further discussion as Hedda returned.

"Well, if the ham and pineapple are burnt, it's her own fault. Theo, open the wine for us. Glasses are in the cupboard beside the TV. I'll get plates and cutlery. Eating out of the box makes me feel like I'm at work."

Before Theo could express the mildest comment about being treated like a waiter, Beatrice picked up her bag and got to her feet.

"Must pop to the loo before we begin."

"First door on the right," said Hedda, indicating as she turned to the kitchen.

Something was wrong, Theo could sense it. He stood still as Beatrice left and Hedda clattered about in the kitchen. Gael was supposed to take a cab from work, not travel half an hour by bus from her own place. At their first meeting, she'd told them she didn't eat meat, so why would she order a ham and pineapple pizza? There was no reason for Beatrice to play it so cagey around Gael's editor, unless she had similar doubts.

He picked up the corkscrew and opened the wine, his mind preoccupied, when Beatrice came out of the bathroom. While still out of Hedda's sightline, she met Theo's eyes with a fierce intensity and jerked a thumb towards the front door. The she re-entered the room with a bright smile.

"This is a lovely apartment. Those tiles in the bathroom are divine! Mmm, this smells good." She sat on the sofa, beaming up at Hedda. "Come along, Theo, pour the wine, I'm eager to tuck in. Have you ever been to Portugal? They have the most wonderful tiles – *azuleijo* – entire stories on a wall. Thank you for the pizza, I admit to being absolutely ravenous. Chin-chin," she smiled at them both and they began to eat.

Her behaviour concerned Theo. She was obviously planning something but he had no idea what. He ate his pizza and took the smallest sips of wine, ready to respond when she gave the signal. What signal and what response, he would have to wait and see.

He'd swallowed two slices of pizza to Beatrice's one because of how much she was talking. It was totally out of character. Where food was concerned, Beatrice gave it her full attention. Hedda waved a glass at Theo to refill her wine and he pretended he hadn't seen it. He picked up a third slice and dropped it instantly as Beatrice started choking. On his feet in a second, he rushed to her side.

She jerked and coughed, red-faced and gasping for air. "Must be nuts," she choked.

Theo's mind raced to catch up. "Your allergy?" he asked, patting her back.

She squeezed his hand urgently. "Epi-Pen, my bag!"

Theo snatched up her handbag and guided her into the bathroom. He waved away Hedda's flappy questions about if she should call an ambulance. Once into the bathroom with the door shut, Beatrice continued wheezing but started typing on her phone.

Gael's phone unobtainable – Hedda lied – kept us here – maybe taxi for Gael wasn't taxi? We go now – say sorry and leave for hotel – must find Gael

Theo kept up the pretence. "Is that better? Can you breathe now? You scared me. Maybe we should skip the pizza, huh? Beatrice, how do you feel? OK, that's better. Let's get back to the hotel. No, no, I'm far more worried about you. Can you stand?"

They emerged together, Beatrice leaning on Theo, him carrying her handbag. He shook his head in reassurance. "Don't worry. Anaphylactic shock but she's getting better. She has an allergy to nuts. Not normally a problem with pizza, so that's weird. Sorry about the debrief, but I need to take the boss home. I'll contact you tomorrow with an update."

"Oh, God, Beatrice, I cannot apologise enough. Let me call you a taxi."

Beatrice squeezed Theo's arm.

"That's not necessary," he replied. "We'll hail one outside. Thanks, sorry for spoiling the evening and give Gael our best. Oh, yeah, don't forget her pizza is still in the oven. Bye, Hedda, apologies and thanks again."

They left her wringing her hands and issuing threats to the pizza company. Theo suspected the second the lift doors closed she would be on the phone. Beatrice said nothing until they exited the building.

"Grab a cab and let's go to the hotel. Do we know Gael's home address? If not, you should go to the newspaper offices. Find out what time she left and in which car. I'm worried about her, Theo. I think her boss is prepared to throw her to the wolves. Think about it – tame copper, leaving the windows open, arranging a car ..."

"... ordering Hawaiian for a non-meat-eater, making sure she knew where we were. I have questions. Why? Who is she working for?"

"TAXI!" bellowed Beatrice and a cab indicated right.

Theo shot a glance over his shoulder. "She can't see us from here, thankfully, otherwise you, Ms Klaxon-Lungs, would have just given the game away."

Beatrice told the driver their address. "You know what I think? We have no idea what the game is. But the stakes just got higher. If Gael really has gone missing, I am genuinely fearful for her safety."

"They wouldn't hurt her, would they?"

"Apparently Hedda has the ear of a senior police officer, which might encourage her or her henchmen to act with impunity." Beatrice gave him a dour look and Theo dug his nails into his palms.

Chapter 17

The same porter at Jeremy's produced Catinca's portfolio from a cupboard behind his desk. She stared at it, breathing heavily. The man gave her a kind smile.

"Would you like to check everything is present and correct?" he asked.

Catinca nodded, not trusting her voice.

The man indicated some kind of cloakroom and although he didn't close the door, he left her in peace. She knelt, unzipped the portfolio and after checking piece after piece, reassured herself everything was still there. All out of order and in no kind of organisation, but each image replaced with respect. She zipped up the leather folder and exhaled a nervy sigh of relief.

"Is anything missing?" asked the porter.

Catinca shook her head. "Can't see anything." She looked at the man and his friendly expression. "When I left that room, stuff was all over the place. Who picked it up?"

"That would be me. I took your call, I remembered your visit and after the occupants of the room had departed, I collected all your sketches and replaced them in the correct repository. I have no expertise in your kind of line, but I can see you have an extraordinary talent."

Catinca's chest heaved but she was unable to form a coherent sentence.

The porter continued. "If I had a talent like that, I wouldn't waste it on the undeserving. Can I get you a glass of water?"

She shook her head again and gave him a tearful look of gratitude. "Gotta go, thank you." She realised this was the kind of establishment where everybody tipped everybody else, like a constant coin-go-round. Before she could even locate her purse, the man held up a hand.

"Please don't. Tipping is a one-way street. I've given you a tip, no need to reciprocate." He glanced out through the portico. "The weather is changing and a thunderstorm looks likely. I would hate your designs to suffer the worst of the rain. Would you accept a club umbrella? It's the least we can do. Or perhaps a taxi should you have further to go?"

There was only one place Catinca could feel safe and that was Boot Street. "Yes, a taxi, please."

The man escorted her out the door, opened the door of a black cab and handed her a dark-green umbrella with a wooden handle. "Just in case. Pleasure to meet you, Ms Radu. Have a nicer evening."

His words echoed in her head as the cabbie grumbled about driving to the East End. "Have a *nicer* evening." As if he knew all about her afternoon.

When she got to Adrian and Will's flat, no one answered the doorbell. The taxi had already gone and she retreated under the porch to wait. Rain hammered down into recently created puddles, splashing upwards again so that water came at her from both directions. She opened the big green umbrella, holding it like a shield to keep herself and her work dry.

A glance at her phone told her it was almost seven. Adrian should have been home two hours ago and Will was rarely later than half past six. As she wasn't expected, they may well have taken Dolly down the pub for a pie and a pint. She was scrolling for Adrian's number when her phone rang. It was Theo. Catinca couldn't answer. His enthusiastic enquiries were too much to bear. If only he were here. She could think of no better comfort than to be enveloped in his arms. She let the call go to voicemail and leaned back against the front door, wondering how life had gone from full beam to lights out in a few short hours.

Without warning, the door opened behind her and she fell backwards into the hallway, the contents of her open handbag spilling across the floor. Dolly started barking and Adrian crouched to pick her up.

"Catinca? What on earth are you doing on the doorstep?"

She scrambled to her feet, tears already welling. "I rang the bell."

"Oh, right. I was blending some soup so I wouldn't have heard ... are you all right?" He held out his arms and Catinca crumpled into a weeping mess. He stroked her hair and kept mumbling reassuring phrases as he led her into the apartment. "It's all right, don't worry, everything will be fine. Wait on the couch while I get your things. Sit, Dolly, sit. Good girl." He handed her some tissues and went into the hall.

Catinca blew her nose and wiped her eyes to see Dolly at her feet, serious brown eyes looking up at her face and her tail wagging occasionally, as if to cheer her up. Catinca stroked her head and the wagging became more regular. Voices came from the hallway. A second later, Will was kneeling in front of her, his expression filled with concern.

"You don't do drama, unlike other people we know." He glanced over his shoulder to the sounds of Adrian carrying in her stuff.

She gave him a wobbly smile but didn't trust her voice.

"That's why I believe this is serious. We could leave you in peace to collect yourself or if you're ready, you can tell us what happened. Just one thing, are you injured?"

She shook her head. "I want to tell you. I need advice. But can I have shower first?"

"Go ahead. You know where everything is. Use Beatrice's

Boudoir. We'll make dinner." He took Dolly and Adrian into the kitchen, leaving her with a sense of both panic and relief. She grabbed her snotty tissues and took her handbag into Beatrice's room. There she stripped off, wrapped herself in a towelling robe and padded down the hall to the bathroom, where she washed away her day.

They were waiting in the living room when she emerged, like two big brothers; concerned but trying not to show it. Her outfit was entirely made up of Beatrice's spares: a pair of brushed-cotton pyjamas, woolly socks and a belted cardigan. Her hair was still in a towel and she had foregone her make-up. They'd probably never seen her so underdressed. Dolly bounded over to greet their unexpected visitor.

"Hello, Dolly dog. Hello, Mister and Mister. Sorry just to turn up like this. I needed to see friendly faces, innit?" She curled up on the sofa beside Adrian.

"No need for apologies," said Adrian. "We have some soup warming on the hob. Classic comfort food, if you're hungry."

"Yeah, that'd be great. Thanks for getting all my stuff in."

Adrian went into the kitchen. "All part of the service."

"Your phone's been ringing," said Will. "I just left it."

"Probably best," said Catinca. She tucked her hands into her armpits. "Don't wanna talk to anyone yet. Apart from you two." She squeezed her eyelids together, determined to suppress more tears. She had to explain what had happened in a clear-headed manner and get Will's take on reporting sexual assault. No time to waste on weeping. When she opened her eyes, Adrian was placing a bowl of soup in front of her, with a basket of fresh bread rolls.

"Anyone want wine?" he asked.

Catinca and Will shook their heads.

"This is my Winter Warmer. Green leafy veg with a touch of truffle oil and mixed nuts. Good for whatever ails you."

She took a spoonful, blew on it and tasted. It was warming, with layers of flavour. The cabbagey, sprouty notes reminded her of her childhood. Usually, she would close that memory door and nail it shut, but tonight, she allowed herself some comforting recollections.

Neither of her companions spoke, giving her time and space. Will complimented Adrian on the soup. Catinca agreed. Adrian offered her the bread basket and told Dolly not to beg. Catinca took a roll and bit into it with gusto. As always, eating chez Harvey and Quinn was better than any restaurant. Where else could you eat fine food in borrowed pyjamas? She finished her soup and smiled.

"You're magic, you are," she told Adrian. "Always got recipe to make me feel better. Remedy, not recipe. Thank you for soup and welcome. Now I gotta another favour to ask. What's best way to report sexual assault?"

She would have held herself together if it hadn't been for Adrian. Without looking at either of them, Catinca managed to get through a dispassionate account of what occurred in Room 467 at Jeremy's. Only when she lifted her head and saw Adrian's eyes brimming with tears did she crack. She covered her face with her hands and cried all over again.

Under his breath, Will said, "Don't," as Adrian took her in his arms. She allowed him to cradle her and they both sobbed into each other's shoulder. The towel fell off her hair and her wet locks fell on his shirt. Eventually she lifted her head and reached for the tissues.

"Don't what?" she asked Will, still sniffing.

"It's nothing, just that after an experience like you had, it's not a good idea to touch a person without their permission."

Adrian blew his nose. "For God's sake, Will! Drop the police handbook for once. One of our best friends has been assaulted and my first instinct is to comfort her. My second instinct is to rip that abusive bastard's bollocks off."

Will did not reply.

Catinca slipped her hand into Adrian's. "You're a good mate. You both are. Thing is, Will's right. I got to do this properly." She released a huge sigh. "You know what else stinks? That was my big chance in terms of career. Best job I ever been offered and now it's gone, all because of some filthy old pervert wanted his jollies. Agnessa loved my designs and wanted me to do her dress, but he went and ruined it."

"Are you sure?" asked Will. "You could still design the dress and only communicate with her father on paper."

"Nah, that ain't gonna happen. I sent Agnessa a message, saying just that. Heard nothing back. Point is, job don't matter. What matters is that over-privileged sleaze ball don't do it again to someone else. I got to report him. Tell me what to do, Will, and I'll do it."

Will stood up and paced over to the window, tapping his index fingers to his lips. Catinca and Adrian both watched him as he stared out of the window. Finally, he turned to look at her.

"Before you do anything, we need to think through all the consequences. I'm going to lay out your options and the potential ramifications of each one. Whatever you choose, I will support you every step of the way. We both will. The situation is particularly shitty because of the guy's position and it will come down to your word against his. He can and probably will make things very unpleasant for you."

"Will! Don't you dare try to put her off reporting this! This is exactly why the shitbags get away with it for so long and why something like the Me Too movement was badly overdue. If Catinca stands up for herself, it might encourage other women to do the same. Face it, there's no way this was a one-off."

Will ignored him and focused on Catinca. "Have you ever met Beatrice's friend Dawn?"

"Yeah, she helped me and Beatrice with that investigation in France. I liked her. Very practical."

"She is. She's been promoted to a DCI with the Essex force now and doing a damn good job. Before that though, she was the Met's go-to specialist when it came to cases of sexual assault. I think it would make sense for you to talk to her, and get some neutral advice from a professional. Listen, Catinca, because this is important. Taking on a family like the Trottiscliffes on your own is a daunting task. They won't think twice about trashing your reputation to make your testimony suspect. I agree with you this guy needs to be stopped. But there's more than one way to skin a cat. Can I set up a meeting for you and Dawn in the next couple of days?"

Catinca wavered. In her mind, it was vital to lodge a complaint as soon as possible. At the same time, it was important to get the perspective of a senior police officer about her chances of success. Will was right about one thing: it was her word against his. Her, a Romanian immigrant and him, a peer of the realm. If she was going to do this, she had to do it right.

"Can I sleep on it? My head's a bit of a muddle at the moment."

"Of course. We should take the dog out now because I can tell Adrian is bursting to shout at me and we don't need to subject you to one of our domestics. Think it over and let me know in the morning. I won't be offended either way."

She smiled. "Thank you." She bunted a shoulder against Adrian. "Go easy on him. I'll go to bed now and think about what the hell I'm going to say to Theo. Thank you for everything. Good night."

She kissed each of them on the cheek and went into the bathroom. Outside in the corridor, clattering claws and excited barks told her Dolly was more than ready for her evening walk. She heard them close the flat door and leave the building, Adrian's voice already rising and falling in indignation. She cleaned her teeth and washed her face, all the while trying out different explanations in her head. There was no way she could tell Theo the truth until she saw him in person. But neither could she ignore his messages and obvious concern. A little white lie would be necessary.

Once settled in Beatrice's Boudoir, she picked up her phone and saw there were three voicemail messages. Two from Theo and one from Agnessa Trottiscliffe. She played the last.

Ms Radu, Ness Trottiscliffe here. Sorry I didn't respond earlier, it's been one heck of a day. I want to say I am completely in love with your dress design and absolutely, we can work on it without involving my father. I gather from your message he's been up to his old tricks again. He means nothing by it, you know, he just gets a bit handsie with attractive women. Ignore the randy old bugger and you won't have to see him again. I'll make sure your invoice is paid and then you can get to work on creating the most divine wedding gown ever. Squeak! Can't wait! Ciao for now.

In dumbfounded amazement, Catinca listened to the message again. 'A bit handsie with attractive women?' 'Randy old bugger?' As Adrian said, this clearly wasn't the first time. On the other hand, the job was still available. Agnessa wanted the dress badly enough to sideline her father. Catinca sat on the bed for so long she heard Adrian, Will and Dolly return. Finally she picked up a phone again and called Theo. To her surprise and a little relief, it went to voicemail.

Hi, it's me. Sorry I didn't call before but I was waiting for some feedback. Turns out the bride-to-be loves my designs and wants me to make her dress. Some problems to iron out first, but nothing I can't handle. Hope you and Beatrice had a good day and can't wait to see you tomorrow. Off to bed now. I miss you.

No lies but not the whole truth. He would be home tomorrow and she could explain. She got into bed and pulled the duvet up to her chin. *Explain what, exactly?* As yet, she had made no decisions and was keeping her options open. In the morning, she would make her mind up about whether to talk to Dawn and whether she was going to make Agnessa's wedding dress.

Tonight, all she wanted to do was sleep.

Chapter 18

For a carer, he didn't seem to do much caring. Axel turned up around eleven every morning, played chess or walked Huggy Bear with Matthew, supervised his lunch preparations then left again. In the afternoon, he arrived just before five, spent another hour chatting in Matthew's study or drinking tea with him in the kitchen, before driving home. He paid Marianne very little attention unless it was to criticise and seemed far more interested in the dog.

It was distracting having him around, especially with his quiet voice, which made it hard for Marianne to eavesdrop. She stuck to his instructions, making healthy lunches filled with fish and vegetables, and cooking warming stir-fries for her father's evening meal, but never received a word of praise. It would be interesting to see how Beatrice got on with this implacable character.

As for Dad, he had taken to his carer instantly. He still had the odd scatty moment, packing for a trip to London or not recognising Marianne when she came through the door, but generally looked forward to Axel's visits. He talked about their conversations with unusual animation. Huggy Bear, the trollop, was completely smitten and flung herself at the Swede the second he arrived. Tanya, Gabriel and even Luke approved wholeheartedly of Axel Zand and his no-nonsense manner.

Marianne was not convinced, but hopefully today would be the last time she needed to work at the cottage as Beatrice was due to return that evening.

When she arrived shortly before nine, she found her father in the kitchen with the contents of a drawer scattered all over the table. He didn't return her cheery 'Good morning!', muttering to himself as he sorted through long-dried up tubes of glue, batteries, keys to doors no one remembered and broken bits of toys. She made them both a pot of tea and stood beside him as he inspected each item in turn.

"What are you looking for?" she asked.

He whipped around to stare at her. "That, young lady, is none of your damned business. Poking your nose where it is not wanted is the height of impertinence."

Marianne took her mug of tea and left him to it. Her inbox contained several interesting enquiries and she worked steadily for a couple of hours. As the clock crept towards eleven, she listened for the sound of Axel's car. While she waited, she popped into the bathroom to brush her hair and add a touch of lip gloss. When the doorbell rang, she stood on the landing, waiting for Dad to let him in. The doorbell rang again. Marianne trotted downstairs, already rolling her eyes at her father, who must have dozed off in his study again.

Axel stood on the doorstep and gave her a curt, unsmiling nod. "The weather is good. Cold, yes, but not wet. We will walk today. How is your father?"

"He was snarky when I first got here, but he might be in a better mood by now. I've just come downstairs. Please come in."

He did so and stopped before taking off his coat. "Where is Huggy Bear? The doorbell is her alarm signal."

Marianne looked around, acknowledging his point. "I don't know. She normally sleeps in the kitchen, by the Aga ..."

Axel walked past her, still in his outdoor gear and knocked on Matthew's study. He opened the door and shook his head.

"Go upstairs and check all the rooms. I will search down here and in the cellar."

Door after door revealed no trace of her father and she ran downstairs to see Axel coming in from the garden. She shook her head, beginnings of panic pulsing in her chest. Her 'office' door was always open so she could hear if he left the house. An idea hit her and she went into the porch. His winter coat was missing, as was the dog's lead.

"He must have gone for a walk, but I didn't hear the front door open, I swear."

"You said he was 'snarky' when you arrived. What does that mean?" Axel's padded bulk blocked out the light.

"He snapped at me when I asked what he was looking for in the kitchen drawer. It's where they keep Sellotape, elastic bands, loyalty cards and all the crap no one knows where to put."

"Loyalty cards? Such as?" Axel's face was in shadow but Marianne could feel his frown.

"Waitrose, the Indian restaurant in Crediton, the pub down the road, the delicatessen in Brampford Speke, you know. Local businesses."

"How many of those are within walking distance?"

She thought about it. "Only The Angel, I suppose. Should I call them and see if he's there?"

"That would be wise."

She found the number in the address book on the hall table, while he stood beside her, unzipping his coat to reveal his tunic.

"Hello, Susie, it's Marianne Bailey here, Matthew's daughter. I was just wondering if you'd seen my dad today."

"Marianne! We were just talking about you. Yes, he's right here, waiting for his fish and chips. He knocked on the door at half ten. We don't open till twelve, but seeing as it's Matthew, where's the harm in serving him a pint? He wants to use a two-for-one voucher which expired five years ago, although I'm not sure why. Unless he plans to share it with Huggy Bear?"

"Can you keep him there till we arrive? We'll be five minutes."

"Not a problem. We're having a chat about the good old days. Take your time."

Marianne replaced the receiver and exhaled a worried sigh. "We have to fetch him from the pub. He's ordered fish and chips and is drinking beer. If we're quick, we can stop him consuming all that crap. Shall we take my car?"

He pulled on his coat. "We take both. We arrive at the pub as if we meant to meet there and behave like it's a social occasion. Matthew can eat fried food today and perhaps we should join him. Then you bring him home and I go to my next job. Remember, we enter his world, not force him into ours. Are you going to wear those shoes in this weather?"

Marianne's annoyance reached breaking point. She stomped into the hallway, unzipped her suede boots and put on a pair of Beatrice's old wellies. She yanked her coat off the peg and glared at him. "Are you going to come or stand around judging me? Because I need to lock the door."

He walked past her without a word and Marianne gritted her teeth. *One last afternoon and then he's all yours, Beatrice bloody Stubbs.*

The pub was not due to open for another twenty minutes, so the bar was completely empty apart from her father perched on a bar stool with his Border Terrier at his feet. He looked over his shoulder as they approached and showed no surprise whatsoever at seeing them.

"One of the reasons I prefer The Angel above all other hostelries in the area is the silence. The Star may have a nice garden and The Toad's menu makes this place look like a workman's caff. The difference is there are no screens showing football or music videos, no fruit machines or piped music and no loud gaggles of holidaymakers here. When one is of a mind to enjoy a pint and a plate of fish and chips, there really is no better welcome than Susie at The Angel. What would you like to drink?"

Axel hunkered down to make a fuss of Huggy Bear. He looked up and asked, "What are you drinking? Would you recommend it?"

Matthew opened his mouth to respond and then closed it again, staring at Marianne. His eyes changed, narrowing in confusion, widening in fear and finally settling on the dog as if she was his anchor. A swell of sympathy rose in Marianne as she understood the storms raging behind her father's face. He was adrift, bearings lost and needed a life belt.

"He's a real ale aficionado, aren't you, Dad? I know both he and Gabriel love a pint of Tanglefoot. Or perhaps there's a special on today? In any case, I wouldn't think warm, hoppy beer would appeal to someone from Sweden. You drink cold lager as a rule, or is that a stereotype?"

For the first time since she'd met him, Axel looked directly into her face. He stood up and smiled, his blue eyes warm. "Tanglefoot? It's not an attractive name and suggests an impediment to sobriety."

"Ha!" Matthew laughed, his focus on Axel. "Impediment to sobriety, indeed. Susie, pour the man a half of Tanglefoot so he can judge for himself. Marianne, would you like a glass of white wine? Highly recommended with fish and chips. Where is the food, by the way? I've been here at least an hour."

Marianne met Susie's kindly gaze as she pulled the beer pump. "I'll have a white wine spritzer, because I'm driving. Dad, Susie was waiting for us to get here. She can't serve lunch until the entire party arrives. That would be very bad manners. Shall we sit at a table to eat? Where would you like to sit?"

Matthew opted for the corner table near the fireplace. Marianne slipped into the wooden settle so she could see the bar. Axel and Matthew occupied the seat opposite. It may have been the height and bulk of the man beside him, but suddenly, her father looked very frail. Her throat contracted and she swallowed several times, refusing to let emotion get the better of her. That was her sister's forte, not Marianne's.

"I do love a real fire," she said. "So does Huggy Bear, obviously. I'll bet it was cold when you two went out for a walk this morning."

"Perishing," agreed Matthew. "That's why we decided to take a break halfway and enjoy some of Susie's legendary fish and chips. Ah, talk of the devil!" He rubbed his hands together as Susie approached with a tray.

In response to Marianne's open-mouthed air of amazement and glance at her watch, Susie gave a brief shake of her head. "We warmed the kitchen up a bit earlier today, that's all. Marianne, I didn't know if you wanted ice in your spritzer, so left it out. Here's your Tanglefoot, Mr ..."

"You can call me Axel. I'm Matthew's assistant. Pleased to meet you, Susie, and the fish and chips look legendary, as Matthew promised. Thank you."

Susie distributed the plates. As she walked away she gave a pointed glance at Axel and a significant look at Marianne. That was typical. Everyone in the local pub was interested in who was seeing who, local disputes, weddings, pregnancies and funerals or anything else that remotely resembled a soap opera. A stranger in the village was a story waiting to be told. Marianne dropped her eyes and picked up a chip. Much as she appreciated Susie's kindness, she had no desire to be the afternoon's gossip fodder.

"It's interesting, I think, that the British national dish of fish and chips is a European import," said Axel. "Fish from Portugal and fries from Belgium." He watched Matthew shake the Sarson's bottle all over his plate. "The vinegar, I concede, is a British addition."

Marianne wondered whether the question was designed to irritate her before she saw her father's face. Matthew responded far better to abstract concepts than practical details. Her instinct would have been to ask him about the morning's walk and where he had been, focusing on the immediate, the here and now. That produced limited results. His responses to such enquiries tended to be confused, aggressive or simply ignored. Whereas Axel appealed to a separate part of her father's brain. His long-term memory and acquired knowledge, not to mention firmly held opinions, were more deeply rooted than whatever had occurred over the last twenty-four hours. Once again, Axel knew her father best.

"The story of fish and chips, as you say, is rooted in our relationship with our nearest neighbours. One could write an entire treatise on how the tastes, the language, the religions and the culture of Albion have been shaped by its interaction with the wider world. There is a widely held belief that the national British dish is no longer fish and chips but what we perceive as an Indian curry. External factors affect our cuisine to the extent that were I to introduce Luke to the weekly diet I consumed as a boy, he would run away in terror." He chuckled and took a mouthful of battered fish. He chewed, closed his eyes and swallowed, releasing a small sound of approval. "I don't know how she does it, but this batter is light as air. Must be the beer. What do you say to the Tanglefoot, Axel?"

In response, Axel lifted his glass to his mouth took one taste and swallowed the lot in one go. "It's an acquired taste, that's true. But I just acquired it. Unfortunately, I have to leave for my next appointment. Susie, can I get a doggy bag? Sorry to rush off, Matthew, Marianne and thank you for lunch. See you later this afternoon. Bye, Huggy Bear."

He zipped up his jacket, threw the contents of his lunch into the takeaway bag Susie provided and strode through the empty bar. Marianne watched him go, thinking about what he had said about entering her father's world. She dipped a forkful of battered fish into the tartare sauce.

"What do you mean by the weekly diet you consumed as a boy? Sunday roast and all that?"

A slow smile spread across Matthew's face as he gazed into the fireplace. "Marianne, I doubt you've ever eaten tripe and onions, or brawn with mustard, or Spam fritters. For your sake, I hope you never will."

The moment they got home, Matthew and the dog toddled off into the conservatory for a 'read of the newspaper' otherwise known as an afternoon nap. Marianne made herself some coffee and was on her way up the stairs when her mobile rang.

"Where have you been? I called the house phone," Tanya demanded.

"Dad went out with Huggy Bear and turned up at the pub at half past ten. Susie humoured him and made fish and chips for us all."

"Us all? You, Dad and Huggy Bear?"

"Yeah, and Axel. Why are you calling in the middle of the afternoon?"

"Aww, Axel. How romantic. Roaring fire, fish and chips, glass of red in an empty pub. There are worse ways to spend an afternoon. Anyway, I'm calling because of Beatrice's email. Did you read it?"

Marianne opened her office door and dumped her bag on the bed. She fired up the computer but was too impatient to wait. "No, I just got in. If she coming back today or not?"

"Not. Something's happened and she staying on till Friday. Have you got plans tonight? Only Gabriel is taking Luke to some candle-making fair so I thought I could bring over a takeaway and have a chat."

A strange impulse seized Marianne and she wondered how Axel would react if she asked him to stay for dinner. In a moment, she shook her head and frowned at herself for being so ridiculous. "Sounds great to me. So long as it's not fish and chips."

Tanya laughed. "Chinese, I was thinking. Lots of veg, not too much spice and light on the digestive system for Dad. Axel leaves at six, right? I'll pick up the food and get there around half past five so I can say hello."

From downstairs, Marianne heard an anguished cry. "Oh shit, what now? Got to go." She shoved the phone in her pocket and hurtled down the stairs. She found her father in the kitchen, on his knees, crying. Huggy Bear sat in her basket, cowed and hunched. On the chair which had once been Matthew's, there was an inert lump of grey fur. Marianne reached out a hand but before she even touched the cat, she could see Dumpling was dead. His yellow green eyes, so practised at the scathing look, were lifeless. He'd passed away in his sleep.

Marianne crouched and placed an arm around her father's shoulders. "I'm so sorry, Dad, I know how much you loved him. At least he went peacefully, the poor old pusscat. He had a good life, you made sure of that."

"The old boy was a very restful presence. I shall miss him dearly," whispered Matthew, his voice shaky. "Whatever does one do next? I wish Beatrice were here. Could you call Gabriel and ask him about… oh, you know… procedures?"

In her mind, Marianne was cursing her godmother.

Where the hell are you, Beatrice Stubbs? This is your responsibility, not mine. You can't just leave them alone like this, damn it! Get back here and take care of the man you love.

She gathered herself. "Yes, of course I can. Why don't you and Huggy Bear go and rest in the conservatory? I'll wrap Dumpling in a blanket and put him in the cellar. Once I've spoken to Gabriel, we can decide how to manage. By the way, Tanya is coming round with a Chinese takeaway this evening. You have a lie down and remember all the happy times with that silly old dough ball." She helped him to his feet, Huggy Bear at his heels. In the conservatory, she draped a blanket over his reclining form, took the soggy tissue from his hand and replaced it with a clean one. Huggy Bear hopped up to claim the space behind Matthew's knees and he reached back a hand to stroke her fur.

Marianne gave the dog a wink. "You look after him," she mouthed. The dog's head sank onto her paws, her sad eyes on Marianne.

She called Tanya to explain the hasty end to their previous conversation and asked her to seek Gabriel's advice when he returned. Tanya cried over the loss of Dumpling. In Marianne's opinion, her sister was overemotional. She ended the call, chose a clean towel and wrapped up the dead cat. The cardboard box which had contained Matthew's latest book delivery acted as a makeshift coffin. Then she took the sad little package down to the chill of the cellar, her heart hurting. Not for herself, not really. Dumpling's significance in her life was not much more than an animated cushion. Even so, she knew how much the fluffy old heap had meant to her father. She closed the door and trotted up the flight of stairs to sit in front of her computer. It was already quarter to three and her work rate was embarrassingly bad. She looked at her to-do list and reorganised her priorities. Then she rested her head on her forearms.

Next thing she knew, the doorbell was ringing and she had drool on her wrist. It was five-fifteen. She jerked upright and listened. The front door opened and Matthew greeted Axel, the tone of his voice conveying the domestic tragedy. Marianne closed down her computer, splashed some water on her face and applied some matte lipstick. She had to give at least the appearance of a busy professional. As she descended the stairs, she heard a female voice added to the mix.

"Why don't you stay for dinner? We always over order and you'd be more than welcome." Tanya's persuasive tones came from the kitchen. "Unless you have another job to attend to?"

Marianne took the stairs two at a time, slowing her pace towards the bottom. It was better not to look too eager. But had she not hurried downstairs, Axel's softly spoken voice would have been inaudible. "I understood Matthew's partner would be returning tonight. Where is Marianne?"

The sound of her name on his tongue was a thrill. "Here I am," she said, entering the kitchen, which smelt deliciously of sweet and sour chicken, chop suey and egg-fried rice. "Beatrice has delayed her return by twenty-four hours. Typical Beatrice, she sent an email rather than call. She always does this when she's working on a case. She's the most unpredictable woman."

"Always has been," said Matthew. "Trying to lure that female was like stalking a snow leopard. Elusive as a pimpernel. Once she'd moved in – that took years, Axel, let me tell you – I thought I'd won. But no. Periodically, she disappears to flirt with danger and I'm left here wondering if she'll ever come home." His face was wistful.

Tanya paused in the act of opening all the foil packages to kiss her father's cheek. "She'll be here tomorrow, you'll see. Now, who fancies what? Axel, please stay and eat with us."

Marianne added her voice. "After eating fish and chips on the go, a sit-down meal would be best. Unless you have other plans?"

"My work is finished for the day. My only plans were to make something to eat and write up my day notes. Yes, please, I will join you. It's a very kind offer. I don't eat meat but everything else is fine. Can I do anything to help?"

The meal was comfortable and relaxing. When Matthew began lamenting the cat, Marianne tried to change the subject, but both Axel and Tanya engaged with him.

"You should find the perfect spot to bury him in the garden. Perhaps near the bench. That way, you can sit together as you always have."

"Have you got a good photo of Dumpling? Because that lady in the village does lovely sketches in charcoal. That would be a nice memento to hang in your study."

"Another thing to do is to jot down or even record a few notes about your pet's personality. It can be painful but also cathartic and something to return to when you want to remember."

"Axel, finish the spring rolls, will you? I told you we always over order. Unless you want to take some home with you? Where do you live, by the way?" Tanya proffered the foil package.

He scratched his beard and shook his head. "Thank you but I'm full. It was very nice of you to invite me to share. Leftover Chinese, in my experience, makes for a pleasant lunch the day after. I have eaten cold chop suey for breakfast, to tell you the truth. I live in Crediton, right above the butcher's shop, which is the perfect atmosphere for a vegetarian." His eyes crinkled and Marianne caught a flash of his white teeth. "The other thing I dislike about living in town at the moment is the obsession with Halloween. It's artificial, based on borrowed cultural iconography and one more excuse to drink too much. If there were more respect paid to The Day of the Dead, I would understand."

"Well said," agreed Matthew. "The whole hype is an act of collective delusion. Utter nonsense commercialised beyond all recognition."

Tanya dabbed a deep-fried prawn into the spicy sauce and popped it into her mouth. "In that case, Mr Scrooge, you won't want to come to Exeter on Saturday with me and Luke for the Harvest Festival?"

Matthew's eyes lit up. "Exeter? I should enjoy that very much." He laid his knife and fork in the centre of his plate. "Yes indeed, most definitely. I enjoyed that meal. One of those occasions where I don't actually miss drinking wine. If it's all right with you, I think I might take Huggy Bear for a stroll down the lane and retire for the night. It's been quite a day."

Axel stood up. "I'd like some fresh air also. May I join you? Thank you so much for inviting me, Tanya, I'll see you tomorrow morning, Marianne. Good night."

He followed Matthew and Huggy Bear into the hallway and

the two sisters waited until the front door closed.

"He. Is. Hot." Tanya sat back in her chair and rested her hands on her stomach. "Tall, sexy, capable, intelligent, long eyelashes, groomed beard, nice smile..."

"... plus judgemental, bossy, arrogant and egotistic," added Marianne.

To her surprise, Tanya burst into a belly laugh. It took her several moments to compose herself and wipe the tears from her eyes. "You do realise you've just described yourself," she said. "You're pissed off because he has a set of skills, such as empathy and a willingness to listen, that you don't and probably never will possess. Not only that, he is unimpressed by your shit. You don't like him because he's dismissed you and that gets your goat." She started laughing all over again and poured herself some water.

Marianne gave her a cold glare, stood up and opened the fridge. Usually, there would be a half-drunk bottle of wine in the door, but since Matthew's diagnosis, it was all elderflower cordial and fizzy water. "I'm going home. You can put Dad to bed because I've had just about enough this week. I'll be here tomorrow, trying to catch up on my work, but then I'm done. If Beatrice isn't back tomorrow, you and Gabriel will have to take over. I have other priorities. Thanks for the Chinese."

She was still upstairs packing her laptop when she heard her father clumping up the stairs, talking to his terrier. As soon as he was in his room, she darted onto the landing and looked out over the driveway. Tanya stood there, talking to Axel. Marianne watched and fumed until the carer got into his car and drove away, Tanya waving him off. How dare she?

Chapter 19

The 08.52 Eurostar departed Brussels for London St Pancras with two reserved first-class seats empty. Theo and Beatrice had stayed up late into the night, trying to locate Gael O'Connell to no avail. She was not at her apartment or the newspaper offices, or answering her mobile. She was either incommunicado deliberately or she had disappeared. At half past one in the morning, Beatrice called a halt and advised Theo to get some sleep. If, and it seemed highly unlikely, Gael turned up at the office the following morning, Beatrice and Theo could take the afternoon train back to London. If not, she was facing what could best be described as a situation.

One of the habits James had encouraged during the therapy sessions was to look inward, rather than out. Beatrice had a tendency to apportion blame and identify external factors as the elements that grieved her. By examining her own reactions to outside elements, she had sometimes, but not always managed to head off a crisis. Now was as good a time as any for a full and frank assessment of her approach to this situation.

She was panicking, frightened witless by the thought that whoever had faked Sonny Das's suicide might have taken Gael. It was far too close to home. Gael was just like her, committed, driven and determined to root out the truth. The woman was simply doing her job. Rather than the fruitless phone calls and ever-wilder theories Beatrice sought as an explanation, she had to face the inconceivable and trust her instinct.

She was accustomed to thinking of journalists as allies. Yet her previous experience with newspaper editors in Spain and Finland made her suspicious of the people who pull their strings. Hedda was no exception, and Beatrice had good reason to mistrust the woman. By her own admission, no one but she and Gael knew the detail of this case. Second, she insisted on leaving the boardroom open when they broke for lunch. Later she made out that Gael often ate pizza with her, working late at Hedda's apartment. In which case, why would she give Gael a card with her home address and order a non-meat eater a Hawaiian pizza? In front of Theo and Beatrice, she had instructed Gael to get a cab from the newspaper offices. Later she told them Gael lived a half-hour bus ride away. Hedda was involved in Gael's disappearance, Beatrice knew it.

Therefore, she should be reported to the police. The question was, if Hedda had the ear of a high-ranking detective, how far did the net extend? Beatrice pressed her fingertips to her eyelids. Her upbringing and training leant towards the hierarchical. If you had a problem with the waiter, you asked for the manager. If an issue arose with a police officer, you took your grievance to his or her superior. Where could you go if you suspected the editor, senior detective and banking board were in collusion? If one didn't trust the bodies charged with holding the general public to account, what was left?

It was three in the morning when Beatrice finally closed the lid of her laptop and prepared for bed. She washed her face, cleaned her teeth and switched off the light. That was when the answer came.

The judiciary.

She got up again and within forty-five minutes, she'd found a name. Elsa di Tutte, senior judge and legal adviser to the European Union. She would do nicely.

When Theo rapped on the door at 09.30 the next morning, Beatrice awoke with a start from a dream about spiders. She rubbed her eyes and pulled on the hotel bathrobe to open the door. Her crotchety expression lifted when she saw her assistant had been to the patisserie and bought two huge milky coffees and an assortment of pastries.

"Any news?" she asked, ushering him inside.

"Gael's phone is still unobtainable. She's not been home nor arrived at work. Still, according to the doorman, she doesn't often get in before nine. Let's have breakfast and give him another call. If she's not there, what next?"

Beatrice fell on the pastries as she'd only had a single slice of pizza since yesterday lunchtime. Between bites, she explained her concerns and the urge to go up a level, where they could be reasonably sure of professionalism and a lack of corruption.

"Aren't you jumping the gun?" asked Theo. "We can't report Gael as missing until twenty-four hours after she was last seen. That means tonight."

"We're not going to report anything. We'll wait to see if Hedda does. If not, she's as guilty as I assume. I want to contact this judge and lay out my theory. If she's worth her salt, she'll start the ball bowling before the alarm is raised. What?" she asked, noting Theo's grave demeanour.

"Do you think something has happened to Gael?" he asked, his voice hushed.

Beatrice chose her answer deliberately. "I'm facing up to that eventuality."

"Me too. I like Gael and admire her ferocity. If they're willing to go after journos ..." Theo took a long draught of his coffee. "Two people on the trail of the story have gone missing. The first one turned up dead. If Hedda and her copper friend …"

"Bent copper friend," interrupted Beatrice.

"… possibly bent copper friend are trying to suppress the

story, there are two other people they need to silence. You and I are connected to both Sonny Das and Gael O'Connell, plus we know a reasonable amount of the detail. That puts us right in the path of danger."

"Exactly," said Beatrice, reaching for a croissant. "That's why I want to send Hedda an email this morning with our invoice attached and a generic well-wishing sign off. As if the outcome of the story no longer concerns us and we are back in London, getting on with our lives. We were only ever advisors on the case, we trust her to hand over to the authorities and have no reason to pursue it further."

Theo's gaze rested on her over his coffee cup. "Whereas the reality would be…?"

"Whereas the reality would be we are still actively working this case, so long as Elsa di Tutte is willing to pay us. Now, whether that's here or in London depends on the circumstances."

Theo looked at his watch. "It's getting on for ten. I'm going to find a payphone and call the newspaper to speak to Gael. If she's not there, let's activate Plan B."

"Capital idea. I'll try to get as an appointment with the di Tutte woman sometime today. Theo, two things. First, be extremely careful out on the street. Two, have you finished your breakfast? Because I wouldn't say no to that *pain au chocolat* if it was going begging."

"It's all yours."

Judge Elsa di Tutte was a very busy woman. Her schedule for the day, indeed whole week, was entirely booked out, according to her secretary. At the risk of being pushy, Beatrice replied asking for a fifteen-minute conversation over coffee break. She alluded to the fact her concerns covered business, journalism and law enforcement. All she could do then was cross her fingers. While she was waiting for a reply, she prepared an invoice and a breezy email for Hedda.

Dear Hedda

My most sincere apologies for rushing off last night. By the time we got to the hotel, I was fully recovered. That nut allergy catches me out at the most inconvenient times. I'm sorry to miss out on the pizza and even sorrier not to say goodbye to Gael. Please pass on my heartfelt thanks for everything she has done. I also wish to extend my gratitude to you for such kindness and hospitality during our stay.

We depart for London today so please find attached our invoice and expenses. Should you require physical receipts, I will pop them in the post. Good luck with handing your findings to the authorities and I hope you both receive the recognition you deserve for such tenacious reporting.

Kind regards

Beatrice Stubbs

She pressed send and noticed a reply from Judge di Tutte's office. The judge was having a working lunch that day and could spare Beatrice fifteen minutes for a coffee at one-fifteen. The secretary included an address and advised her to arrive several minutes early to clear security. In the eventuality she were late, the judge would be unable to accommodate her.

She confirmed immediately and waited until Theo returned before making any further plans. The second she opened the door, he shook his head.

"She's not at work, she's not at home and her mobile is still unobtainable. I really don't like the look of this. They wouldn't do another one, surely?"

"Depends how big this is. My belief is she's being 'talked to'. Person or persons unknown have removed her from her usual habitat and will be applying persuasive techniques to get her to drop the story."

"Persuasive techniques?" Theo asked.

"That's not a euphemism," said Beatrice. "They will begin

with a carrot, offering all kinds of inducements and rewards if only she will comply. If the girl has any sense, she will do just that. If she doesn't, they might use the nasty stick. I'd rather not think about that. The fact she has not yet returned is a very bad sign."

A loaded silence fell on the room until Beatrice focused on the task in hand. "Listen, we need to check out this morning and I got an appointment with the judge at quarter past one. She'll only give me fifteen minutes so I must be pitch perfect. Then we can get the 14.50 train to London. If I'm nippy on my toes, I could be home with Matthew for bedtime cocoa."

"What about Gael?"

"That's why I need to be pitch perfect. The justice department has to join the dots and connect Gael to Sonny Das. If they get involved, Gael will be far too hot to handle and returned to her desk by tomorrow morning." Beatrice sounded more confident than she felt. "How about a practice run with you after my shower? I want you to play an irascible old judge who can't wait to get rid of me. We'll rehearse till it's perfect and then head for the chambers. Oh, did you manage to get hold of Catinca?"

Theo's frown smoothed. "Yeah, she's pretty confident but the gig's not in the bag yet. Go have your shower. I'll sit here and get into character."

By midday, they were as ready as they would ever be. In the taxi across the city, they were silent. Beatrice mentally went over her pitch for the fiftieth time, recalling Theo's constructive criticism. 'Stick to the facts'. Her spiel was down to four minutes, giving an overview of the whole situation. 'Don't draw conclusions for her'. If required she could elaborate on particular points for another six, allowing the judge five more minutes for questions. 'Give her all the documentation with an executive summary.' She clutched the paperwork and checked her watch for the tenth time since they got in the cab.

"What do you want me to do while you're in there?" asked Theo.

"Find out a bit more about Gael. I know you looked into her professional background but try to find out who she is as a person. Partner? Family? Career trajectory? Something about that girl encourages trust and I want to know more. Oh my God, is this it? It looks bloody terrifying."

The Palais de Justice stood on Place Poelaert smack in the centre of the city. The word 'imposing' came nowhere near expressing its impact. A mixture of both grandiose and austere, even by gazing on it one felt judged and found wanting. She paid the driver and said goodbye to Theo, swallowing as she ascended the steps. Imagine if she were here to face trial, not just for a quick chat with a judge. The security procedure only intensified her nerves, even if it took no more than a few minutes.

The inside was no less dramatic. The main entry hall reminded her of New York's Grand Central Station with a gallery above, monumental staircases, Doric columns and a bust of Themis, Greek goddess of justice. Much as she would have loved to explore the majesty and intricate minutiae of the place, she was far too jittery about her imminent meeting to concentrate.

She announced herself at a reception desk and a pleasant young man gave her directions to the offices she sought. She was far too early but actually relieved about it. Better to sit half an hour on a wooden bench than come racing in, hot and stressed at the last moment. She found the wing which housed the judges' chambers and sat down nearby. A desk sat at a diagonal to the entrance, where presumably she was expected to announce herself. A secretary looked up at her. Beatrice gave her a polite smile then turned her attention to her phone.

Rather than re-reading her notes on the current case, she brought up a different set of pages: mantras suggested by James. These aphorisms were rescue remedies for the mind. When feeling panicky, insecure, threatened, numb or reckless, she could reach for a calming thought to recalibrate her thinking. Only effective when the first flutters occurred, these words could head off a spiral. However, if she really could not regain her balance, she would need more powerful weaponry.

The one she needed jumped out at her immediately. 'I do the right thing. For myself and for the whole world.' She closed her phone, bent her head, allowed her eyelids to fall and muttered the phrase over and over again.

"Are you talking to yourself?"

Beatrice's eyes shot open to see a short woman peering at her through a pair of owlish glasses. She wore a black two-piece with pearl buttons with tailored black trousers and lace-up ankle boots. Her grey hair was swept up into a pleat and in her earlobes were a pair of pearl earrings. Beatrice recognised her face from last night's research and got to her feet.

"Yes, I was. Well, sort of. That was a mantra to control my anxiety. You must be …"

"What are you anxious about?" the woman asked. Her tone was more practical and matter-of-fact than soft and empathetic.

Beatrice searched for a vapid reply but none came. "Meeting you," she said, lifting her gaze to the woman's deep-brown eyes. "I'm Beatrice Stubbs."

The woman's unsmiling stare bored into her. Of all the questions Beatrice expected, this one took her by surprise. "Have you eaten?"

"Not yet."

"Good. Come with me." She beckoned Beatrice to follow her. They passed the secretary, walked along a carpeted corridor at a rapid pace and stopped outside a door which could have been part of a mediaeval castle. Yet rather than wielding a wrought-iron key, Judge di Tutte pressed a key card to a pad and ushered Beatrice through the portal to the inner sanctum. Inside stood a dining-table with six chairs in front of two windows each opening onto a tiny balcony. Bookshelves lined every wall and the sounds of a string quartet came from hidden speakers. The sense of retreating from the world already soothed Beatrice's mind.

"When I've had enough of people, I take a working lunch. Only my secretary and I understand that means I want to enjoy an hour alone, uninterrupted by the chatter of imbeciles. It's my moment to shut out the world, maybe listen to a violin concerto, rally my strength and savour the act of eating. You look to me like the opposite of an imbecile. Perhaps we can share my seafood platter with brown bread and butter? While we eat, you can share your ... ah, here he is."

She answered the door to a knock Beatrice had missed, and thanked the man in French. Beatrice could understand enough of their exchange to know the judge was ordering something more. Di Tutte wheeled the trolley in herself and laid various platters on the end of the dining-table.

"My appointment," Beatrice began, "was scheduled for after your lunch. I had no intention of trying to steal your time or your food."

"That much I know. A professional always covers her tracks. When having a 'business lunch', I always order enough for two so I can legitimately claim I was having a meeting. I take the rest home in my lunchbox." She looked over her glasses. "Law-abiding, you see? That means we can eat, converse and if Henri chooses wisely, appreciate a glass of Chablis. Please sit down and make yourself comfortable. I understand you have something to tell me."

Beatrice's well-prepared pitch clocked in at just over four minutes. The remainder of the conversation took almost forty. Di Tutte asked quick-fire questions and Beatrice had to find the relevant information in her prepared folder without hesitation. Only when the judge was reading the documentation she had demanded could Beatrice snatch a bite to eat.

Henri returned with a half bottle of white wine, but Beatrice stuck to water. Her concentration could be nothing less than 100%. She swallowed a mouthful of mackerel pâté and gave di Tutte her full attention.

"Where do you think this journalist is now? Is she in danger?"

Beatrice shrugged. "I honestly don't know. My assumption is that she's being warned off. Everyone has a weak spot. Children, family, pets, that sort of thing. If Gael refuses to obey, they'll threaten someone or something she loves. I'm trying to find out more about her background as we eat."

Di Tutte winkled out a whelk, her expression thoughtful. "What do you expect me to do?"

For that one, Beatrice was ready. "In your position, you have access to neutral, unbiased investigators who are not on anyone's payroll. I want to hand over this information to someone I trust to use it effectively. In all honesty, when I first accepted this case, I believed we were dealing with a single fraudulent bank which bumped off a whistleblower. Now I fear this network is spread wider and is more deeply embedded into the fabric of society that I suspected. A private investigator and a journalist are no match for the scale of this operation. As a retired police officer and senior detective, I am placing my faith in the law. Everything I read describes you as a fearless prosecutor who invokes the full weight of the European Court of Justice when required. I couldn't think of anyone better with whom to share our findings." Exhausted by her speech, she reached out for her glass of water.

Di Tutte poured a second glass of wine and passed it over the table. "In that case, we should drink to justice."

Beatrice lifted her glass, unsure as to what the woman meant, but joined in the toast regardless. "To justice."

They ate in silence for another minute, then di Tutte patted her lips with her napkin. "I will open an enquiry. At this stage, not public and extremely discreet. So discreet, in fact, we will be a team of three. We will proceed with caution and release no smoke signals to alarm our targets. For your usual fee, I would like to retain you as an advisor, working with one of my finest prosecutors. Can you remain in Brussels for a few days, at least until we establish the inquiry?"

She'd delayed her return already and should really be in Upton St Nicholas supervising Matthew's care. But this was a gear change she had not seen coming. "Yes. I can extend my visit until Sunday and then I must progress with my other cases." *Whatever they might be.* "I'm at your disposal."

Di Tutte's face brightened and half her mouth lifted. "My secretary will arrange accommodation. I have a meeting in fifteen minutes for which I must prepare. Here is my card so you can contact me directly. Thank you for trusting me. I think I will enjoy working with you. Have a good afternoon and I will contact you soon."

Beatrice said goodbye to the small figure backlit by October sunshine, leaving her casework on the table. On the way down the stairs, she read the judge's card and raised her eyebrows. Rue de Champs Élysées 12A, 1050 Ixelles, Brussels. Champs Élysées, how very chic. If it was anything like the one in Paris, at least. Seemed being a judge was a nice little earner.

If Theo was to get the train home that afternoon, they had to hurry. Another mad dash across the city in a cab, during which they spoke in semi-code.

"Any news of our friend?" she said, as the driver pulled away.

"Some, but nothing contemporary or relevant to the current situation. Did you deliver the package?" he asked.

"I did and it was well received."

"So we are free to go?"

Beatrice nodded. "Sort of. You can go home today and I'll return on Sunday. My services are required in an advisory capacity. I hope you'll continue with your tasks remotely. Keep digging into her personal life. Until further information comes to light, that could be vital."

He clasped a hand around her wrist. "I'm not comfortable leaving you alone."

"I'll be very careful. Plus I have a heavyweight in my corner. Quick now, go check in or you'll miss the train. Take care, keep in touch and give my love to Catinca."

He jumped out into the cold, blew her a kiss and ran into Brussels Centraal. The taxi driver gave Beatrice a suspicious look in his mirror. He probably interpreted their conversation as sufficiently suspicious to mark them as spies or drug dealers or worse.

"*Merci, monsieur. Maintenant, Place de Marolles, s'il vous plaît.*"

To her delight, di Tutte's secretary had booked her into Apartements Minimes, a five-star self-catering establishment, no more than ten minutes' walk from the Palais de Justice. Beatrice adored apartments. Hotels always carried a low-level of guilt – all those sheets, towels, cleaners – whereas an apartment was a temporary home. Her bedroom, living-area and kitchenette became hers in a matter of minutes. And this level of luxury surpassed all previous experiences.

After the customary cooing and exploration of her new environment, Beatrice attended to her worries in order of urgency. Where was Gael? How was Matthew? Why had the judge chosen to retain her as an advisor? Was Matthew's carer up to scratch? Which angle of enquiry should she take, or none at all until di Tutte gave instructions? What possible excuse could she offer to Marianne and Tanya? Was communication between her and Theo secure?

She plugged in her laptop and accessed the hotel Wi-Fi. Fifteen emails. She skimmed the lot and found nothing of importance. Gael took priority. She grabbed her phone, hid her number and called the paper. Gael O'Connell was 'working remotely' according to reception. Her mobile still responded with the unobtainable message and there was nothing from Hedda in response to her latest. She scrolled news sites for any developments in three languages, but nothing had broken on the subject of Sonny Das, Banque Franck et Schneider or Gael O'Connell. She chose not to use a search engine for any of those names, just in case anyone conflated her curiosity with persistence.

Instead, she called home. Of all the voices in the world, she wanted to hear Matthew's.

"Hello, Bailey speaking."

"Matthew! It's Beatrice. Just checking in to make sure you're behaving yourself."

There was a silence.

"Matthew, is everything all right?"

"I'm sorry to break this to you over the telephone, but I have sad news."

Beatrice clutched her throat, her pulse beating at an alarming rate. "What is it? What's happened? Matthew?"

"Our dearly beloved Dumpling has departed. I was not present but I believe it was peaceful. The funeral will take place tomorrow, after school. Luke has written a eulogy which is at once heartfelt and forward-looking. Poor old chap."

"Oh, no! That's so sad. He was in fine fettle when I left."

"Exactly. No signs of any ailment that I could see. He wasn't the most active creature and yet a very soothing companion. I shall miss him. But as Gabriel said, he had a jolly good innings. Where are you now?"

"Still in Brussels because I have been asked to stay on until Sunday. We've been forced to escalate this case. I'm afraid I won't be able to make the funeral."

"Sunday! That's another three days!"

She squeezed her eyes shut. "I know. My intention was to

return home this morning, but complications arose. Theo is on the Eurostar right now, heading for London. How are you getting along with your home help?"

Matthew released a profound sigh. "Naturally, she changes the subject. Axel is a most reassuring presence. Very well read, you know. We have the most stimulating discussions. Even Marianne seems to be defrosting. I think you'll like him. I most certainly do."

"In that case, how could I not? Is Marianne there? I'd like a word about the weekend."

"She is. I'll give her a shout. Hurry home, Old Thing. Without you, I find every obstacle twice as challenging."

"I will, I promise. Take good care, my love and see you on Sunday."

It took some cajoling but Marianne agreed to stay over for the weekend. Beatrice ended the call with a familiar sense of guilt, as though she was evading her responsibilities and expecting other people to pick up the slack. Probably because that was nothing more than the truth.

Chapter 20

From the train, Theo called Catinca twice. She didn't pick up. He made up his mind to go to her shop and refused to worry. He spent the rest of the time reading what he could about Gael O'Connell. Her social media activity turned up a significant other. She was still close to a university friend called Mikhael Vakala. Theo sent him a direct message, expressing his concern for her welfare and asking the guy for a chat. The response was swift. Vakala blocked him. Another dead end.

Rather than go home, he took the 205 bus to Liverpool Street, heading for Spitalfields. He couldn't shake the sense of discomfort about the lack of communication between him and Catinca since yesterday. Then he reprimanded himself for such egotistical thinking. Her mind was elsewhere, focused on the job of a lifetime instead of him. She must be on tenterhooks, waiting for confirmation of her new commission.

He strolled up Bishopsgate, ignoring the Halloween decorations lighting up the afternoon gloom, keenly anticipating the look on Catinca's face when he walked into the shop. As he drew closer, he saw the lights were off and blinds drawn. Radu was shut? At half past four in the afternoon? He knocked on the door in case she was in the atelier upstairs but no one answered. Next door was a coffee shop where Catinca often popped in for an oat milk latte. He didn't remember the names of either hipster behind the counter even though he'd been there on several occasions.

"Hi. My name's Theo, a friend of Catinca's. I just dropped by to see her and the shop is closed. Have you seen her today?"

The two men looked quizzically at one another and back to Theo. The one with the tallest hair spoke. "Do you know, I don't think I have. She's certainly not been in for her usual. Come to think of it, I don't think I saw her yesterday, either. Unless I missed something. Al?"

Al, the one with the dense beard, shook his head. "No, her shop has been closed all day, which I thought was odd. Last time I saw her was yesterday morning when she was opening up. I shouted a good morning as I cycled past and she wished me the same."

"Right. I'll swing by her flat and see if she's there. Thanks for your help."

Despite the cold and his aching leg, Theo decided to walk up the road to Shoreditch. He tried her mobile one more time, reluctant to turn up unannounced because she might be too busy for visitors. Once again, no reply. By the time he got to her building, rush hour was in full swing. Pavements were crowded, traffic was stop-starting its way along the street and everyone seemed to be in a desperate hurry. On top of all that, it started to rain.

Catinca's new apartment was a real step up from her previous lodgings. Instead of sharing a first-floor flat above a supermarket with two nocturnal games designers, Catinca had a one-bedroom place to herself on the sixth floor of a new build. It even had a balcony with views over the city and was close enough for her to walk to work. He rang the buzzer, half expecting another dead end, but she answered.

"Hello? Who is this?"

"It's me, Theo."

"Theo," she said, her voice oddly flat. "You'd better come up."

He got into the lift, now convinced it was not his imagination. There was something wrong. Could it really be all over before it had started? What had he done wrong this time, apart from dashing off to Brussels right after their second date? The lift doors opened with a ping and Theo stepped out to see Catinca's apartment door open just a crack.

When he moved into the light, she opened the door fully and Theo stopped short. In all the time he'd known her, he had never once seen her without full make-up, accessories and stylish clothes. But now her face was scrubbed clean, her hair pulled back in a loose ponytail and she wore an oversized sweatshirt and tracksuit bottoms. On her feet were slippers shaped like some kind of animal. Theo wasn't sure if they were supposed to be mice or baby seals. He looked at her face, which was pale and drawn.

"Are you OK?" Theo said, in a low murmur, afraid of the answer.

Catinca shook her head and gestured for him to come in.

He crossed the threshold and dumped his rucksack on the floor. More than anything, he wanted to take her into his arms but something made him hesitate and let her take the lead.

"What is it? Are you sick?"

Without answering, she led the way into the living room and pointed at the armchair. She sat on the sofa and judging by the state of it, she'd been there for a long time. Her laptop was open on the coffee table, surrounded by mugs and glasses and scrunched-up tissues. On the sofa were a duvet and a pile of pillows. She nestled into them and folded her arms. She couldn't seem to meet his eyes.

"I'm sorry just to turn up like this, but I couldn't reach you on the phone and the shop was closed. I was worried."

"Yeah, I know. Sorry for avoiding your calls. Something happened and I had some thinking to do. I couldn't be distracted. Still not decided what to do yet." She sighed. "Just listen for a minute and please don't judge me. OK?"

"Of course not." His mind scrambled to find an explanation. She had met someone else. The wedding dress commission had fallen through. She changed her mind about having a relationship with him because of his job. The shop had been burgled. She was leaving Britain to return to Romania. Devastating news regarding her health had come in that morning's post.

"Yesterday afternoon, I had my interview. First part went brilliantly. Bride fell in love with all my designs and agreed to hire me. Ten minutes after his daughter left, Lord Tobias Trottiscliffe sexually assaulted me. In struggle, I fought him off and gave him a nosebleed. He told me I'd regret that and I ran out of there as fast as I could. Later, when he was gone, I went back to get my portfolio. Then I turned up at Adrian and Will's place. Mostly to see friendly faces but also to ask how to report sexual assault." She gathered herself with a shaky breath.

Theo's whole body chilled. He'd seen that guy on TV. A big bloke, fat and heavy, with a sense of smugness. As if he didn't play by everyone else's rules. Compared to Catinca's stature, he was a gorilla. To use his physical bulk and celebrity status to molest this vulnerable woman made Theo both enraged and nauseous.

Catinca took a sip of water and continued. "Thing is, on top of his groping, I thought I lost the job. But his daughter still wants me to make her dress. Adrian wants me to report him to protect other women. Will wants me to talk to a Met officer about what happened. And I … I want two things. I want to stop him doing that to women. But I want to create that dress. See what I mean about some thinking to do.?"

His disgust for Trottiscliffe made Theo open his mouth before he had thought about what to say. "No, I don't. It's obvious what you have to do. I can't stand the idea of him pawing at you. I'm glad you made his nose bleed. He deserves a lot worse." He stood up and paced towards the window. "You can't let people like that get away with it, no matter who they are. You should report that macho prick as soon as possible. You should have done it yesterday."

Catinca was silent for a long time, watching Theo pace. His emotions were in such a state of agitation, it took him a while to register the stony expression on her face. He replayed his words and realised he had not stuck to his side of the bargain. *Don't judge me*, she said. What had he done? Judged her, made it about himself and told her what to do. No expression of sympathy for what she had suffered, just an insensitive selfish response to his own feelings – so who was he calling a macho prick?

He came back to the armchair and looked across the table into her cold eyes. "Catinca, I'm sorry. You've just suffered a physical invasion of your personal space and the first three people you trust with that information tell you what you should do. I'm sorry for my shitty reaction but I'm a hundred times sorrier that you had to suffer that in the first place. I wish I'd been there so it had never even happened. I just hate the thought …"

Her eyes flashed with anger. "It's not all about you. Anyway, now you know why you couldn't explain over the phone. I'm gonna need some time to process this and decide how to move on. I'm meeting that copper friend of Beatrice's in the morning. The down payment for the wedding dress should be in my bank account first thing tomorrow. My problem, no one else's. My decision, no one else's. Look, you better go now and I'll call you when I'm ready."

"Catinca, listen, please. I want to apologise."

She got out of her duvet nest and walked towards the door, her huge sweatshirt swamping her body. "Give me the weekend to think things over. Right now, I need some time alone."

She handed him his rucksack and he took it, frantically trying to think of some way to rescue the situation. "I'm so sorry," he said.

"Me too," she replied and closed the door behind him.

Theo trudged along the streets, his mood as grim as the skies above him. His anger had nowhere to go. He hated Trottiscliffe, despised himself and for someone dedicated to pacifism, struggled with an urge for vengeance. As if goading him, the weather kicked him while he was down. With so many tall buildings either side of the street and the roads themselves clogged with traffic, you'd think the streets of London would protect you from the weather. Tonight, that was not the case. The wind cannoned into bus stops, spun litter into mini tornadoes and lashed pedestrians as if intent on giving them a good thrashing. The beads at the end of Theo's plaits struck his face more than once and when one particular gust shoved him sideways, two plaits whipped into his eyes. He sheltered in a doorway, wincing and pressing a palm over his face. The pain subsided after several seconds and he wiped away involuntary tears.

In his cross-body bag, he found a beanie hat which would keep his hair from assaulting his face. The wind cranked it up a notch and threw in some threatening rain. A woman walking ahead of him opened an umbrella which immediately blew inside out and flew off across Commercial Street to splay itself against the windows of Superdrug. Theo powered on, ignoring that small part of his brain which recalled the sunny streets and mellow beaches of northern Mallorca.

He turned onto Wheler Street, past the graffitied hoardings and speed-walked towards the railway bridge. Five minutes to home. The bridge sheltered him from the rain for a minute and he wiped his face with a cold hand. The growl of a big bike echoed around the brickwork and to Theo's disbelief, it mounted the pavement and drove right at him, forcing him to leap into the street, into the path of a pizza delivery van. The driver slammed on the brakes and swung the van right, missing Theo but catching his bag with the wing mirror. Theo was jerked onto the bonnet then slid to the ground. The driver got out, rushing to help him up. Once they'd established Theo was unhurt, they agreed in the most colourful terms that the bike rider was of limited intelligence and shouldn't be allowed on the streets. The pizza driver wished him a good evening and Theo, wet, bruised, shaken and sad, made his way home.

Chapter 21

Late into Thursday evening, Beatrice's mobile rang while she was watching a television programme in French. She couldn't understand more than 50% of it, but it was a nature programme about wildcats so the pictures spoke for themselves.

The voice on the other end was also French accented but speaking English to a level which put her own vocabulary to shame. Monsieur Hervé Corbusier was a senior prosecutor on Judge Elsa di Tutte's team, assigned to investigate a possible instance of institutional corruption. His comprehension of the facts was completely accurate and his analysis impressive. He could only have learned of the detail that afternoon yet his mind had taken mere hours to get up to speed with what Beatrice, Theo and Gael had unearthed over several days. He was charmingly polite, apologised for disturbing her so late and invited her to a breakfast meeting at the Palais de Justice the following morning.

She agreed eagerly and he insisted upon sending a car, no matter how many times she assured him she could walk. After he had wished her an excellent evening, she put down the phone and looked forward with anticipation to the next day. Then she returned to her wildcats.

Before she went to sleep that night, she spent a moment writing in her mood diary, took her medication and lay in the blackness to remember a tatty old grey cat with absinthe eyes.

The sound of her mobile dragged her from the deepest of sleeps. It took a second to recall where she was and she reached for the phone on the bedside table. The display said 06:15 and the caller was H. Corbusier. Beatrice blinked at the screen. Their meeting was for nine o'clock. Waking her three hours ahead of time was ridiculous.

"Hello?"

"Ms Stubbs, I profoundly regret disturbing your rest. I would never have presumed to intrude at such an hour had not news reached my desk of the most extreme urgency. May I entreat you to join me at the Palais at your earliest convenience? A car has been dispatched to your apartment block and will be waiting as soon as you are ready. Please accept my sincere apologies for the rudest of awakenings."

"Um, oh. Yes, I'll be there ASAP. This news ... I don't suppose you can tell me over the phone? Or give me a hint if it's good or bad?"

"Your supposition is correct. This is why I was forced to summon you to the Palais at this ungodly hour. There we can be assured of secure communications. Regarding the nature of my information, I believe you have a saying in English: 'Good news waits till morning.' Currently, it is still dark. I look forward to meeting you in person."

Beatrice threw off the duvet and headed for the shower, her mood grim.

The driver must have been waiting for half an hour in order to drive her from her apartments to the Palais, a journey of fewer than two minutes. He dropped her at a rear entrance and she thanked him with a blush at the extravagance. He simply wished her a good day. Her door opened and a security guard helped her out. She followed him through silent halls and echoing corridors until they reached the annex she recognised from yesterday. The guard swiped her in and showed her to a room several doors down from that of Judge di Tutte.

A man opened the door with a relieved smile. "Ms Stubbs. Hervé Corbusier. I am delighted to make your acquaintance." He bowed and she did likewise.

He was much younger than she expected, early thirties, perhaps. His hair was black, so dark it was almost blue, cut short on the back and sides, but slicked into place at the top. His suit was blue and his shoes black. For someone dragged out of bed in the wee hours, he seemed fresh and well rested. He gave her a broad smile and his dark eyes crinkled with real warmth.

"Same to you, Mr Corbusier. After last night's conversation, I can see you have a fine mind. I'm grateful to the judge for allocating you to the case."

"The privilege is mine, let me assure you. This way."

She followed him into the boardroom and placed her handbag near the end of the twelve-seater table, which was polished to a gleam.

His heels made an odd hollow sound on the parquet floor as he walked over to the coffee machine. Beatrice guessed he wore elevator shoes.

"About this news ..."

"Yes, you must be impatient to hear, that I understand. One cappuccino and a glass of water, then we will waste no more time." The machine gurgled away and the scent of freshly brewed coffee reached Beatrice's nostrils, acting like a balm.

He placed a little tray in front of her containing a cup of coffee, a shot glass of water and a dinky little biscuit in cellophane. "Thank you. I need this like you can't imagine."

"I believe I can. Without my morning espresso, I barely function. To the news. As I implied during our telephone conversation, the information I received two hours ago was not positive. A woman was killed in a hit-and-run accident late

Wednesday night in a troublesome suburb outside Brussels. It took the police a while to identify her, as she had no personal possessions. But a few hours ago, I learned they matched her appearance to a recent missing person's report. That report was filed by us and the dead woman's name is Gael O'Connell."

Beatrice clasped her hands together. "No!"

Her dread about the impending news – was it Theo? Was it Gael? Was it Judge di Tutte? – owed much to an overactive imagination. To discover one of her grimmest fears had been realised seemed implausible. Gael. Earthy, lively, obsessive, animated Gael could not possibly be dead. Beatrice's skin cooled and she placed her hands over her eyes.

"I'm afraid so. My condolences. You had worked closely with her on this case and this must be a terrible shock. Do you need a moment?"

Grief and shock were no help. Action was needed. Her sadness for Gael would have a moment of its own. "No, I need some answers. This stinks. Sonny Das blows the whistle and suddenly runs to Bruges where he hangs himself. Or someone else does it for him. Gael follows the same trail, learns enough to deliver a massive exposé and winds up dead when she should have been eating a pizza with us. Two other people assisted on that investigation – my assistant Theo Wolfe and yours truly – where does that leave us? Our first line of enquiry must be into Hedda, Gael's editor. She is as dodgy as they come. Does the judge know about this?"

A soft knock came at the door and an older man wheeled in a trolley, filled with delicious aromas. But Beatrice was too angry to be hungry.

"Monsieur Corbusier, we have got a tiger by the tail and must be prepared for a very dirty fight."

Corbusier thanked the trolley man for unloading the platters and waited for him to depart before replying to Beatrice.

"That is where our opinions diverge, Ms Stubbs. This

enquiry must be as transparent and clean as possible. To that end, I have a proposal I would like to present to Judge di Tutte tomorrow morning, subject to your approval. Please, help yourself to some breakfast. Our kitchens have a well-deserved reputation for pastries. There is also yoghurt and fruit should you prefer something lighter." He bit into something that looked like a sausage roll covered with nuts and made a few notes on the papers beside him.

The raspberry tarts did look enticing. Beatrice placed one on a plate along with one of the nutty things, just in case she liked it. "Your proposal, Monsieur Corbusier?"

He finished chewing and took a swig of coffee. "My proposal is to call for the cavalry. The investigation into the death of Ms O'Connell will be carried out by our own police, here in Brussels. However, the enquiry into malfeasance at Banque Franck et Schneider, at the newspaper and possibly into senior levels of police or politics, should be a European-wide initiative. We need the support of experienced investigators across the continent. You know as well as I that this operation is international and therefore requires a unified response. If Belgium clamps down, they will move to one of the other EU countries, maybe as far as Switzerland or Turkey. This is why I believe we should employ a task force. By which I mean a team of experts who can take your excellent ground work to another plane. This is no longer an exposé but a wide-ranging criminal investigation. If the judge gives me permission to proceed in this direction, I would very much like your advice as an experienced senior detective with a track record across Europe. Our task force must be hand-picked for their expertise and professionalism. That's the only way we can break open the inner circle."

His words sent a thrill of excitement through Beatrice. If Corbusier was serious about an international team, he must have access to considerable funds. On a previous case, Beatrice had discovered connections between various arms of a French family business. Even though she'd been on her own, supported by a young Romanian fashion designer, she had indeed brought the organisation to justice. This was on a different scale. They needed forensic accountants, lawyers, detectives, experts in digital communication, financial analysts and pan-European jurisdiction. Their only hope was the court of law and Corbusier had an air of confidence.

"That sounds like a brilliant plan. Expensive, but brilliant. Do you think the judge will really throw her weight behind such a proposal? This exceeds my expectations."

Corbusier allowed himself a quiet smile. "Also mine. The judge will support us if we can present her with a coherent, realistic and practical plan with full costings. This is where I think we can box clever, Ms Stubbs. To hire freelancers for every aspect of this case would be risky in both financial and security terms. My instinct is to ask for collaboration from other countries by loaning us their experts. Politically and in the eyes of the media, this has all the hallmarks of why the bloc is a force for the good. Do you see where I'm going with this?"

She gave a nod, barely able to form her exploding thoughts into speech. "I certainly do!"

"Each expert operates on a need-to-know basis, reporting directly to the directors of the enquiry." He flicked a finger between them to indicate who he meant. "They do not communicate with one another and have no idea there are other specialists working on the same case. Only then can we guarantee discretion."

"Makes sense. Any information beneficial to other operatives can be passed via us. No idle talk and absolute confidentiality."

"Exactly. There is an additional reason I want us to work hand in glove," said Corbusier. "I'm interested in how a detective's mind works. By the way, is your assistant going to join us?"

"Theo? No, he's gone home to London. I'm not sure a detective's mind is very different from that of a prosecutor. What do you think I can add?"

Corbusier brushed crumbs from his fingers. "A prosecutor would never have considered returning to that hostel in Bruges, for example. Which is where your assistant took a witness statement from a resident, I understand. Very thorough and I commend you. It would not occur to someone like myself to visit Banque Franck et Schneider either. Your dogged persistence is an education. I sit here, fuelled by caffeine and chocolate, feeling very pleased with myself. Circumstances that usually prove fatal. Where am I going wrong? What have I missed? Tell me your concerns about this proposal and let us shape it into the most perfect form before presenting it to the judge. Would you like more coffee? I can see you appreciate our patisserie, so you must try the brioche."

The sun had risen and spilled a rosy light across the table. Beatrice took a slice and Corbusier poured her coffee. "Well, even if you did drag me out of bed at an appalling hour of the day, you were absolutely right to do so. I think our collaboration could prove most fruitful. Let's take it step by step, make a risk assessment and formulate an optimum outcome. Good gracious, would you listen to my hot air! Next thing you know, I'll be standing at the whiteboard brandishing a laser pen. Although, that's not a bad idea. We are looking for links, connections and as a result, influence. Where do you want to begin?"

With a few taps on his tablet, Corbusier managed to make a screen rise from the centre of the table. It took several minutes before Beatrice realised what he was doing. His fingers dabbed and punched and swiped his tablet while the screen filled with images, lines denoting connections and groupings to show where one individual's work, life, history overlapped with another's. She was enthralled. It was like a brain sketched out on a widescreen.

"It's immensely complex. Someone must have designed all this. Corruption like this isn't organic. There has to be a mastermind, or mistress-mind, a puppeteer pulling all the strings," Beatrice mused.

"You're right. An architect is directing operations. Whoever he or she is, they feel invincible, assured of their position and laughing at all attempts to shut their criminal activities down. Probably holed up in Monaco or Belize, I expect. Or am I being over-imaginative? I do watch rather too much James Bond."

"No such thing as too much James Bond. My money is on the CEO or chairman of the bank. The man who originally employed me, Christopher Sheldon, is just a lackey whereas we need to track down the monkey grinder."

Corbusier seemed to chew over her comment, then said, "Lackey or not, we should look very carefully at Mr Sheldon's role." He tapped the screen. "For example, he has a helicopter licence. What on earth for? A junior role can sometimes reveal more than we think. That reminds me, I would be interested to talk to your assistant. Might I have his contact details?"

Beatrice found one of Theo's cards in her handbag and passed it over. "My primary concern is Gael's death. Are the police treating it as murder?"

"If not, I shall certainly instruct them to do so. Now to our task list. Here's how I think we could make best progress."

Corbusier shared duties between them and seemed to undertake the more menial tasks, while giving Beatrice the more exciting job of choosing specialists she personally recommended. They worked side by side the whole day, as their plan took shape. Their single-minded focus energised Beatrice and she found herself liking Corbusier as a colleague. If only there had been more men like him when she first started out. She liked him even more when he ordered a robust lunch to be served in the boardroom.

In the afternoon, they worded a cagey email to police forces Europe-wide, asking for the loan of suitable personnel for a potential collaborative project. Once it was sent, they sat grinning at each other across the table. Daylight was fading and Corbusier switched on the lights. He glanced at his watch and the computer screen in disbelief. "It's half past five! You have been here far too long and deserve a rest. Judge di Tutte will hear our proposals at nine tomorrow morning. Are we fully prepared, do you think, Ms Stubbs?"

"We are ready, Monsieur Corbusier, and I for one cannot wait to get started."

The man beamed at her with such warmth, it came across as a hug. "Five minutes and I will call for a car to take you to your quarters. I know you think it bureaucratic foolishness, but I have your welfare in mind. It might be better if you don't leave the hotel this evening. Buckle up, Ms Stubbs, we're in for quite a ride!"

She laughed at his eager enthusiasm, wondering who he reminded her of. Probably every officer of the law the second they caught the first whiff of pursuit. Quite a ride, indeed. She just hoped the legal profession provided safety belts.

Chapter 22

It was tempting to stay on the Tube. Sort of fitting, in a way. She could go round and round the Circle line, just as she had done on Wednesday, after Lord Tobias Trottiscliffe had tried to coerce her into an intimate act. Sort of fitting in another way in that her thoughts bounced between the same few points over and over again, making no progress and hitting the same dead ends as if her brain were a pinball machine.

She wanted to talk to someone and ideally that someone would not be a man. Her conversation that morning with Dawn had been quite different to the others she'd had on the same subject. Adrian, Will and Theo were all too close and their affection for her made them want to act. She knew that and she appreciated it. But Dawn listened dispassionately, offered questions about her feelings, made no judgements and asked Catinca what she wanted to do. She *asked* Catinca, not told her. And when it came to a realistic assessment of the facts, Dawn pulled no punches.

You're a great witness, clear about what happened and accurate on detail. If you wanted to press charges, you'd have a decent chance of convincing a jury. But it still comes down to your word against his, your brief against an expensive legal team who will go all out to find anything that makes you look unreliable. There's a chance your going public will trigger other women who've suffered at his hands to come forward but that's not something you can count on. Even if they did, would they crack under pressure or accept a pay-off for their silence?

All this is hypothetical because if you take on the commission to make his daughter's wedding dress, you've got no chance. You accept his money, but accuse him of sexual assault? This is how these abusers operate. Attractive lure – I can make you famous! – then sexual harassment and sufficient legal back-up to make sure you've got nowhere to turn. Catinca, I'll give you all the support I can, but this is one occasion where you can't have your cake and eat it. Take him down or make the dress. It's up to you.

As soon as she got to her shop, she checked her bank account online. Sure enough, the Trottiscliffe down payment had been received. She was five grand better off than she'd been that morning. Not once in her life had she possessed so much money. If she proceeded, she would be paid double that. Years of dreaming, fantasising about making her passion her career, and here it was. Hard work had earned her the big break, the golden opportunity and all the other clichés about grabbing the one chance. She scowled at her own choice of vocabulary. Not grabbing, not snatching but accepting a well-paid assignment. Pocketing the cash and promoting her career.

Pocketing the cash of a man who felt entitled to grope and fondle anyone who took his fancy. Keeping quiet about his inappropriate behaviour meant enabling him to continue. As Dawn had told her that morning, the more they got away with it, the further they would go. She couldn't do it. She stood up and looked out of the window at the rainy street.

She had to do it. Her designs were making if not quite headlines then column inches. All the work she put in to get this far could not be thrown away on her prissy principles. Anyway, she need never see the guy ever again. With five grand in her bank account, she'd cooperate with Agnessa on the condition her father was never present, and reap all the glory of making the bride look the most beautiful she would ever look in her life.

Her thought processes were no straighter since getting off the Tube. People were looking at the shop window, maybe even considering coming in. She switched on the lights, turned the sign to 'We're Open!' and waited. By five o'clock, she'd sold three scarves, a printed shirt and one of her most beautiful dresses, and nipped next door for an oat milk latte. It was crunch time. Now, she needed a female friend to listen, to hypothesise and to help her work out exactly what she was feeling.

She called Tamsin.

Friday night rush hour in October was no fun at the best of times. But now temperatures had dropped to an unpleasant 5° from last weekend's balmy 18°, it was unrelentingly miserable. Thankfully, she only had to walk a few streets to Dionysus and then she was halfway home. Because she used to be assistant manager and was responsible for the original design concept, whenever she turned up at Dionysus, she was welcomed like a local celebrity. That's why she rarely visited during the day if she wanted to have a quiet chat with a friend. But the evening bar staff and wine emporium employees were largely recent hires and few had a clue who Catinca was. Adrian would have left for home and Tamsin was due off shift at six. The Shoreditch clientele would be far too busy talking shop on Friday night to come and bother two women having a quiet chat in the corner.

Tamsin had reserved them a barrel-table in the alcove. Far enough from the bar to be private and with sufficient distance from the kitchen to deter casual chatters. With their two dark heads bent over a bottle of rosé in confidential conversation, only a crass git would dream of interrupting. She opened her arms to hug Tamsin. Their embrace was warm and lasted a few seconds longer than usual.

"Missed you," mumbled Catinca.

"Missed you too. You OK, babe?"

"Gimme a minute. Hair's looking good."

Tamsin twirled. "Found a place in New Cross what does the best braiding I ever seen. You like the colours?" Each braid bore a thread of bright synthetic hair, subtle but stunning.

"Your hair is work of art. Gives me design ideas, innit? What we drinking?"

"Pink bubbles. Sit down. I ain't gonna rush you, so we can talk about the weather, Ezra's cringe-worthy shirt or my fabulous hair. My personal preference is your take on my festive theme."

Every other pub in the area sported rubber bats, fake cobwebs and cheap witches hats to tip a cheesy wink at Halloween. Tamsin had gone all-out Mexican Day of the Dead. Painted sugar skulls, silk roses, the specials blackboard chalked like a gravestone, battery-powered candles in red holders and an 'altar' displaying a selection of framed photographs, but rather than lost souls, each depicted a member of staff cradling a bottle of wine.

Catinca was amazed. "You outdone yourself! It's classy but wicked. One of these days, I'm gonna poach you to work for me. What is it with Ezra's shirt?"

"You tell me, babe." She poured them both a glass.

Catinca looked across at Ezra, his sculpted beard, quiffed hair and shirt, a patchwork of Tarantino movie posters. "It's an insult to anyone with eyes," she observed.

"Taste-signalling from someone who ain't got none," agreed Tamsin. "He said it was a statement."

"Mate, he's a nice guy but a fashion fuckwit."

"I arksed him what the statement was. He said it was open to interpretation. I told him I interpreted it as textile vomit, know what I mean?"

Catinca snorted with laughter, which somehow managed to release tears. She patted a napkin to her lower lids, hoping to rescue her make-up, and blurted out the whole story.

It took a long time. Two glasses of sparkling rosé long, to be precise. When she'd finished, Tamsin reached a hand over the barrel.

Catinca took it and their fingers intertwined. "Babe, that is fucked up. But I gotta say, giving him a Glasgow Kiss? You are my queen."

They sat in silence, clutching hands for a moment until a shadow loomed over their table. Ezra placed another bottle of rosé on the table, pressed his fingers to his lips, waved a palm over the bottle like a magician and walked away.

"Twat," said Tamsin.

"Twat," agreed Catinca. "Still, more pink bubbles so I ain't complaining." She sighed, a certain weight dropping from her after telling Tamsin everything, even the nasty details she'd only been able to share with Dawn. Maybe the more she talked about it, the less power it would hold. She smiled at her friend. "You're a good listener."

"Listening and drinking? I'm a natural. Question is, what you gonna do?"

Catinca screwed up her face. "Whole situation is sodding mess and whichever way I jump, I'm in the shit. Report him, go to court, bring him down and wreck my reputation. Don't report, make dress, take his cash and enable pervert to keep messing with women. Anyway, it wasn't Glasgow Kiss. I used back of my head and not on purpose."

"Not in my version, babe," Tamsin replied. "In my version you were wearing DMs and stamped on his hand-tooled loafers then cracked your forehead right on the bridge of his nose. While he lay bleeding on the floor, you spat on him and kicked him in the bollocks."

Catinca couldn't laugh. "No, it wasn't like that. He's impressive and powerful and I seen him on telly. I froze and tried to be polite. He knew I wasn't going to fight because he's Sir Tobias sodding Trottiscliffe. Listen, Tamsin, I replayed it over and over and tried to rewrite the script. But it don't work. He was bigger, posher and held all the cards. I can't win. He didn't physically screw me, but in real terms, he already has. No happy endings here."

All the humour left Tamsin's face. "He scared you, didn't he?"

Catinca closed her eyes. "Still does."

They sat in silence for a several minutes, sipping their bubbles, both lost in thought.

"You got the cash, yeah?" asked Tamsin, her eyes reflecting the brake lights from the wet street outside. "They already paid you?"

"A down payment. I signed the contract electronically so I got a third of the money in my account. If I change mind, thirty days to pull out and same goes for them. Next step, they release next third for me to buy materials. Final third when I deliver dress to bride's satisfaction. I either return cash and make complaint now, or it's too late."

"What do you want, Tink?"

The nickname made Catinca smile. "To make the dress. To stop that bastard. Can't do both. Gotta choose what's most important to me. Both are most important to me."

Tamsin leaned over the barrel and caught Catinca's hand again. "Let me arks you a question. What if you could do both? Make the dress *and* stop that bastard? That way, you'd tear down his reputation and walk away with his cash. It's just a matter of timing, babe. You've got contacts, know what I'm saying?"

Catinca stared at her. "What do you mean?"

"You're friendly with a copper, an ex-copper and a private detective. Handy, that. You're also best mates with one of the most devious minds in the business. And she's got a wicked plan." She held up her hand for a high five.

They slapped palms. "I got no idea what you're talking about, but I feel better already. What wicked plan?"

"Not here and not now. You free tomorrow night or are you seeing Theo?"

Catinca shook her head. "I told him I needed weekend off. You want to come over and I'll cook?"

"I'll come over but I'm cooking. We'll have ackee and salt fish and plan our strategy. We're gonna nail that git, don't you worry. Time for a toast, babe." She raised her glass and noted Ezra doing the same from behind the bar.

They turned to him with broad smiles, chinked their glasses together and both muttered the same word out of the corner of their mouths. "Twat."

Chapter 23

By seven am on Saturday, Beatrice was impatient to start her day. She had worked until ten in the evening last night, sifting through all of the proposals received from police forces across the continent and forwarded to her by Corbusier. The meeting with the judge was scheduled for nine, and Beatrice buzzed with optimism and energy.

Her conscience had kicked her awake just before six. Overnight, thirty new applications were waiting to be read and evaluated before making her way to the Palais de Justice. Apartment hotels were all very well in the sense of privacy and independence. The only problem was there was no such thing as room service. Since Beatrice had been absent all day yesterday, there was no food whatsoever in the fridge. Just a half-drunk bottle of orange juice and a litre of milk. She made herself a milky coffee and opened the files sifting them into piles of yes, no and maybe.

The activity made her feel very old and out of touch. With a whimsical fondness for her previous career, she imagined she might recognise at least one or two of these names. Not a single one. She wondered if she would be allowed to lead one of the teams. After all, it was her work that had brought them this far. Fantasising about a collaboration with the justice department made it a struggle to keep concentration but finally she placed all her files in her work bag and checked the time. Nearly eight. A car would collect her at 08.45 so she had forty minutes to shower and dress. God knows when she was likely to get any breakfast.

On impulse, she sent a message to James. If there was an outside chance of talking to her counsellor on a Saturday, she would take it. A whining from her subconscious was growing harder to ignore. To her immense relief, he replied immediately, offering her half an hour over lunch. She agreed with gushing gratitude and set an alarm for 13.30.

Elsa di Tutte heard them out, her chin resting on her knuckles. Her sharp eyes flicked back and forth between her prosecutor and Beatrice, who both stood for the only reason that no one had invited them to sit. The judge asked Corbusier to type up his recommendations ready for her signature. At the same time, she gave permission for them to send acceptances to European police departments for offers of specialist assistance. No information to be released regarding the enquiry itself but those individuals would be briefed upon arrival.

"Warn them that the time frame is as yet unspecified. That said, we are unlikely to require their services for longer than three months." Her mouth gave that little half smile again. "Thanks to the efforts of Ms Stubbs." The smile disappeared and she placed a hand to her throat. "And in no small measure to Gael O'Connell. May she rest in peace. We will find out how she died and the perpetrators will be brought to justice."

Beatrice looked at the carpet, envisaging Gael's expression as she said '*Pommes frites* to die for, am I right?' The judge was very fair in her praise so Beatrice did the same. "Gael had come a long way on this trail before my assistant and I showed up."

"You have an assistant? The Robin to your Batman, I assume." She gave her little half-smile and turned to the prosecutor. "Monsieur Corbusier, I congratulate you," said di

Tutte. "I believe you have selected six individuals from across the continent who can bring the highest levels of skill to our enquiry. You were quite right to insist on taking this role. Ms Stubbs, your contributions have been most valuable. It was a pleasure to work with you. Would you send M. Corbusier your invoice which he will settle on receipt?"

Her comment took Beatrice by surprise. She was under the impression that once they had set up a complex system of investigations into connected cases, her role was just beginning.

"Ah. Am I not taking a role in this enquiry? I'd rather hoped to see it through to the end."

Di Tutte gave her a look of amused surprise. "To the end? That will take months, Ms Stubbs, if not years. Justice is a slow-moving beast but indefatigable. We will never give up. No, as a private detective, your participation is inappropriate. For a start, you are not bound by the same codes of conduct as your fellow officers. Monsieur Corbusier is capable of taking over from here. On a personal note, I appreciate your trust and efficiency thus far. We are grateful and I wish you a safe journey home to London. Have a good weekend."

Di Tutte had employed her as an adviser, nothing more. At this stage, all Beatrice could do was hand over to international law enforcement. "I see. Thank you. Same to you."

The judge left the room and Corbusier phoned for a car. He walked her to the gate, his hollow heels knocking over the flagstones like horses' hooves.

"I wish you every success with your investigation, Monsieur. Thank you for being the perfect host."

Corbusier took her hand. "I sincerely regret your departure, believe me. I very much enjoyed working with you and wish we could have gone further together. Unfortunately, the judge is right. This is a matter for the justice department. Please inform me when you intend to leave and I will ensure a car transports you to the station. It is the least I can do. *Bon voyage* and as you're

British, I believe it's appropriate to say Happy Halloween. Goodbye, Ms Stubbs!"

Back in her room, Beatrice could not quite hold it together. Tears leaked from her tightly closed eyelids. She couldn't even say why she was crying. Perhaps it was a mixture of professional disappointment and a wish to avenge lives taken too soon. She owed it to Sonny and Gael, whose codes of honour led them to pursue truth at their own risk. Both were dead and although she had no official confirmation, she suspected the same was true of Bikram.

Appreciate it now, because you never know how fast it can disappear.

There was nothing to keep her in Belgium any longer. She would take the train and leave the grey and icy skies looming over the Brussels skyline. Not that she had any real idea of the temperature out there since she had been confined to her hotel room, inside a car and holed up in the Palais de Justice for the last two days. Time to get out and enjoy the fresh air. Tomorrow, she would wake in her own bed. Free to stomp around in woods and fields, run after the dog and stroll down the lane with Matthew for a pint at The Angel.

Her mood brightened along with the sky. She booked a seat on the 14.50 Eurostar, packed her suitcase and debated whether to inform Corbusier. No, she needed to walk the streets and engage with reality. The second question was whether she should give Matthew the good news or turn up on the doorstep as a surprise. She opted for the latter.

After checking out, she left her suitcase with reception, tucking her passport and ticket into the zip-up flap for ease of check in at the station later. Then she wandered along the maze of streets around the Marolles flea market, looking for a lunch venue. A friendly looking place offering omelettes caught her eye and a waitress showed her to a window table.

When her herb and Gruyère omelette arrived, she tucked in and gazed out at the street where a sparrow pecked at crumbs. The bird triggered a niggle at the back of her mind and she replayed the morning's conversation. 'You have an assistant? The Robin to your Batman, I assume'. She'd never mentioned Theo to the judge, sticking purely to the facts. So how come Corbusier knew Theo had visited Hostel Herribert? That information was nowhere in the dossier. Why did he need Theo's details?

She dug out her phone from her bag, intending to ask Theo if he'd heard from the prosecutor and noted a new email.

To: admin@beatricestubbs.com
From: mensana339709@biz.in
Subject: Sonny D

Dear Ms Stubbs

I am no longer in Europe but follow the news and business pages, searching for some proof Sonny's death was not suicide. Nothing reassures me and his existence seems to have been wiped from history. You were the only person who seemed interested in what really happened to my friend. My conscience will not leave me in peace until I share with you what I can recall from our conversations. I warn you now, it's not much.

Sonny found evidence of fraudulent accounting at BFS as I mentioned. He followed the paper trail and uncovered a money-laundering system used to pay off whistleblowers. His belief was that potential informants, media, police and lawyers had all benefitted from turning a blind eye. Not just in Belgium but all over the continent.

He did not run away, Ms Stubbs. Oh yes, he ran, but like a bloodhound. He was hot on their heels. The hostel where he died was a piece of the jigsaw. He tried to tell me but I refused to listen. Because I am a coward and Sonny was not.

This is why I write to you today with my warmest wishes and faintest hope that you will find out who was responsible for the death of my friend.

This email address accepts no replies and will no longer exist as of tomorrow. As I said, I am a coward.

Yours in all sincerity

Bikram Ghosh

Her omelette was going cold. She ate it quickly, her mind bouncing in all directions. Her relief at knowing Ghosh was alive and safe was soon overcome by two elements of his email. Hostel Herribert was a piece of the jigsaw? And the payroll included lawyers. She scribbled some notes on a napkin and collected her thoughts.

When her alarm beeped in the quiet restaurant, she jumped. Her counselling appointment! She'd completely forgotten. She threw some Euros on the table and thanked the waitress, then hurried outside to call James.

"Hello, Beatrice. It's good to hear from you. Are you in Devon?"

"No, Brussels, at the moment. We took on a missing person's case which turned out to be something else entirely."

"When you say 'something else entirely', is that in a good way?"

"No, definitely not in a good way. Two people are now dead, both of whom would be alive if it wasn't for me. On top of that, Matthew had a fall and I should be there with him. I feel I'm being irresponsible and at the same time, I'm afraid of being responsible in case I mess it up."

"Let's take this a step at a time. The deaths you mentioned. Is either of those connected to a lack of responsibility on your part?"

The rumble of passing traffic made it hard to concentrate.

Beatrice sat down on a bench to consider the question. "Not directly. I thought I was doing the right thing but I should have asked more questions rather than take things at face value."

"So would say you acted in good faith?" His voice was gentle and reassuring.

"Blind faith, perhaps. I've been thinking about this for some time but now it's impossible to ignore. I'm past it, James. I can't do this anymore, but neither can I adequately care for Matthew. I'm not up to it."

"Let me see if I understand what you're saying. The private detective agency is too much for you in terms of emotional and physical strain. But giving up the agency to stay at home with your partner would substitute one set of strains for another."

"Yes, that's it precisely."

"Would either option feel more manageable if you had some kind of assistance, do you think? At our last session, you mentioned how well Theo had fitted in. Might you consider giving him more responsibility and taking a supervisory role? As for a helping hand at home, you could ..."

"We already have," Beatrice interrupted. "The family interviewed and employed a carer to support Matthew. He seems very capable."

"I see. In that case, what do you think is at the root of your concerns regarding the domestic issues?"

She took a long time to formulate an answer. "I'm worried about being judged and found wanting. That's always been an issue in the work environment, but the idea of failing in the role of Matthew's partner is very hard to bear."

"Have you met the carer yet?"

"No. He's only been in position for two days." A group of masked and caped fancy-dress people were cavorting and howling further up the street. She was itching to end the call and get to the station, but it was she who had asked for an emergency consultation.

"Do you have any reason to believe he will 'find you wanting', as you put it?"

"I'm projecting my own fears onto him, I suppose. Maybe I should meet the man first before getting in a tizzy before the event. Oh, hell, these bloody Halloweeners are getting on my wick. Listen to me, moaning about passers-by when we've only got a few minutes to go. As for the usual, I am taking my stabilisers and I am keeping my diary. Thank you for taking time out of your Saturday to listen, James. You're very good at helping me focus."

"You are welcome. One thought to leave with you. Our sessions, your medication and the understanding of your partner have always been the three struts of your support structure. Now that the latter role is in a state of flux, it may be the perfect time to seek practical assistance, taking the pressure off. Other people may have skills better suited to the circumstances. Remember, you do not have to manage everything alone. When are you returning home?"

"In about an hour's time."

"Have a good journey and I look forward to our regular session next month."

She released a long sigh, grateful for James and his steadying words. The wretched party people drew closer, making an unholy racket. She stood up with a scowl. They were grown adults. What possible reason would they have to dress up and make such a ridiculous noise in the middle of the day? There was nothing frightening about this Dracula, an overweight red devil and two prancing individuals with skeletons painted on black tracksuits. They came closer, capering and laughing, completely surrounding her. 'Dracula' swept his cape over her face and she brushed it away in annoyance. Then he did it again and the two skeletons grabbed her by the arms and marched her forward, screaming like banshees while the devil laughed. In a matter of seconds, they threw her into the back of a transit van where two men were waiting, dressed as scary clowns. Before she could even scream, a gloved hand covered her face and she inhaled the unmistakeable smell of chloroform.

Chapter 24

The idea of taking Matthew shopping had to be Tanya's. Much as Gabriel had a generous nature, battling his way through crowds of Saturday shoppers would fill him with as much joy as a cricket match would enthral Marianne. But Luke was excited, Tanya glowing with enthusiasm and Matthew the most positive he'd been since Dumpling died. Gabriel merely looked resigned. They gathered all their things and departed around eleven, leaving Marianne and Huggy Bear in a suddenly silent kitchen.

"So what do we do now? You've already had a walk, I'm not working on a Saturday out of principle and they won't be back till teatime. I suppose I'd better start cleaning." She tidied away all the breakfast things, loaded the dishwasher and pulled out disinfectant, polish, oven cleaner and dusters from the corner cupboard. The minute she wheeled the vacuum cleaner into the hall, Huggy Bear slunk into the living room, her hatred of domestic appliances well known.

Marianne began in the kitchen, the most-used room of the house. She tied her hair back in a scrunchie, donned rubber gloves and put on the radio so she could hum along as she worked. It was strangely satisfying to do the kind of labour which gave instant results. Kitchen complete, she started work on the conservatory, her father's favourite spot. She was vacuuming the hallway when Huggy Bear came tearing out of the living room, barking her head off.

A shape was visible outside the front door and Marianne went to answer it, expecting a delivery man or the postie. Axel stood on the doorstep, his face showing no surprise at her appearance or at the excitable terrier bouncing around his feet.

"Good afternoon, ladies. I hope I'm not interrupting."

"No, not really. Dad's gone into Exeter with Tanya, Gabriel and Luke. I thought I'd do some cleaning while they're out from under my feet. What are you doing here? You don't work on Saturdays."

"Nor do you and you're still on duty. I came to ask you out for lunch. But I can see in the middle of something. What about a compromise? I'm very good at cleaning so between us we can get everything done in the next hour and still be in time to get a meal somewhere local. How far did you get?" he asked, walking into the house.

Her surprise at his attitude rendered her speechless for a moment and she closed the door behind him. "Well, I am about halfway through downstairs. You don't have to ..."

"No I don't, but I do want to take you out for lunch. I'll start on the bedrooms and when you are finished with the vacuum cleaner, I'll do the floors. Do you like pizza? They have a new wood-fired oven at The Star. One of my Italian colleagues tells me the taste is genuine. Would you like to try?"

He picked up the cleaning fluid, cloths and polish, heading for the stairs.

"Yes, why not? My lunch plans involved leftovers and toast. A pizza sounds nice. Umm, I only have one pair of rubber gloves which I don't think would fit you."

He turned back with a smile. "I'm a professional, Marianne. I never go anywhere without my own pair of rubber gloves. Will you bring the vacuum upstairs when you're ready?"

With that, he trudged up the stairs, followed closely by Huggy Bear. Marianne caught sight of herself in the hall mirror:

no make-up, a towelling headband holding her hair out of her eyes, flushed face and a bobbled jumper which had seen better days. She switched on the vacuum cleaner, determined to finish the job and jump into the shower before going out for lunch. As she worked, she ran through the limited possibilities in her wardrobe upstairs. Thank goodness she kept an emergency make-up pouch in her handbag.

"I'm going to choose the most simple pizza on the menu. That way I can judge the quality of the dough, the tomato base, the cheese and whether the wood-fired oven makes any difference or not. I am inviting you and I wish to make it clear that means I am paying for lunch. I know you British invite people somewhere and then expect them to pay for themselves." He shook his head. "A strange country, in so many ways. I'm driving so I am going to have one glass of red wine and half a litre of water. You order whatever you like."

It was a long time since Marianne had visited The Star. If she was honest, it was a long time since she'd been to a restaurant with anyone other than her family members. When she and Jago were together, they thought nothing of driving across the county to experiment with a new fish restaurant, or taking the train into Exeter to attend the opening of a five-star celebrity chef's latest project. She shook herself, refusing to allow all those memories of last-minute cancellations and furious rows in the past to spoil the present.

"That's very kind of you. I should be treating you, seeing as you helped me clean the house on your day off."

"Don't be ridiculous. I helped you clean the house so that we could go out for lunch. And if I invite you to lunch and you pay, how can we consider that a date? Once again, just to be clear, I am paying and this is a date. Will you please choose your food because I'm very hungry?"

Due to the complete absence of a suitable reply, Marianne

scanned the menu. "Right, fine. To drink, I'd like a large glass of red wine. And to eat … here's one I've not tried before. Pizza Forestière. Rabbit, prunes, mushrooms and rosemary. Sounds adventurous."

"Sounds disgusting. It's a good thing I don't plan to kiss you today," said Axel, raising a hand to a waitress. "Excuse me, we have chosen what we want to eat." He gave their orders and asked her to repeat them back. Once satisfied, he turned to Marianne with a curious expression.

"Do you like taking care of your father?"

She hesitated, still processing his most recent comment. *No plans to kiss me?* Her opening gambit would have been an admiration of the log fire. She marshalled her thoughts. "The circumstances suit us all. I can work from home, keep an eye on Dad, Beatrice can …"

"I didn't ask you to repeat what you said on my first day. The practicalities are clear. My question was about your feelings towards the situation. If you don't want to talk about it, why not say so?"

Marianne bridled at his bossy tone. Pragmatic and down-to-earth behaviour was appropriate when dealing with her father, but she did not appreciate a blunt grilling from someone employed for a very different role. "It's not easy to manage his condition. Aside from the physical demands, watching him deteriorate can be upsetting." Those two sentences had taken her a surprisingly long time to articulate. "You see, his mind has always been his defining feature. That, and his strength of will. It's as if he's a balloon with a slow leak. Gradually and inevitably, he's going to shrivel in front of my eyes."

To her horror, tears filled her eyes and she scrabbled in her pocket for a clean tissue. Embarrassment and annoyance competed for pole position as she asked herself why on earth she'd been more honest to this near stranger than she had with their own sister. She pressed the tissue into the corner of her eyes and did not look up. "Sorry, sometimes it creeps up on me."

"Two red wines?" asked the waitress, placing the small glass in front of her and the large glass in front of Axel. "And one bottle of water. Can I get you anything else?"

Axel switched the wine glasses and smiled at the waitress. "Thank you. No."

He poured the mineral water into his glass, focused on his task. Marianne sniffed and lifted her face. "Thank you for the invitation. Cheers." She held her glass towards him.

He raised his to meet it, his eyes fixed on hers. "Thank you for accepting. Cheers."

They tasted the wine. Marianne made some half-hearted attempt at sounding knowledgeable about Sangiovese and in the ensuing silence, she thought once again about commenting on the blazing hearth.

Axel raised his chin to the ceiling and scratched his beard. "Yes, I understand that. This is why managing a parent's mental deterioration within the family is a double-edged sword. Of course it's reassuring for the person with the condition to be around familiar faces. But the family dynamic changes when accepted roles are reversed. Your father does not seem a particularly authoritarian figure, but he is the patriarch. When his daughter is unable to drag him out of the stream, for example, both people need to make an adjustment. The majority of attention is focused on him, his health, his comfort, his safety. At the same time, his closest family are coming to terms with the fact that they, as you put it, are slowly losing someone they love."

Marianne couldn't speak and took another chug of her wine.

"Caring for your father is not simply a matter of practicalities. You need to recognise your own emotional reactions and make sure you're looking after yourself, your sister and the elusive Beatrice Stubbs. Is she coming home tomorrow?"

"As far as I know, yes. Things tend to be unpredictable

around Beatrice. When you meet her, you'll understand."

Axel made a noncommittal grunt and looked past her out of the window. He appeared different out of his carer's tunic. He wore a blue jumper with a zip-up neck, which framed his jaw and intensified his eyes. He caught Marianne staring and she glanced away.

As a result of his last speech, a thought occurred to her. "Is that what this is all about? Your taking me out to lunch is what you see as your pastoral duties to your client's family?"

He drew his chin into his neck. "Pastoral duties? I have no such responsibilities, but I do have plenty of opinions which I give freely. That is why I told you to look after yourself. No, I invited you to lunch because I would like to get to know you better. If it goes well, I will probably ask you to see a film next weekend. After that, who knows? It's the wrong time of year for a romantic picnic, but I'll think of something seasonal, like a carol concert or a snowball fight." He gave her a frank look and his eyebrows twitched upwards. "Those are my intentions and I hope they are acceptable to you."

To cover her confusion, Marianne took another sip of wine. "You seem to have it all worked out," she said. "How do you know I'm not ... spoken for?"

"Because I've done my research. Your sister is a very good source of information and kindly agreed to the shopping trip today, leaving the way clear for me to make my move."

Despite her bewilderment, Marianne laughed. "And what if I'd said no?"

"I would have given it a few weeks to impress you with my charm and asked you again. I can be very persistent when I want something. Ah, here's the pizza. We should order you another glass of wine as you've practically thrown that one down your neck. Another large Sangiovese, please, and do you have any black pepper?"

The food looked and smelt delicious. It wasn't what she'd

planned for lunch but today was full of surprises. She smiled at the man opposite. “Actually, I’m very glad I said yes.”

He grinned back at her. “So am I.”

Chapter 25

Three sensations dominated Beatrice's consciousness. Firstly, the cold which penetrated as far as her bones. Secondly, pains. Her head throbbed, her left hip and shoulder ached where she had been lying on them, her mouth was dry and her throat sore. And bringing up the rear but becoming increasingly urgent was the need to pee. She opened her eyes to see nothing but black and lay perfectly still, trying to comprehend where she was.

After several minutes, either her eyes were adjusting to the darkness or the room was becoming perceptibly lighter. She turned her head to look over her right shoulder and saw a long rectangular window high up on the wall. Weak sodium light illuminated the room to the extent that Beatrice could make out her surroundings: a cellar with stone walls, a dusty concrete floor and against the wall opposite, a rough stone staircase leading up to a closed door. In the space beneath the staircase was a pile of objects. They were difficult to distinguish in what little light came through the narrow window, although it looked like the usual detritus one kept in the cellar: a pile of bricks, a bucket, paintbrushes and a metallic suitcase.

She sat up stiffly and looked to her left. Nothing there but dust. To her right, more of the same. She realised she was sitting on a blanket, the kind you might throw over a horse. The urge to pee increased to discomfort and she looked around for somewhere to relieve herself. There was nothing else in the cellar but a mound of rubble a few paces from the bottom of the stairs.

Beatrice checked her watch. It was five to two in the morning on Sunday the first of November. She had been unconscious for over twelve hours. She thought back to the partygoers in costume. Those idiot pranksters had abducted her and shut her in a cellar, presumably to frighten the life out her. She closed her eyes, not even convincing herself. Those people were no pranksters and they intended a lot more than a fright. She had to do something instead of sitting there petrified.

Heaving herself unsteadily to her feet, she looked up at the strip of night sky visible through the only window. The first thing she had to do was find a bathroom. She dusted herself off and climbed the staircase. It was no surprise to find the door locked, but fumbling around on the wall, she located a light switch. The harsh glare from a single bulb made her squint for a second. Rather than bang and shout to draw attention to herself, she retreated and assessed her options. If she didn't find something fast, she'd have to pee on the floor.

Her eyes fell on the bucket. She fumbled with her trousers and knickers, squatting over the bucket in blessed release. She had just finished relieving herself when the door at the top of the stairs opened and a shadow fell on the steps. Under the staircase, Beatrice was invisible to her visitor.

"Hello?" came a woman's voice from the doorway.

Beatrice righted herself and stepped into the light. "What's going on? Who are you? Why have you brought me here? Do you know who I am?"

The torch shone into her face. "Yes, Beatrice Stubbs, we know who you are. I brought you some tea." With that, the figure retreated and closed the door behind her.

"Wait! I asked you a question!"

There was no reply other than a key turning in the lock.

Beatrice climbed the stairs and saw a tray on the top step, with a pot of tea, a mug and plate of brownies. She took it downstairs to the blanket to think. This was no prank. A group of people had snatched her from a busy street, shoved her into a van and knocked her out. Her handbag was missing and with it, her mobile phone. No one was expecting to see or hear from her until later that afternoon, seeing as she'd told no one her plans. The thought was both dreadful and insufferable, adding to the pain in her aching head. She hunched inside her coat, tucking her hands under her armpits. Everything seemed to hurt and she couldn't think clearly. An unpleasant smell permeated the room which was nothing to do with the bucket. Decay, mould and rot. It reminded her of something but she couldn't identify what.

"Fat lot of use you are," she said to herself, and the sound of her voice brought reality crashing down. Up until that point, circumstances had seemed bizarre, almost dreamlike. Now, she was wide awake and heaving great sobs. Sonny Das. Gael O'Connell. Beatrice Stubbs. All three asked too many questions and had to be silenced. She breathed deeply, trying to calm herself out of her crying jag. *Think practically*, she told herself. *The most important thing is to get out of here, so how are you going to do it*? Wild fantasies of fashioning a skeleton key from the teapot were not rational.

The teapot. She stared at it, a faint wisp of steam rising from the spout, as if taunting her. She was so very thirsty. She lifted the lid and sniffed the contents. It smelt of peppermint and herbs and most importantly, it was warm. She poured a sip and tasted it. Quite delicious and refreshing, even if they hadn't provided any milk. Typical bloody Europeans. She filled the mug and eyed the brownies. With one finger, she pressed the one on the top. That too was warm. Who on earth baked at two o'clock on a Sunday morning?

Beatrice took the smallest nibble. Chocolate brownies, rich, moist and comforting. Cake and tea, the most comforting partnership. Not just the fact they satisfied her needs, but the tray and the blanket were a good sign. If these people planned to get rid of her, why take such care? The other factor which buoyed her hopes was the voice. Whoever made these cakes and served her tea was a woman. Not to say her own gender was incapable of murder or cruelty, but something about a female voice gave Beatrice confidence. She would appeal to the woman's better nature. There was still a way out of this.

A presence came to sit opposite. Head bent, it wore a mask. Yet this differed from the cheap plastic disguises of the Halloween crowd. This looked permanent. In the shadows, all Beatrice could make out were ears and a snout. In the hollows where its eyes should be, was an infinite blackness.

Appeal to her better nature? Are you really that naïve? Your pathetic hopefulness will make it worse when you face the inevitable. Always the optimist, until the bitterest end.

"Shut up!" she said aloud. "You are not helping. In fact, you never do. Leave me alone. I won't give up."

Voices came from the floor above for the first time. Beatrice ceased chewing and listened. Too muffled to make out words or even language, but it sounded like some men asked questions and a woman answered. But she couldn't listen because it was speaking again.

How many more have to die at the altar of your ego?

The masked figure was now hairy, its jaws open and tongue lolling as it panted, but no spark of light shone from its eyes.

You should have ended this years ago. I did warn you. People will suffer and people will die, all because of you.

Beatrice picked up a brownie and hurled it at her tormentor. The cake tumbled into the air in slow motion, sprouted wings and performed a butterfly ballet around the beast's ears. It was painful to watch the beauty of motion around such ugly stasis. With a sudden snap, the pigdog's tongue whipped out and caught the brownie butterfly, swallowing it whole. Beatrice could hear the little creature's screams. She recoiled, pointing a finger at the masked horror which showed its yellow teeth in a smiling, slavering snarl.

"Go away. I don't want you here. GO AWAY!"

How could you, Beatrice? We were best friends. I'd never leave you.

The door opened at the top of the stairs and footsteps descended.

"Go away. You can't be here," she hissed.

The apparition opened its mouth wider and wider until it turned inside out and disappeared. The pigdog was gone. But she could still hear its voice. She could always hear its voice.

It's my turn now. I've waited such a long time.

Three people and the sound of trotting horses made her scuttle backwards, knocking her teapot on its side. A werewolf, a green ghost and a bloodied, bandaged zombie crouched to look into her face.

"Three blind mice," said Beatrice. But their eyes were not blind, looking into hers with intense curiosity.

The zombie spoke and she knew his voice. She trusted his voice. "*Bon, ça suffit.* Do it now. You'll leave immediately? Good work."

The horse clopped its way over the floor and up the stone stairs. Beatrice didn't know zombie horses climbed stairs and now the pigdog had vanished, she couldn't help but laugh.

Only her middle bit worked. Her arms and legs had gone, maybe taken by the werewolf or eaten by the zombie. She was floating and the sky was bright with millions and billions and trillions of little tiny stars. The water kept splashing over her head. She was sinking and she didn't want to sink because then she couldn't see the stars. She waggled her middle bit, the only bit still working, making a motion like a maggot to get her head above water. Each time it got harder and she grew so tired she could have fallen asleep.

Then it came. She recognised the snuffling in her ear, its hot breath and familiar embrace.

You didn't think I'd miss this, did you? I'm here to help. Relax, I've got you now.

Wings enveloped her and she laid her head on the cushion of its chest.

No more fighting, the battle is over. We're together at last. Let go, give up.

Justice never gives up, thought Beatrice. Who said that? The judge, probably. Or was it the architect?

A wave submerged her head and her lungs heaved and she bucked herself to the surface, spitting water from her nostrils. She yelled and lashed out at the creature behind her, only to find it was no longer there. Instead, a light shone from above, silhouetting a figure with open arms.

Chapter 26

Freezing air penetrated Theo's lungs as he entered Nunhead Cemetery. He always came south of the river on November 1st to visit her grave. A day to pay his respects to the woman who had changed his life. He placed some silk roses on her headstone and crouched to picture her laughing face. Her voice in his ears was as loud as if she were behind him, lecturing him on how to live. "Don't waste time, Theo. Life won't wait so don't leave it too late."

"Miss you, Grandma," he whispered and blew her a kiss. "Every day." Then he zipped up his jacket and set off at a run. The size and wildness of the cemetery made it the perfect place for a jog, even today when evidence of last night's Halloween parties spilled from the litter bins.

He kept his eyes on the path ahead of him, watching for patches of ice. To either side of the strip of tarmac, blades of grass wore frosty coats turning the fields a dusty sage rather than cricket green. The run turned out better than expected. Not just his first attempt since the ice-skating fall, but after drinking a whole bottle of red wine to himself last night. No matter how tired his legs were, a wild and reckless energy drove him on. His plan to consolidate the bond between him and Catinca was in motion. He had invited her for a walk in the park that afternoon, just him and her, so he could apologise and listen to whatever was on her mind. She accepted. He would win her trust, he was determined.

At the halfway point he passed the ruined Anglican chapel and checked the time. His pace was not its best probably because his mind was elsewhere. He sped up to make sure the second half of the run would compensate for the first. Legs pumping and arms working like pistons, he overtook a family group carrying flowers, forcing himself into fifth gear. The muscular pain took second place to his lungs, heaving huge gulps of icy morning mist. He pushed on until he reached the viewpoint from where he could see St Paul's Cathedral and came to a halt, hands on his thighs. He was about to gauge his time and pace on his mobile when it vibrated, alerting him to an incoming call.

The display flashed up a number he did not recognise but he answered anyway. Just in case.

"Theo Wolfe?"

"Good morning. My name is Doctor Janssen. I am trying to contact the Beatrice Stubbs Private Investigation Agency. Your office answer machine gave me this as an alternative number."

"Oh, right. Yeah, I work for the agency. The office is closed today. It's Sunday."

"Yes, it is Sunday here also. I'm calling from AZ Sint-Jan Hospital in Bruges. An emergency patient was admitted this morning, after nearly drowning in a canal. She's not very coherent but insists her name is Beatrice Stubbs. I did a little detective work of my own and found your private investigation agency. The patient is around sixty years of age and speaks English. Do you think you know this lady? I can send a picture?"

Theo's mind seemed to be on go-slow. "That sounds like my boss. She was in Brussels this weekend but I had no idea she'd gone to Bruges. Yeah, a photo would be good."

"One moment." The image arrived in seconds. Beatrice, in a hospital gown, a net over her hair and her pupils so dilated it seemed her eyes were black.

"That's her! Is she OK?"

"The cause of her confusion appears to be marijuana. She ingested a substantial quantity and must have fallen into the water."

"Marijuana! Beatrice? What water?"

"As I said, she fell into a canal and was rescued by the owners of a houseboat. Her drug consumption may have been unintentional. She wouldn't be the first person to make an innocent mistake. Her health is good but her state of mind is such that we would need a family member or friend to take responsibility before we can release her."

"My name's Theo Wolfe and I'm her assistant. Send me the address. I'll be there this afternoon."

"That would be extremely helpful. She's awake at the moment but not especially lucid. Could you try and talk to her?"

"Of course. Put her on." Theo was already striding along St Asaph Road towards Brockley Station.

Her voice came on the line. "Hello, who is this?"

"Beatrice! It's Theo. What happened? Are you OK?"

"I'm very well, thank you for asking. And who are you exactly?"

Theo hesitated and answered truthfully. "My name is Theo Wolfe. I'm Beatrice Stubbs's assistant at her private investigation agency."

She let out a little gasp. "Theo? Where are you? Have you found anything?"

"I'm in London. Something did turn up, but I'm more worried about you."

"Never mind that, I'm perfectly all right. What is it? What did you find?"

"Well, remember you asked me to dig a bit deeper about Gael's past and work? Something bothers me."

"Tell me. Quick."

"Some stories Gael wrote were never printed. The editor killed them. All those pieces alleged corruption in positions of power: financial irregularities at private banks, political influence on the police, and the extent of corporate fraud, government lobbying and continental if not international tax evasion. What's interesting is that one particular name keeps cropping up."

"Whose name?"

He told her.

"Call the judge, Theo. You must call ..."

He waited for her to finish. Nothing came.

"Beatrice?"

She'd gone. He heard voices in the background and the doctor returned.

"The lady is a little confused but we're keeping an eye on her. I'll send you a message with the hospital address. When you have an estimated time of arrival, please inform me. Don't worry too much, she's in good hands."

"Thank you, Dr Janssen. I'm on my way."

Call the judge, she said. Even if he could find the woman's number, what should he say? *You're a detective, Theo,* he reminded himself. *Work it out.*

A London Bridge train was approaching. Theo sprinted over the bridge. The thud of his trainers on the platform beat a two-syllable rhythm in his ears. Bea-trice. Bea-trice. Bea-trice.

Once aboard a near-empty carriage, Theo took out his phone and dialled.

"Hi, Catinca, it's Theo. Sorry, but I need to cancel our appointment. I have to go to Brussels. Someone just tried to kill Beatrice."

The Eurostar from St Pancras International to Brussels was due to depart at 12.58. The screen showed no delays. Still smarting from his call with Catinca, Theo checked in and found his seat. He gazed out at the platform, trying to calm his thoughts.

Even if I find the judge's number, what do I say? Beatrice was insistent I call the woman, but didn't say why. She was still off her head. I can't even be sure she knew who I was. No need to panic. Beatrice is in hospital, in safe hands. Get there, take whatever action necessary and bring her home. If all goes to plan, I should be at her bedside by six o'clock this afternoon. Give the doctor a bell. He can let her know I'm coming.

"Janssen?"

"Hello, Dr Janssen, Theo Wolfe here. We spoke earlier regarding your patient Beatrice Stubbs. Just to let you know, I'm about to leave London and will be at the hospital around six this afternoon."

The doctor did not reply.

"Dr Janssen?"

"I am sorry, Mr Wolfe, but I have bad news. Beatrice Stubbs is missing. She left her room at some point this morning and we have so far been unable to locate her. In her current state of mind, we are extremely concerned."

"How can that happen? Have you called the police?"

"Yes, the police are involved and would like to speak to you. I will inform them of your arrival time. I must go now." The phone went dead.

Theo rang off and faced facts. Either Beatrice left her hospital room half-stoned in a hospital gown or someone had taken her.

Chapter 27

Lucidity was proving elusive. One minute, Beatrice was clear-headed and sharp, the next fuzzy and tangential, wandering along random thought paths until she was completely lost. She tried again, starting with the facts.

She was in a hospital bed, wearing a hospital nightie. People in nurses' uniforms and doctors' coats came in and out and examined her. The logical assumption, therefore, was that she was in a hospital. They asked her questions, most of which she couldn't answer. The staff spoke to her in English but to each other in a language she didn't recognise. Perhaps she was still in Belgium. But hadn't she bought a ticket for the Eurostar? What time was it?

She looked at her wrist, where her watch should be. Nothing but bare skin. Bear skin. Bare bearskin. The Queen's Guards wear bearskin hats. Made from the fur of real black bears which gets in their eyes and they never smile even when the tourists try to make them laugh. Poor bears. She closed her eyes and tried to remember the words to 'Teddy Bears' Picnic' and when she opened them again, a doctor was looking at her.

"Good morning, how are you feeling?"

"Today's the day ... pardon?"

"How do you feel? How are you?"

"Very well, thank you. And yourself?"

"I'm fine. What were you going to say about today?"

"Today's the day they have their picnic."

The doctor gave her a pleasant smile. "Who's having a picnic?"

"The teddy bears. What day is it today?"

"Sunday. The first of November. I think it would be a good idea for you to eat something. Would you like some soup?"

"Yes, please. Could I have a bread roll with it? Did you say today is Sunday?"

"Yes. Today is Sunday and you can have some bread with your soup. I'll be back later. Try to rest after you've eaten, OK?"

"OK. Sunday the first of November. That's a good day for a picnic."

"It certainly is. By the way, what is your name?"

"Beatrice Stubbs."

"Beatrice Stubbs. And where do you live?"

She stared at him. "In the woods?" she suggested. By the look on his face, that was the wrong answer.

The nurse brought her some vegetable soup and a slice of dark bread which was not what she had ordered but it was extremely tasty and so heavy it filled her up. She finished the lot and decided to have a nap. Just what the doctor ordered.

Sunday again? When she'd woken up in that cellar it was Sunday the first of November. All Saints' Day. Memories flapped around her mind like bats released from a cave. She'd woken up in a cellar with no saints but monsters. A werewolf, a pig's head, a horse. Her eyes flew open. The horse! That was what she'd been trying to remember. The horse was at the centre of things and she had to call ... she squeezed her eyes shut, trying to concentrate. What was the matter with her today? It was as if her mind was full of mush and gibberish. There was something incredibly important she had to tell them. Something about the horse ...

She heard the sound of a camera clicking and opened her

eyes. The camera clicked again.

"Mrs Stubbs?" The doctor was standing in front of her, holding a mobile phone. "Good news. I have your assistant on the phone. He's coming to take you home."

"What? Who?"

"Your assistant. Would you like to speak to him?"

Beatrice took the phone, more than a little paranoid as she had no idea who was on the other end.

"Hello, who is this?"

"Beatrice! What happened? Are you OK?"

"I'm very well, thank you for asking. And who are you exactly?"

There was a pause. "My name is Theo Wolfe. I'm assistant to Beatrice Stubbs at her private investigation agency."

Clarity hit her like a flash from a camera. "Theo? Where are you? Have you found anything?"

"I'm in London. Something did turn up, but I'm more worried about you."

"Never mind that, I'm perfectly all right. What is it? What did you find?"

"Well, remember you asked me to dig a bit deeper about Gael's past and work? Something bothers me."

"Tell me. Quick."

"Some stories Gael wrote were never printed. The editor killed them. All those pieces alleged corruption in positions of power: financial irregularities at private banks, political influence on the police, and the extent of corporate fraud, government lobbying and continental if not international tax evasion. What's interesting is that one particular name keeps cropping up."

Before he even spoke, she knew what he was going to say. She was right.

"Call the judge, Theo. You must call ..."

The name escaped her as did all sense of urgency. She

dropped the phone on her cover and addressed the doctor. "I'm still waiting for my soup, you know." Her head sank into the pillow and her eyes closed. She was awfully tired today.

When she awoke, everything looked different. The sun shone through her window and the room sparkled and gleamed as if freshly washed. She threw off the covers and swung her legs to the floor, but when she stood, a wave of dizziness swept over her and she sat down on the bed once more. From the table by the bed, she poured herself a glass of water and drank the lot. It was vitally important she get dressed and find a telephone. A delay could prove fatal. She pressed the buzzer for the nurse.

"Good afternoon, Mrs Stubbs. How do you feel?"

"Much better, thank you, and I'm ready to leave now. Do you know where my clothes and handbag are?"

The man gave her a strange look. "I will go and ask."

After he'd gone, Beatrice attempted to stand, holding on to the bedside table. This time she was more successful. Her brain raced at the speed of light, in comparison to how she'd felt a few hours ago. But now she understood why. Her suspicions were correct and Theo had confirmed it. Somewhere buried in a layer of her subconscious, she'd known all along. Now she had to warn the others.

Steadying herself with the bed frame, she turned to the window and saw the other bed in the room was now occupied. She couldn't be sure, but she didn't recall seeing another patient before. It was a teenage girl, rather overweight, with bandages around both wrists. Her puffy face was filled with piercings and traces of sooty make-up shadowed her eyes. As Beatrice stared, the girl looked up with a resentful scowl.

"Hello," said Beatrice. "I'm your neighbour."

The girl turned her head away.

With a light knock, the doctor came in, smiling. "On your feet already? That is a very good sign. But unless you need the bathroom, I suggest you return to your bed. There's a danger of dizzy spells or a return of your previous confusion."

"I'm fine now, thank you. Can you tell me what I happened? The last thing I remember was eating some brownies and drinking herbal tea. Judging by the effect they had, I assume the brownies were hash cakes and something dodgy was in that tea."

The doctor checked her charts. "Yes. My best guess would be that tea contained psilocybin, a hallucinogenic better known as magic mushrooms. Combined with the hash cakes, that's quite a debilitating combination. If you were unaware those items contained drugs, you should report the purveyors to the police."

"Oh, I will. Have no doubt."

"At the very least, they should have taken proper care of you when you became intoxicated. As it was, you fell into the canal and are lucky to be alive. The houseboat owners heard your cries and managed to get you out of the water before it was too late. They were telling the story on the television this morning and we are fielding calls from journalists enquiring after your wellbeing."

Beatrice stared at him in horror. If the news was public that a woman had been rescued from the canal, she was in trouble. She had to get out of the hospital and speak to the judge. It could not wait. "Please can I have my things? I have to leave now."

"I'm afraid that's not possible. Your assistant will be here some time after lunch and only then we can discharge you. For now, I recommend rest." With a quick smile he turned his attention to the girl and said something in another language.

"Doctor, I'm sorry to interrupt, but it is essential I have my handbag. If you won't let me leave, I must make a phone call. It's a matter of the utmost urgency."

The doctor seemed puzzled and even the teenager paid attention.

"We don't have your handbag, Mrs Stubbs. When you were brought in, you had nothing but your clothes. Not even a coat.

Without any form of ID, we had to wait for you to tell us who you were. You can use the telephone by your bed at any time, of course."

He wished them both a good afternoon and left.

Beatrice sat down and thought, her pulse rapid. She didn't know the judge's number but she could call the Palais de Justice. Except it was Sunday and the judge wouldn't be there. The chances of getting her home phone number out of the Palais staff were nil. She clenched her fists in frustration and pressed them against her eyes. Somehow she had to speak to di Tutte.

"What's the matter?" The girl was watching her.

Beatrice lifted her head. "I have to speak to someone but I don't know her telephone number. It's extremely important."

"If you know her name and address, you can find the number online," said the girl, chewing at her lip.

"I don't know her ..." She stopped as a realisation hit her. "Yes, I do. She gave me her card. Rue des Champs Élysées. I remember thinking about the one in Paris. As for the number, I have no idea." She tried to picture the card. Two digits and a letter. "It might have been 10A," she said aloud.

The girl reached into her bedside table. "We can check." Her thumbs moved over the phone screen at speed. "There's a Rue des Champs Élysées in Ixelles, in Brussels. Is it that one?"

"Yes!" said Beatrice, coming to stand beside the girl's bed. "Can you find 10A and see if there's a phone number?"

The girl shook her head. "No 10A on that street. Number 10 and 11 but no 10A. You know, it could have been 12A. People often use 12A instead of 13 because it's unlucky. Yes! There is a 12A!" Her face fell. "But no number listed. Some people don't want their number made public. Sorry."

Beatrice dug her fingernails into her palms. The people who drugged her could be on their way to the hospital to finish the job while she sat there fretting about Directory Enquiries. "I have to go there in person. But how the hell am I supposed to do that with no money, no clothes, no shoes or coat? Oh, this is so bloody infuriating!"

She sat on her own bed with a thump. What about Theo? The doctor said he was on his way. She could call him and tell him to go to the judge. But Theo's number was programmed into her phone and she didn't know it by heart. If she called Matthew and asked him to ...

"I can help you." The girl blushed under her messy make-up. "I've got money you can borrow. Clothes and shoes too. Right there, in the cupboard. My name's Emma."

Beatrice exhaled through her nose. "I'm Beatrice. That's very kind of you, Emma, but I don't think that would work."

Suddenly animated, the teenager sat up in her bed. "What shoe size do you take?"

Twenty minutes later, a figure emerged from the hospital dressed completely in black. Black tights, two baggy black jumpers, a black mini-skirt, black knitted hat covering her hair and black DMs, with tissues stuffed into the toes as they were one size too big. She caught the bus to the city centre, walked to the train station and bought a ticket to Brussels. Her hunched posture and downcast eyes attracted no attention as she shuffled through Brussels Midi station and out to the taxi rank. In just over two hours since leaving the hospital, Beatrice got out of a cab at Rue des Champs Élysées, number 12A.

The pretty pink terraced house had blue shutters and a forbidding-looking gate hiding a garden. Beatrice rang the bell and waited, whispering 'please be home, please be home' in a constant mantra. The ornately-carved wooden door swung open and there stood the judge, wearing jeans and a red cable-knit jumper.

"Judge di Tutte, I'm sorry to turn up at your home on a Sunday, but I have very important information I must deliver in person."

"Beatrice Stubbs?" Her tone was incredulous, taking in her Goth outfit. "What on earth?"

"May I come in?"

The judge led her into the house, which smelt of roasting meat. She showed Beatrice into a study with a view of the garden and faced Beatrice across her desk.

"Now. What was it you wanted to tell me?"

She'd practised what to say but it all came out in a rush. "Yesterday afternoon, some people snatched me from the street in broad daylight. They gave me drugs and dumped me in a canal in Bruges. I believe the people responsible are the same ones who killed Sonny Das and Gael O'Connell. We know there is a mastermind behind the fraudulent activities at the bank, the cosy relationship between police and newspaper, plus the powerful influence on more than one European government. That person wields immense influence. To the extent he is willing to kill to keep his secrets. The investigation you set up will never track down the individual concerned, I can promise you that much. The man you are seeking will make sure the enquiry goes round in circles until it runs out of money or you run out of patience."

"How can you be so sure?"

"Because that person is Hervé Corbusier."

The judge did not blink. "You mentioned someone gave you drugs?"

"Just let me explain."

Elsa di Tutte heard Beatrice out then stared at her desk, massaging her temples. "Hervé did argue most persuasively for the opportunity to lead the enquiry. His knowledge of all the various angles was surprisingly accurate. And yes, I recognise what you say about the distinctive noise his shoes make. But none of this is sufficient to warrant suspension from the enquiry, let alone an arrest. He has been one of my best prosecutors for many years and never a hint of unprofessional behaviour has ever reached my ears."

"That's because he considers himself clever. He practically told me himself. When I surmised there was a mastermind behind it all, he said I was right. There was an architect directing operations, laughing at our attempts to pin him down. An architect! Only when coming round this morning did I make the association. Le Corbusier.

"My assistant dug up some stories which were never printed, written by Gael O'Connell. His name comes up again and again. The editor must have refused to run anything which pointed the finger in his direction. That's how he does it, that's how he got away with it for so long. He wields his influence like a weapon.

"But he's not as clever as he thinks. The cellar where I woke up could have been anywhere. Nothing distinctive about it and I couldn't see out of the window to identify the street. There was only one thing that made it stand out. A smell. Sort of cabbagey and composty with a synthetic overtone. I recognised it because I'd smelt it before. If you send police to the cellar of Hostel Herribert in Bruges, you will find traces of several people's DNA, including mine and I guarantee it, that of Hervé Corbusier."

Di Tutte rested her chin on her index finger. "And if you're wrong?"

"I've made both of us look foolish. But if I'm right, we've got evidence that your prosecutor charged with exposing a network of corruption is and always has been right at its heart."

"I need to make some calls."

"So do I. Would you have a phone I could use?"

Several calls later, Beatrice finally reached Theo. The news that he was en route cheered her enormously. She redirected him to meet her at Rue des Champs Élysées. Then she informed the AZ Sint-Jan Hospital that she was safe and well, and asked them to pass the news on to her ex-roommate. Di Tutte spoke to three different police forces and asked a detective inspector to come to her home in order to take Beatrice's statement. Telling her story to the police took ages and when she emerged from the study, Theo had arrived. She shed a few tears at his visible relief and more of laughter when he took in her outfit. The judge made tea, loaned Beatrice a pink woollen tracksuit with a pair of Uggs and went off to organise their return journey.

"I'm so glad you're here. The chances that anyone would try to bump me off again are pretty remote, but I still have to go back to the apartments for my suitcase and I don't want to do that alone. How did you find those articles with Corbusier's name?"

"You told me to keep digging, right? So I located a friend of Gael's in the States, a guy called Mikhael Vakala. At first he wouldn't talk to me, then I guess he must have confirmed for himself what happened to Gael. We spoke on the phone and he sent me all her investigative stories the paper refused to run. She trusted him to use that info if anything went wrong. It was her insurance policy. But you already had Corbusier marked, didn't you?"

"Yes, but too late," said Beatrice. "He said a couple of things, about you visiting the hostel and my turning up at the bank which he couldn't have known from my paperwork. He must have had other sources of information and now we know who they were."

The judge re-entered the room. "I sent a driver to collect your valise who will then take you to the Eurostar terminal. Two tickets on the 19.05."

"Thank you," said Beatrice. "The whole time Corbusier was watching me, amusing himself like a cat playing with a mouse. It's not a pleasant feeling." She turned back to Theo. "I wonder why he didn't send someone after you?"

"I can't swear to it, but I think he did. A motorbike came pretty close to knocking me under a pizza van on Thursday."

"What?" Beatrice exclaimed. "How come you didn't tell me?"

"At the time, I had other things on my mind. It's only now I put two and two together."

The judge looked at the wall clock with a frown. "The key players will soon be under arrest and their minions will go underground. The aim was to keep you quiet. It's too late for that now. I believe it unlikely there will be further attempts on your lives. That said, I advise extra caution."

Theo agreed. "You'd better stay at mine tonight and I'll put you on a train tomorrow morning. Do you think Sonny's flatmate is safe?"

"Yes, I do. Bikram Ghosh isn't stupid. He won't take any chances. I doubt we'll ever hear of him again and for his sake, that's a good thing."

Judge Elsa di Tutte tweaked the curtains to peer into the street. "The car is here."

She came to the door to see them off and took Beatrice's hands.

"The first time I saw you, I knew you would be interesting. I underestimated just how much. I will take over this enquiry personally and I swear I'll do it justice."

Beatrice believed her.

Chapter 28

It hurt, putting Beatrice on a train at Paddington on Monday morning. It was an intense moment for them both as she was determined to thank him for rushing to Belgium at short notice. Theo had a tough time holding on to his emotions. He was overtired after sleeping badly on the couch and still processing the stress of the previous day.

"Are you sure you'll be OK?" he asked again.

"I'll be fine, don't fuss. It makes me feel very old. You go home, get some rest and call your gorgeous girlfriend." She hugged him again, went through the ticket barriers and gave him one last wave before she boarded the train.

Go home, rest and call your girlfriend. That was exactly what he intended to do, just in a different order. He stood at a bus stop on Praed Street, phone pressed to his ear.

Catinca answered on the first ring. "Theo? Where are you? How's Beatrice?"

"She's … Beatrice. I've just put her on a train at Paddington. We got in late last night. How are you?"

"Pretty good! Got loads to tell you. What you doing this afternoon?"

"Getting some kip. Do you fancy a drink tonight, maybe?"

"Yeah! Let's go to Dionysus. It's always dead on a Monday. Eight o'clock?"

"OK. Catinca, is everything all right? Between you and me, I mean."

Catinca gave a husky laugh. "We're more than all right. Sorry I shouted."

"I deserved it. Right, the bus is coming so I'll see you at eight."

"Brilliant. Have a good kip." There was a loud smacking kiss and she laughed.

He shoved the phone into his jacket and got out his Oyster card. Although the thought of seeing her later that evening thrilled him to his bones, the one thing right now he needed far more than his passionate, beautiful, almost-girlfriend was his bed.

She was right about Monday nights. Dionysus had more staff than customers. Tamsin was working in the shop section but when she saw him enter the bar, she gave an excited wave. He waved back and went to the counter to order a bottle of wine. Because the start of the week tended to be so quiet, Monday nights were a good opportunity to train new members of staff. Theo nodded a greeting to Jed, who was instructing two new barkeeps, and ordered a bottle of cava with three glasses from a young girl with a whole lot of tattoos.

He'd only just settled into a window seat when Catinca burst through the door with her usual flamboyance. She blew kisses to Tamsin and Jed, then scampered across the floor and threw her arms around Theo. He hugged her and was surprised when she drew back to look at his face and planted a kiss right on his mouth.

"What was that for?" He asked.

She gave him a lofty look "I don't need to provide reason for spontaneous displays of affection. You got cava! I was gonna suggest we drink fizz. What's the time? Five to eight, so Tamsin gets off any minute now. Quick, before she gets here, tell me everything what happened in Brussels." She shrugged off her coat and Theo was strangely pleased to see the old Catinca had returned. She wore a ruffled blouse in burnt orange, amber earrings and a black pinafore dress with a wide flared skirt. Her make-up was sculptural and her eyes sparkled in tones of ginger and gold. He didn't even need to check her feet. He knew what was at the end of those black tights.

"Five minutes won't cut it. Let's save that conversation for later. The main thing is we're all safe. Beatrice arrived in Devon a couple of hours ago and is already planning our next job. She never lets up."

"She ain't the only one." Tamsin appeared beside them, pulling off her dark green apron. "All right, Theo? You sorted Belgium out, then?"

"Hi, Tamsin." He rose to kiss her cheek. "How come you're on the graveyard shift?"

"'Cos I'm the in-house designer and it's the best day to make changes. What do you think of the Christmas display?"

Theo hadn't even noticed, but Catinca enthused over the silvery baubles and white paper chains, admired the faux 'footprints in snow' and raved over the crystal tree in the window. Now that he paid attention, the atmosphere was stylish, classy and enticing.

"That was quick. You did a great job. Very Dionysus. You want some cava to celebrate?"

"Won't say no to that." She stuffed her apron into a ball under the table and prodded Catinca. "You told him yet?"

"Nope. I was waiting for you."

"I'm here now. Let's go. Thanks for the fizz, mate."

Catinca raised her glass. "To best friends!"

Tamsin chugged her cava and launched into her speech. "Imma keep this short because we don't want cause this girl no more grief. Sir Tobias Tosser took advantage of his position and assaulted our mate. She talked to the police who told her the truth. His word against her word. If Catinca presses charges, they will destroy her business. If Catinca accepts their commission, her own conscience will destroy her. Unless … we get his cash *and* his reputation. I got an idea. Listen up, Mr Private Detective, 'cos we got a job for you."

Theo listened up and judging by Catinca's eager posture, she knew what was coming.

"The man's got a weakness for pretty girls, right? We put him in a situation where he thinks he can take advantage of a young, star-struck female and we give him enough rope to hang hisself. Catinca accepts the commission and works with Agnessa." She rolled her eyes. "What kind of a man would saddle his daughter with a name that sounds like an ailment? A tosser, that's who. Anyway, Catinca suggests a meeting to select perfect fabrics with bride and her father, hosted by her gorgeous assistant, Taz." She flicked her hair over her shoulder and gave them both a supermodel pose. "That's me, in case you're wondering. With some sort of ruse I ain't worked out yet, we get Agnessa to leave first, leaving me alone with him. Stunned by my beauty and innocence – hey, I can act – Tosspot tries it on. We record the whole thing and shop him to the papers."

Catinca clapped her hands. "And we already hooked Trottiscliffe. I messaged Agnessa to view some fabrics and told her if she wanted to bring her dad to sign off on expenses, my assistant would do demo. She confirmed immediately. Her and Tobe the Tosser want a private showing on Wednesday at five o'clock."

She and Tamsin were bursting with excitement, so Theo hid his dismay as best he could.

"Wow! That's fast work. That means in less than two days from now, we need to have everything in place to lure the target into a sting. It's gonna be a stretch."

"I know," said Catinca, reaching out to place a hand on his arm. "But two important things. First of all, meeting is in my workshop. Home turf. Second, we have another pair of hands.

Yesterday, I was pissed off with you, I admit, for running off to Brussels. So I went for a walk with Adrian instead, to moan about it. He was in same position with Will working the weekend. Anyway, I told him our plan and he wants to help."

This time Theo could not hide his exasperation. He scrunched up his eyes and shook his head. "No, no, no."

"What!" demanded the women simultaneously.

Theo opened his eyes and looked from one indignant face to the other. "I'll start with a question. Has either of you two got any experience in running undercover operations? Have either of you pursued any kind of private investigation to a successful conclusion before now? Do you have any idea how vital it is to be discreet at every stage of the process so as not to incriminate yourselves or anyone else involved? Don't answer that. I already know. Listen, I'm not dick-waving here but I'm going to be a bucket of cold water if this involves any element of unnecessary risk. Tamsin, I confess I think this is a dog's breakfast of a plan. But because you're willing to put yourself at risk to help a mate, against my better judgement, I want to help." The women formed a mirror image, both frowning with their arms folded.

"But you got to do it right. On top of setting the lure before the trap is laid, you included somebody else whose reputation for discretion is not the best and who happens to be married to a detective inspector. If Will gets even the faintest scent of this from Adrian, he'll close us down. And rightly so. This kind of sting requires months of preparation and discreet communications. For example, every case Beatrice and I handle has a codename so that we don't sit around in public bars loudly trumpeting the name of the target." He pressed his fingers against his eyelids and rubbed.

Tamsin snorted. "Pretty shitty attitude there, considering it's not even your problem. Catinca wants to get this guy and I'm ready to help her. If our methods aren't up to your usual standards, tough tits. We got a chance to nail this geezer and you can either help us or take your negativity somewhere else." She glared at him over her glass of cava.

To his horror, Catinca's eyes had filled with tears. She saw this as a betrayal and it cut him to the core.

"Sorry we're late! Will came home from work just as we were leaving the flat and I couldn't possibly rush off out." Adrian and Dolly had come through the door unnoticed while Theo was lecturing Tamsin and Catinca. He seemed completely unaware of the atmosphere at the table and released Dolly from her lead. Catinca made a fuss of the dog, which enabled her to hide her face.

"Tamsin, I applaud you. The decorations are sublime. How you managed all this in a single day is beyond me." He glanced at the wine cooler on the table. "Jed! Could we have a bottle of Veuve Clicquot over here, when you have a minute?" He sat down beside Theo. "I spoke to Beatrice this afternoon and heard all about your Belgian adventures. Poor Beatrice, thrown in a canal! To think what could have happened! Let's finish the cava and celebrate with a glass of champagne."

Catinca's head snapped up. "What are you talking about? Beatrice in a canal?"

Adrian turned theatrically towards Theo. "You mean you haven't told them?"

"See, this is exactly what I'm talking about." Theo covered his eyes with his hand for a moment to compose himself. "What happened yesterday is part of a large and complex case. It will take months to resolve, and any wins or losses along the route must be kept quiet. I'm sure Beatrice said the same to you, Adrian."

Adrian looked offended. "Of course she told me I shouldn't talk about it, but we're among friends here. Beatrice is dear to us all and Catinca deserves to know about attempted murder."

"Who's attempting murder?" asked Jed, placing a bottle of Veuve Clicquot in an ice bucket on the table. He held up his hands in surrender. "No need for that, I'll bring you some nibbles without a gun to my head. Do you want fresh glasses?"

"Just one for Adrian, please," said Theo, taking control of the conversation. "Hey, your new staff members look pretty keen. I guess you need all the help you can get before party season."

"Too right," said Jed. "The problem is they lack experience. I don't suppose you fancy coming back for a few weeks?" He started twisting the cork out of the bottle.

"You can leave that, Jed. With four Dionysus old hands at the table, one of us might remember how to open a bottle of champagne. As for a shift behind the bar, Beatrice is keeping me far too busy, but thanks for asking."

"You'd be welcome any time. I'll send someone over with a fresh glass and something to tickle the taste buds. Have a nice evening."

They wished him the same and he glided back to the bar. The atmosphere remained uncomfortable and no one spoke for a minute.

Theo gathered all the diplomacy at his disposal and spoke in a low urgent voice. "Just before you arrived, Adrian, I was trying to impress on Tamsin and Catinca the importance of discretion. I've got more to say on that subject but before I do, one thing takes precedence." He turned to Catinca and met her eyes. "I want to help you do this and make that person pay for what he did. I want to see him face public humiliation and ideally justice. Believe me when I say I will do everything I can to make that happen. What I will not do is rush into a badly planned ambush which could result in our target getting away, managing a repeat performance or turning the tables on us." He fell silent as the tattooed girl brought a wooden platter of tapas and a spare flute to their table.

They smiled their thanks and only when she had returned to the bar did Theo continue.

"Attempting to pull this off in under forty-eight hours is

frankly insane. That said, we have an opportunity to get the target into a space which we control. It can be done but in order to do this as professionally as we can, I'm going to insist on a few conditions. I'm not being a macho arsehole because if Beatrice was here, she would say exactly the same. Unless we do this on my terms, I won't be able to take part." He faced three stony expressions and decided to press on while he had their attention.

"Let's look at this backwards. Imagine that in several months' time, this goes to trial. Defence lawyers will want to see all our phone calls and emails, as well as investigating personal backgrounds to see if they can discredit us in any way. They will dig into our private lives and look for a reason why we might have a vendetta against our target. You," he looked at Catinca, "need to be very careful about what you say and to whom. I suggest deleting any communication between you and Tamsin over the past few days, but making absolutely sure you keep the professional trail between you and your client. In particular, the one making reference to how you don't want to be physically present at meetings with the person paying the bills."

He took a sip of wine and addressed Adrian. "Beatrice told you to say nothing about what happened in Belgium, right? And the first thing you do is walk in here and tell Catinca and Tamsin what happened, overheard by Jed. I know you think you're among friends. What if Tamsin also feels she's amongst friends and shares the story with one of her colleagues? Just wait a minute, Tamsin, this is hypothetical. What if Jed reads something about the story in *The Guardian* and tells someone else he has the inside track? My point is, if we're going to do this sting, we tell no one. I won't consult Beatrice even if she does have the know-how. Adrian, you're not going to tell your husband. Tamsin, don't say a word to Jed or Ezra."

"As if!"

"Listen to me. This stays between the four of us. I mean it, we tell no one. Unless you promise me that, I'm not getting involved."

Three heads nodded and each muttered a promise.

"Right, Adrian, you might as well open the champagne. Let's tackle damage limitation. You just promised me you'll tell no one else. Now you'd better own up. Who have you already told?"

Everyone started speaking at once. Theo released a weary sigh and helped himself to some nuts.

Chapter 29

For the first time in her life, Marianne was acting like a mature adult. Her inner child, or if she were honest, her inner attention-seeking teenager, wanted to dress up and put on some slap and perfume to turn up at Matthew and Beatrice's cottage around half an hour before Axel arrived. But she didn't.

Instead, she checked in with Beatrice on the phone. After hearing Matthew had spent a peaceful night, she made a decision. She was taking a day off for herself. Since being made redundant and setting up her own business, she had worked seven days a week and when not working, she was caring for her father. Last night was the first time she had slept in her own bed for days. Her plan was to enjoy a leisurely breakfast, answer any urgent emails, go out for lunch and indulge in a little retail therapy.

Her reasoning was not entirely selfish. When Axel arrived at the cottage today, it would be the start of a new normal. His interaction with Beatrice and Dad would create a dynamic of its own, so Marianne's presence was an unnecessary distraction. Axel and Beatrice were going to be the key players in Dad's future. It was in everyone's best interests for Marianne to butt out. She showered and changed and on a whim, dialled her sister's number.

"Marianne? What's wrong?" Tanya's voice was edgy.

"Nothing, everything is fine. Beatrice came home yesterday morning, Dad's delighted, Huggy Bear is hysterical and Axel will be there as usual. I'm going to keep a low profile to let them work it out for themselves. You got plans for lunch?"

"Apart from a hot date with a Cornish pasty, no. Where do you want to meet?"

A Truckle of Cheese was a new delicatessen-cum-wine bar one street away from Tanya's office. Like so many others of its ilk, its brand was traditional authenticity at a premium price. Marianne's initial reaction was to be impressed until she saw it through Axel's eyes. She could almost visualise him shaking his head and rolling his eyes at the slate plates and mini buckets of hand-cut fries. She opted for a table near the window, ordered a coffee and waited for her sister while observing the High Street. Freedom was a strange feeling. On one hand, she was uprooted from routine, drifting and listless like a jellyfish. On the other, she was liberated from the daily grind, able to make her own decisions and take Tuesday off. Her peripheral consciousness, otherwise known as eyes in the back of her head, had not switched off. At least every twenty minutes, she needed to remind herself her father was safe and under the care of others.

Tanya was late and Marianne decided to treat herself to a glass of wine. Retail therapy could wait or be done online. Today, she would go with the flow and attend to every whim as she wished.

The little waiter delivered her glass of red and asked if she was ready to order.

"Thank you. I'm waiting for my sister … oh, here she is. Could you give us five minutes?"

Tanya bundled through the door, wrapped in a duffel coat and scarf which made her look like Paddington Bear. Her cheeks were pink and her forehead sweaty. "Typical, isn't it?" She unwound her scarf and unbuttoned her coat. "Nothing all day apart from a couple of time-wasting phone calls and just as I want to go out for lunch, a couple came in looking for a retirement property. I had to fob them off with a few brochures and asked them to come back tomorrow. What are you drinking?"

"A large glass of red, because frankly, I damn well deserve it. I've taken the day off from work, from Dad and from everything else. What you want?"

"A duvet day with nothing else to do than binge-watch Netflix and stuff myself with Cornish pasties." She smiled up at the waiter. "Hello, could I have a peppermint tea, roasted vegetable polenta without the blue cheese and a portion of salad?"

Marianne deliberately flared her nostrils. "I'll have the polenta with blue cheese, please and chips instead of salad. Could we get two portions of ciabatta as a starter?"

Once the waiter had taken their order, Tanya seemed to relax into her chair. "We're going to see Dad tonight, all three of us, but just for an hour. Axel says visitors should not stay too long and certainly not interrupt his routine. I trust his judgement, so we'll leave before they have dinner. He mentioned you had lunch the other day?"

Marianne could see where Tanya was going but played dumb. "I have lunch with Dad every day. All right, all right, yes, Axel asked me out on a date and we're going on another one tomorrow evening. Before you ask, I don't know. He's nice, if a bit bossy, and I think the whole carer circumstance is going to make things awkward. We'll just have to see how it goes."

The waiter had hardly placed the breadbasket on the table before Tanya tore into a chunk off and stuffed it into her mouth. "He likes you. I would have guessed even if he hadn't asked all those questions about your tastes. Plus he has got a fantastic arse."

Despite herself, Marianne burst into laughter at her sister's direct attitude. "As you say, he has got a fantastic arse. The thing is, there's so much more to a relationship than … wait a minute. You're not drinking alcohol. You're not eating blue cheese, your go-to dish from the Indian in Crediton was always prawn tikka masala and now you've turned to vegetable korma. Why does it take me so long to spot these things? You're pregnant, aren't you?"

In a complete reversal of the first time Marianne had spotted her sister's condition, Tanya's smile split her face. No tears this time, no panicky whisperings about the father, no doubts about whether the child was welcome. "Yes. Sixteen weeks. We were waiting for Beatrice to get back before making the announcement."

Squealing expressions of affection in a small town would set tongues wagging so Marianne reached a hand across the table and clutched her sister's, knowing her facial expression could convey all the joy she wanted to express. "Congratulations. I couldn't be happier for you and Gabe because you're already the most perfect parents. Does Luke know?"

"Yeah, we told him first. The only hassle we've had since then is trying to shut the little sod up. He wants to be the first to tell everyone. The plan is to tell Dad and Beatrice on Friday night." Tanya's face lit up as if imagining the scene.

The waiter brought their lunch and Tanya's tea.

"What about Heather? Surely Gabriel's mum deserves to know as one of the first?" asked Marianne.

Tanya gave a laugh and a shrug at the same time. "Heather already knows. We didn't need to tell her, she spotted it around the tenth week and I wasn't even showing then. I can't believe this is happening. I have a lovely family, the best husband and a son I adore. After all the mistakes I've made, I can't quite believe I deserve this."

"Shut up and don't jinx things. Do you know the gender yet?"

Tanya shook her head. "Don't want to know till he or she

arrives."

"Good. Spare us one of those cringe worthy gender-reveal parties. But even if you don't know whether it's a boy or girl, I'll bet you've already got a shortlist of names."

"More like a long list. If you're going to be there on Friday night, I'll show you then. The only thing I'm a bit worried about is how Dad's going to take this. He's losing his grip on the family members he already has, leave alone introducing a new one." She prodded at a slice of aubergine, her face losing some of its animation. "How was he yesterday?"

Marianne raised a hand to attract the waiter's attention and pointed to her wine glass. "Up and down, but mostly up because he knew Beatrice was coming home. Although I did find him in the cellar looking for Dumpling just before lunch. Thank you very much," she said to the waiter who topped up her glass. "Axel offered to go looking for the cat, which seemed to reassure Dad. My reaction was to sit him down and explain that the cat died last week, but as Axel explained, that would come as a nasty, unnecessary shock. That guy knows what he's doing."

"Yeah, he really does. The trouble is, we don't. Marianne, what are we going to do?"

Marianne leaned forward to look into her sister's eyes. "You are not going to worry or get stressed about the situation, especially now. Let's celebrate your good news and enjoy Friday night. Next week, why don't you and I take Beatrice out for lunch, leaving Dad under Axel's beady eye. We can't make any decisions for her, but she needs to realise Dad requires twenty-four-hour supervision. With a newcomer on the way, you'll have enough to do and I want to devote some time to my own life. Anyway, that's next week and the most important thing right now is for you to look after yourself. That means body and mind, so no worrying. Are you listening to me?"

Tanya nodded. "Yeah, but it's hard not to worry. If only there was some kind of distraction. Perhaps you can take my mind off it by telling me all about your date with Axel." She gave Marianne a wicked grin.

"You're a devious cow," said Marianne, unable to hide her own smile. The truth was, she couldn't wait to talk about Axel.

Chapter 30

There was no denying the man was good at his job and evidently had a warm rapport with Matthew, but Beatrice found Axel Zand just a little presumptuous. He had his own key to the house and on Wednesday morning, when Beatrice did not answer the door immediately because she was downstairs hanging out washing, he let himself in. He disapproved of the lunch she had prepared, even though Matthew had specifically asked for a jacket potato with cheese and beans. Worse still, he asked her directly about her plans for her partner's long-term care. Fortunately, a crash from the kitchen called a halt to the interrogation. Matthew had knocked over the teapot. By the time Beatrice shut Huggy Bear in the conservatory and Axel swept up the pieces of broken china, it was time for him to leave.

"I will be back at four-thirty and I hope we can find time for a conversation then. Goodbye, Matthew. Have a nice afternoon and don't forget to let the dog out of the winter garden." He closed the door behind him and moments later, his car splashed down the drive.

She joined Matthew at the dining-room table as he finished his apple pie. "Well, he seems very nice," she said, without conviction.

"He is quite marvellous. I mean, I'm pleased you're home, of course, but Axel's visits are the highlight of my day. Such stimulating company. Has the rain stopped? Huggy Bear is due a walk. Where is she, by the way? We can't have both dog and cat disappearing."

Beatrice stood up with a guilty start. "I shut her in the conservatory while we were clearing up. She's only just dried off after this morning's drenching, so let's wait until the sun comes out. Anyway, you usually like a post-prandial nap and I need to prepare some stuff for the post." She crossed the hallway and opened the conservatory door to release the excitable Border Terrier who dashed into the kitchen and then found Matthew in the dining room.

Matthew's voice reached her, welcoming the dog as if she'd been away for weeks. While he was occupied, Beatrice popped into the study to finish preparing a package. Freshly laundered black clothes, a polished pair of DMs, a black coat and a handwritten letter of thanks wrapped around two fifty-Euro notes were all packed and ready to be sent to Bruges. The phone rang and she snatched it up.

"Hello, Will. Did your contact find anything?"

"Yeah. Word is that Hostel Herribert is part of a money-laundering operation. On paper, expenses are legit. The fact a one-star hostel is paying five-star prices for goods and services attracts very little attention and the money is washed, starched and ironed. The fraudsters have probably got pizzerias, dry cleaning businesses, hotels, hairdressers and a chain of shops selling ludicrously overpriced tat through which they can process their illegal income. My guess is Sonny Das didn't do a runner at all. He went there for a closer inspection of the set-up. He even checked in under his own name, right?"

"Right. Which is where I located him and informed his bosses exactly where he was. They got there first and took him out. Oh hell, I had no idea we were handing them his head on a plate."

"How could you have known? Anyway, I've emailed you what

my mate found regarding financial records so you can share with Judge di Tutte."

Her phone vibrated again. Theo was trying to reach her. She would call him back when she'd finished with Will.

"Thank you, DI Quinn. I knew I could count on you. How's your first week as detective inspector going?"

"Great. Although the coffee is still shite. Listen, something's come up here and I wanted to pick your brains. Have you got a minute?"

The clock in the hallway struck four and with a sense of emerging from a rabbit hole of calls and emails, Beatrice realised there was just half an hour to go before Axel returned. She was thirsty and frustrated and not at all ready for a serious conversation on healthcare. After all her efforts, she still hadn't reached the judge, who was in court all afternoon. She got up, intending to check on Matthew and make herself a glass of elderflower squash. Before she had even opened the study door, her mobile rang and she snatched it up. Caller display showed Theo's name.

"Theo, hello and sorry. You rang earlier and I had every intention of returning your call but it's been a busy afternoon. Sorry to be rude but is there any chance I could phone you back in half an hour or so?"

"That might be a bit too late. Look, I wasn't going to tell you about this, but circumstances have changed. This afternoon, I've set up a sting operation to expose a high-profile figure. Now it looks like we can get a respectable broadsheet to run the story. My thinking is we could get some great publicity if it was under the agency's name. But obviously I need your go-ahead before claiming it as one of ours."

Beatrice sat down with a thud and kicked the study door closed. "I think you'd better explain."

When he'd finished, her shoulders were stiff and her mouth

sticky. All she could do was wish them luck and remind Theo of protocol. If only she could be there! She went into the kitchen to make herself a cup of tea. Once the kettle was on, she put her head around the living room door to ask Matthew if he wanted to participate.

He wasn't there and neither was the dog. She went into the conservatory to see if he was reading in the late afternoon light. No Matthew, no Huggy Bear. On her way across the hallway, she checked if the dog's lead was still hanging in the porch. It was. So where were they? The kettle was boiling. She switched it off and jogged upstairs. Finding no trace of man or dog on that floor, she checked the cellar.

The doorbell rang and before Beatrice got up the stairs, a key turned in the lock. In the doorway stood Axel, Matthew and a sopping wet Huggy Bear. The dog scampered inside, shaking herself and creating a cloud of droplets while leaving muddy paw prints across the chequered tiles.

"There you are!" exclaimed Matthew. "We've been everywhere looking for you. I thought you'd gone back to London without telling me. Then the weather turned parky and I forgot my coat. As luck would have it, Axel was passing and gave me a lift home. Jolly good job as my wellies have sprung a leak. What do you say to a pot of tea and a toasted teacake?"

Beatrice looked at his feet in sodden carpet slippers, taking in his wet hair and dripping cardigan. "Yes, I'd say tea is just the ticket, but first you need to get out of those damp things. Come upstairs ..."

"I'll help Matthew into some dry clothes," said Axel. "You put the kettle on and make the tea. You might need this." He handed her a brown paper carrier bag, spattered with raindrops, and guided a squelching Matthew up the staircase. Inside the bag was a new teapot. It was bright red and bore a delightful design – The Strawberry Thief – the sort of thing that could not fail to cheer one's heart. She placed it in the kitchen, put the kettle on and went in search of an old towel with which to dry the dog.

When the two men returned, Beatrice had prepared a tea tray with jam tarts, hot buttered toast, a pot of Earl Grey and Matthew's medication. They sat in the kitchen, Huggy Bear stretching out in front of the Aga and Matthew regaling her with stories of his afternoon's adventure. Axel asked him questions and engaged with his tales, but Beatrice was too embarrassed about letting him wander off while he was under her charge.

Axel checked his watch and noted that it was time for the evening news. As if it was a matter of routine, he placed a jam tart, two triangles of toast and a refilled mug on a tray and escorted Matthew to the living room. Beatrice sat where she was until the carer had settled Matthew in his armchair, switched on the TV and placed the remote control within his reach.

She braced herself. He sat opposite, his expression neutral.

"I'm truly sorry about this afternoon. A friend called for some advice and I spent some time looking into that. Then someone else rang with a problem ... well, never mind. I left Matthew and the dog asleep in the living-room and had no idea he'd gone out. I didn't hear him."

"Probably because you were on the phone."

"Yes, probably. It might be wise if I lock the front door when we're both at home."

Axel did not reply, but waited patiently for her to continue.

"You asked about my plans for the future. My hope is to continue working as long as that is possible, supported by you and the family when I can't be present."

"From what I understand, you have been back and forth to Belgium in the past two weeks, and ended up in a life-threatening situation. You left Marianne to take care of Matthew, with some help from Tanya and Gabriel. He fell into the stream and she was unable to help him out. At this stage of Matthew's development, he needs routine and familiarity. He needs you to be present."

Beatrice rubbed at the space between her eyes. "I know he needs someone with him, but how am I supposed to run my agency if I can't leave the house?"

"That is not my concern. My role is to advise on the practicality of home care. If you are unable to care for him, we must look at alternatives."

"Oh, go and boil your head," shouted Matthew from the living room. "Lying through your teeth, you tuppenny-ha'penny charlatan."

"It's all right," Beatrice reassured Axel. "He always does this when he's watching the news."

"Yes, I know. He has some creative names for the Prime Minister. Regarding the future, I expect you want to discuss the situation with Marianne, Tanya and Gabriel, as well as Matthew himself. Can we agree to talk further on Monday morning?"

Beatrice hesitated. "So soon?"

"The sooner, the better." He got to his feet. "I must go now because I have a date. Thank you for the tea."

"Thank you for the teapot. It's very kind of you to replace it."

"Don't mention it. Matthew told me more than once how he admires William Morris. It seemed the obvious choice. Have a good evening."

"You too. Are you going somewhere nice?"

"The farmer's market at Exeter Cathedral and then a drink afterwards."

"Oh, that sounds perfect for a first date. How romantic!" she enthused, picturing the pretty little stalls dotted with fairy lights.

"It's a second date, actually. Then I need to choose something a little more serious for the third time. Perhaps a coastal walk and a decent restaurant. Do you have any recommendations?"

"Apparently Chez Bruno is very nice and it has a Michelin star. I remember Marianne raving about it when Jago took her there."

Axel frowned and shook his head. "That sounds pretentious.

A country pub with a fire would be better, I think. I'm going to say goodbye to Matthew. See you tomorrow."

Strange man. Abrupt and impatient, yet with a warm and generous side he was unashamed to present. She couldn't work him out. She looked at her watch. Four forty-five. Only quarter of an hour before Trottiscliffe was due to arrive at Catinca's atelier. She hoped to heaven it would work out as Theo had planned. Beatrice crossed her fingers and sent powerful good luck vibes in the direction of Spitalfields.

Chapter 31

It was in everyone's interests to carry on as if everything was normal. Theo had insisted Adrian and Tamsin went to work as usual on Tuesday. During the day, Adrian invited Tamsin to join him on a vineyard visit, in earshot of other employees. Catinca opened her boutique, managing the shop floor herself to present a picture of normality. Meanwhile, Theo spent all day setting up a surveillance system in Catinca's atelier. There was no way of predicting where Tobias Trottiscliffe would pounce, if indeed he pounced at all. The cameras had to cover every possible angle, the microphones had to be strategically placed and the timing rehearsed to the second.

Theo banned anyone from entering the room while he prepared and that included Catinca. He joined her for lunch at next door's coffee shop and they chatted about politics, the weather, the idea of a mini-break somewhere other than Bruges and said goodbye in the street with a kiss. Catinca returned to her shop and Theo went around the back alley to climb the fire escape and access the atelier.

He tested, checked, changed angles and altered volume levels then tested once again. Once satisfied with the recording equipment, he spent an hour and a half arranging the best place to conceal himself. He had to be completely invisible to anyone in the room but at the same time, close enough to prevent any harm coming to Tamsin if things got out of hand. Eventually, he settled on creating a hide between several rolls and bolts of cloth. He created half a tepee against the wall by placing three tall rolls of black or navy fabric at an angle, draping some black netting with a constellation design as a substitute curtained entrance. From there, he was close enough to hear and observe everything that went on in the room while remaining out of sight. If anything went wrong and he was required to act, he would be out of there in under a second. He waited until six o'clock, long after Catinca had locked up and gone home as per their agreement. With evening light and indoor illumination at the level it would be the following day at the same time, Theo checked everything again. When he was satisfied, he switched everything off, locked the workshop and returned home.

The other three, who he had begun to think of as his team, each had their own duties to perform on Tuesday evening. Catinca was coaching Tamsin in how to present fabrics to their client. Adrian had Theo's permission to speak to his friend from Gay Men's Choir who happened to be an investigative journalist with one of the best known London broadsheets. Theo scripted the entire operation and tried to envisage every aspect that might not go to plan. The urge to call Beatrice nagged at him to such an extent he actually picked up the phone more than once. But he had made them all promise to say nothing and to avoid all electronic communications between themselves on the subject. He couldn't be the one to blab. Instead, he meditated for half an hour, concentrating on everything Beatrice had taught him. No stone unturned.

On Wednesday morning, each arrived separately. Theo was on site by 08.30, making a full assessment of the electronic equipment. Tamsin arrived at twenty past nine with two coffees. Theo was relieved to see she'd taken his advice and woven her hair into a braid around her head. Her long plaits were too risky when trying to entrap a sexual predator. The thought of an attacker pulling her hair made Tamsin every bit as nervous as Theo was.

"He ain't gonna get that far though, is he? You're right, though, I shouldn't take the risk. Know what? I quite like this look even if I couldn't fit my cycling helmet on this morning. It's sort of Ride of the Valkyries, if only one of the Valkyries had been black."

"It does suit you actually. Let me show you how this is gonna work." He walked through the entire workshop, explaining the location of all cameras and microphones and pointing out the optimum area to get herself assaulted.

As soon as he said those words, he rested his forearms on the cutting table and clasped his hands together. "I can't believe I'm asking you to do this."

"You ain't. Stop stealing my thunder 'cos you know this was my idea. Theo, give me a break. You're a professional and you know what has to be done. Let's just do a proper job and show who that bastard really is. Know what I'm saying? No time to be squeamish. Here's Tink!"

Catinca entered the room, looking more beautiful than he had ever seen her. To call such a goddess 'Tink' was unthinkable. She wore a gold trench coat, a black polo-neck sweater and cigarette pants above her black Converse trainers, as if she'd just stepped out of a Philip Marlowe novel. Her make-up was dramatic, enhancing her beautiful features, and her hair cascaded in ringlets down her back. He stood in undisguised admiration as she sauntered across the floorboards.

"All right? Adrian's downstairs, changing and getting into character." She widened her eyes. "Mr Director, you've got a right diva on your hands. Tamsin, lemme look at your hair! You're a lucky bitch. That face, that hair and that sodding amazing figure! Trozley the Tosser is gonna be putty in your hands. We ready then?"

Theo couldn't speak. The reality of what they were about to attempt terrified him, but these two women stalked into battle, shoulder to shoulder, convinced of victory. Valkyries indeed.

"Ms Radu, I'm so sorry to disturb, but Elton wants the whole line of S/S 21 and he's not taking 'hang on a minute' for an answer." A vision Theo could never have imagined flounced across the room. Adrian strutted across the parquet floor in a pair of nude platform boots, cerise culottes, a pink button-down shirt with a set of pearls around his neck and his hair tied into two mini Björk-style buns. He twirled and Theo noticed the back panel of the shirt was transparent.

With one hand on his hip, he said, "Hi, I'm Ludovico. Follow me."

Tamsin burst into delighted laughter.

Theo stared, slack-jawed in admiration. "You look ... I don't know what you look like."

"Like a fashion icon's assistant? Because that's the impression we were going for. What about the pearls? Too much?"

"Nah, keep 'em on," said Catinca. "Wish I could put whole look on Instagram. We ready to rehearse then?"

They walked through the scenario half a dozen times, with Catinca playing the role of Agnessa and Theo himself playing the role of Trottiscliffe. Although Theo was uncomfortable with how much Catinca and Adrian were enjoying their performances, he chose not to dampen the levity. Just so long as they stuck to the script, remembered what to do and when to do it, they could laugh as much as they liked, at least in rehearsal.

"Daddy darling, I really must run. Can I leave you to sort out paperwork? Thank you so much, Taz, and please send my best regards to Ms Radu. Tatty-bye!"

"I'll see you out, Ms Trottiscliffe. Is it all right if I lock up now, Taz? It's gone five-thirty and my spinning class starts at six." Adrian looked at Theo. "Does it have to be a spinning class? I feel my character would be more into Zumba."

Theo face-palmed and Tamsin and Catinca burst into giggles, while Adrian clutched his pearls, a pert expression on his face.

"Just get on with it," said Theo, forcing an indulgent smile. "You go downstairs, see Agnessa off the premises, lock the door and come back upstairs are silently as you can. Let's go."

He heard them clumping down the stairs, ad-libbing nonsense and finding each other hilarious. He closed the door and turned to Tamsin. This was the bit he found the most awkward.

"So then you get the paperwork out and point out the detail, encouraging him to get close to you. Keep it as professional as you possibly can and maintain the politeness even if he does start leching. Then when he … tries it on, you tell him to stop. Make it clear you don't want his attention. You have to say no more than once and then make the decision when to scream. He has to go far enough that it is a sexual assault but obviously I don't want him to, oh, you know."

Tamsin nodded slowly, her expression serious. "It's a tough one to call, know what I mean? Let's go. You do the creepy shit and I'll try and find the right moment. Theo? You all right?"

He wasn't. He couldn't think of anything more repulsive than trying to force himself on an unwilling female, but there was no way he could say that to a woman who was voluntarily exposing herself to sexual assault.

"Yeah. Just trying to get my head around it." He took a deep breath and assumed an upper-class accent. "Well, young lady, I understand you need my autograph on a few papers. Shall we?"

Tamsin withdrew the papers Catinca had prepared. "Certainly, sir. I have copies printed for you and for Radu Designs. As you can see the materials breakdown is on this page and the estimated labour costs are on page two. If I could have your signature here and oh!" She recoiled as Theo ran his hand down her spine towards her backside.

"Please don't do that. It's inappropriate."

He loomed over her with a slimy grin. "You are a very attractive young woman. You make it hard for a man to resist." He reached out a hand to cup her neck and draw her towards him. "Come here."

"No! I'm sorry but I really don't want you to touch me." She pulled away and walked around the other side of the cutting table. "I don't mean to be rude. All I want to do is my job. Would you please sign these papers, Lord Trottiscliffe? That's all I ask."

Her clarity of message and sense of self-preservation hit Theo like an elbow in the solar plexus. He wanted to apologise and run from the room. Forcing himself to proceed according to the script, he leered and reached across the table as if to take the pen, but caught her hand instead.

"Come along, now. Let's not get all stroppy. You'll find I'm a friendly kind of man and in a position to do a lovely creature like yourself some favours."

Tamsin spoke louder. "Maybe I didn't make myself clear. I'm here to do a job, that's all. I try to be pleasant and polite with all our clients unless they cross a line. If you're not willing to sign the papers today, I can have my colleague deliver them to your office later this week."

Theo moved around the table, covering the distance between them in half a dozen strides. He caught her by the waist and pressed her body against his. "I'm not interested in your colleague. But you fascinate me." He bent his head as if to kiss her and she screamed, a bloodcurdling shriek in his ear.

Right on cue, the door burst open and in came Adrian. "Taz! What's the hell is going on? Let go of her! Get off, you dirty old man!" Adrian pulled Theo's shoulder and Tamsin wriggled free. "Did he hurt you? Should I call the police?"

Both Theo and Adrian looked at Tamsin, who simply stared at the floor, as if hypnotised.

"Tamsin?" asked Adrian, more gently. "Remember the script.

You're supposed to tell me that involving the police isn't necessary but you want him to leave immediately. Isn't that right, Theo?"

In a second, Theo saw how well Adrian was managing the situation. By dropping his fake persona and addressing both Tamsin and Theo by name, he was taking all of them out of character and restoring normality.

"Exactly," he agreed. "It's all going perfectly so far. Let's walk through the rest of it because we have to get him out as fast as possible. Ready to carry on?"

"OK," Tamsin muttered. She gave a shiver and raised her voice. "It's not necessary to involve the police. But thank God you came back otherwise I'm not sure what would have happened. I'd like you to leave now, Lord Trottiscliffe. We'll send the paperwork to your office in the next few days. Goodbye."

The speech was stiff and lacked the plausibility of her earlier performance. Theo threw a half-hearted glare at her and Adrian, and then stalked out of the door. Catinca was waiting outside, an expression of concern greeting a face.

"Is she all right?"

"Don't know." He returned to the workshop, applauding with cupped hands. "Great performances all round. Tamsin, you were incredible. Sorry, that sounds arseways. What I mean was you were completely credible and gave an awesome performance. I believed you, one hundred percent."

Tamsin gave a brief smile and a thumbs-up, but Theo could see something was wrong. He made a split-second decision. "Adrian, can you and I run through the timings? I want to check how long it takes to go downstairs, unlock the door and creep back up."

They left the room, closing the door behind them and walked to the ground floor in silence. Once inside the shop, which was strangely gloomy with the blinds down, Adrian gave Theo an enquiring look. "What was that about?"

"That's what I hope Catinca will find out. My guess is Tamsin's just realised what it means to have some bloke pawing her. If she says she wants out, we have to support her. Shit, playing the dirty old man shook me, so God knows how she feels. Let's give them a bit of time. Want to go next door for a coffee?"

"Looking like this? Yeah, right. Why don't you go and get four caramel macchiatos and bring them upstairs? Theo, do you really think we can pull this off?"

Theo answered truthfully. "There are a whole lot of variables. But there's also the slimmest chance we can." He unlocked the front door and went out into the windy street with a strong sense of foreboding.

"Thanks, Theo," said Tamsin, giving him her usual grin as she accepted her coffee. "The role-play weirded me out a bit. See, I wanted to hurt you. It took every scrap of self-control not to punch you, kick you, and knee you in the bollocks. And you're a mate of mine. It's a bit harder than I thought, but I promise I can do this. She's trying to persuade me out of the idea." She pointed at Catinca and shook her head. "Not a chance. Good job we done the run-through. Now I know what to expect." She grinned at Adrian. "Your timing was bang on, geezer. I reckon we can do this."

Theo checked Catinca's expression. There was concern but also optimism in her eyes. He decided to state the facts.

"There are so many things about this operation that could go wrong. They might cancel at the last minute. Agnessa might come alone or she might not leave at the appointed time. Yes, I know she's agreed to meet you in a wine bar down the road," he said to Catinca, "but she might change her mind or forget or even refuse to leave him alone with a young woman. Trottiscliffe may not take the bait. You are beautiful, Tamsin, any fool can see that but there's no accounting for tastes. If he doesn't fancy you, or if he's in a hurry, or a bad temper, he might just sign the papers and piss off. Adrian might fall off his platforms when tiptoeing upstairs, the technology might fail us or I might sneeze in my hiding place and give the game away. The chances of all elements falling into place are remote and we shouldn't get our hopes up. Give it our best, sure, but don't pin all our hopes on catching this bloke in the act. If anyone wants to pull the plug now, I can live with that."

He expected a moment or two of silence while they digested his words so was surprised to see Tamsin fold her arms and shake her head before he finished speaking. Catinca copied the gesture and after a second's hesitation, Adrian did the same. Theo suppressed a convulsion of laughter. The three of them looked like a still from *Grease* – The Pink Ladies.

"I'll take that as a no. All right, it's twenty to one and I'm hungry. Let's break for lunch and come back here for three o'clock. Call me paranoid, but I don't think we should be seen together. I'm gonna get some street food from the market and go for a walk to clear my head."

Adrian unclipped his pearls. "I'll get changed and go home to walk Dolly. Poor darling dog has been alone for three whole hours. Tamsin, do you want to come with me? It's a bit far for you to travel home and back before three."

"Or you can stay here?" offered Catinca. "I could order a takeaway for us both?"

"No, but thanks for asking. I'm going home for some of last night's chilli. It only takes me twenty minutes on the bike. Back by three and promise not to fart."

On the pretence of checking all the equipment once again, Theo waited for Adrian and Tamsin to leave so he could have a moment alone with Catinca. Something about her witnessing his sleazy behaviour towards Tamsin bothered him, even if it had been an act.

She was in the shop, locking up after Adrian when Theo

came downstairs. Her face softened into a smile and she walked towards him, her hands outstretched. "You're amazing to do this for me. Everyone's amazing, but you? You don't believe it's going to work, but still, you throw in everything you got. What kind of crazy man are you?"

He took her hands and gazed into her warm eyes. "People do the craziest things when they're in love."

Her eyes widened and her lips parted. "Did you say what I think you said?"

"Yes. I did. Just so there's no confusion, I'm going to say it again."

A hammering at the window made them both start in alarm. The guy from the coffee shop next door was pointing urgently at something out of sight. Catinca ran to unlock the door.

"Al? What is it?"

"Your mate, the black girl? She just got knocked off her bike. We called an ambulance because she's out cold. The van driver's in a right state."

A knot of people surrounded a prone form beside a pile of bin bags. Catinca forced her way through, clutching Theo's hand. A young man in a white uniform knelt beside Tamsin, two fingers pressed to her neck.

"Is she OK? She's a friend of mine, she just left the shop five minutes ago. Is she all right?"

"She's breathing and she has a strong pulse. We need to wait for the paramedics to know more. I'm a dental hygienist with some medical training. Could you get these people to stand back? It's not great to have everyone breathing over her."

Theo and Al shooed the onlookers away and created a human cordon by directing people into the street and off the pavement where Tamsin lay. The sound of the siren reached Theo's ears before he saw the blue flashing lights. The van driver was pacing up and down beside his vehicle, its hazard lights still blinking, telling everyone what had happened.

"I didn't see her. I was coming out of the junction and I saw a FedEx van indicating right so I thought it would be fine to pull out of his way and next thing I knew, there was a crunch. She was right in front of the van but I didn't see her until it was too late. She flew off the bike and landed in those bin bags. The bike had lights but it was right in front of the FedEx van, which is why I didn't see her. She wasn't wearing a helmet but I think she had a soft landing. It was an accident. I didn't see her."

She wasn't wearing a helmet. Because she couldn't fit it over her hair that Theo had suggesting weaving around her head so that the potential rapist she was about to face could not use her long plaits as a means of manipulation. What the hell did he think he was doing?

Catinca accompanied Tamsin to the hospital, leaving Theo with the keys to the shop. He walked around the market, feeling sick and ashamed of himself. He should call Adrian and warn him that the sting was off, but he didn't want to use his phone in case Catinca called. The market seemed an assault on all his senses; competing smells from food stalls, clashing colours, reverberating noise and people brushing past as if they'd never heard the expression 'personal space'. He walked out onto Brushfield Street and along to Christ Church. He sat on the steps in a patch of sunshine, staring miserably at the smokers standing outside The Ten Bells pub. Inertia weighed him down, making it impossible to move, even though the cold of the stone steps penetrated his jeans. He took out his mobile and phoned Beatrice. There was no answer.

His mobile rang. Catinca.

"Hey. How is she?"

There was a lot of noise at Catinca's end. "She's all right. Mild concussion is all. We're in a taxi on the way to her house. Her boyfriend's coming round to look after her. She's fretting about her bike."

Theo released a long breath of relief. "Good news. I was really worried about her. Tell her the bike is fine. I took it upstairs to the workshop along with her backpack."

"Brilliant. She'll be happy to hear that. As soon as I dropped her off, the taxi will bring me back to Spitalfields so I should be at the shop by three, easy."

"No rush. We got no choice but to cancel the plan. I'd better call Adrian and let him know."

"No, don't cancel! I got an idea. OK, we just got to Tamsin's. I'll see you in a bit." She rang off before Theo could protest.

He stood up and stretched, smiling in the knowledge Tamsin had not been badly hurt and aware of a hollow feeling in his stomach. The only question now was whether to have an Akara burger with fried plantain from Tasty or grab a meze box from The Real Greek.

"No way. There are so many things wrong with this idea I don't even know where to start. It was bad enough putting Tamsin in harm's way. You must be out of your mind. The answer is no."

Catinca had a stubborn set to her jaw. "Why are we doing this?"

"We're not," said Theo. "We're not doing anything. The game is up."

"We put two days' planning into setting a trap for this guy. Why? He gropes and sexually harasses women because he thinks he can get away with it. It's time we put a stop to that. Everything is ready and with one small change, we can still make this happen."

Theo grasped his forehead in exasperation. "Number one, he has already assaulted you once. Quite apart from the fact he is bound to recognise you, you'd have to put yourself through that experience again. It upset you enough the first time. Two, if we take this story to the press, which was the intention, you'd have to make the accusation. And bang goes your commission. There was a chance you'd have lost it anyway with Tamsin accusing him of harassment. But there's no way Trottiscliffe's daughter can wear a Radu dress when Catinca Radu herself exposed her father's sexual misconduct. Number three, you're supposed to be meeting Agnessa in the wine bar at half past five. How the hell do you plan to be entrapping Daddy and swigging Chardonnay with Nessie at the same time? It's not going to work, Catinca. Just give it up."

"No. Answer me one question. What is my greatest talent? I'll tell you because we ain't got much time. Self-transformation. I can do hair, make-up and clothes and look completely different to the woman he met last time. He won't recognise me and neither will she. As for commission, they can stuff it. This is more important. We stick to plan exactly as we rehearsed and we get that bastard. It means everything to me that you and Adrian and Tamsin want to shame him in public. I'm not giving up now."

Adrian looked from one to the other, his hands clutched together like a priest. "It is true," he said tentatively, "that she can disguise herself so that even we wouldn't recognise her. We also have confirmation a major paper is ready to run the story."

Theo shot him a look and Adrian held up his hands in surrender.

"You're avoiding the key issue. I have no doubt you could transform yourself into Catinca Radu's assistant well enough to fool the Trottiscliffes. I believe you when you say the commission is less important than blowing the whistle on this guy. But I cannot get my head around the fact you would voluntarily let that sleaze ball do it again."

Catinca dropped her voice almost to a whisper. "I would. Because this time will be his last. Not saying that thought ain't scary, but worth the risk." She reached out to catch his hand. "We've come this far. Please, Theo. Do this for me."

Both Adrian and Catinca looked at Theo, waiting for his

capitulation. He was boxed in and no way could he refuse.

It took her an hour and a half to complete the change, but the transformation was extraordinary. As she sashayed across the room, Theo could have sworn he'd never seen this woman before in his life. Rich chestnut hair grazed the shoulders of a figure-skimming pink satin shirt dress with an oversized collar and floppy cuffs. Her eyes were now green and her lips the same scarlet as her stilettos. Somehow, she had even managed to change the shape of her face, so that her cheekbones seemed sharper and her chin became the point of a heart. Nothing about the outfit was overtly sexy, but the way she moved and the fabric shifted over her body held Theo spellbound.

"I can't do sodding stairs in these heels, so you'll have to let them in, Adrian. What time is it? We better get in position, they'll be here in half hour."

"Theo, cat got your tongue?" asked Adrian.

His attention monopolised by the sight of Catinca, he had barely registered Adrian's make-up. His eyes were rimmed with kohl and his lips shone with pale pink gloss.

"I need to call Beatrice," said Theo.

They continued setting the scene as he murmured his concerns to his boss. When he finally put down the phone, he opened his mouth to summarise her advice when the shop doorbell rang. The three of them stared at one another, frozen. It was ten to five.

"Into position. You know what to do. Good luck!" Theo ducked into his observation point and set the camera running behind the gauze. His heart was pounding too fast and his breathing must surely be audible from the workshop. He concentrated on the tiny screen showing the solitary figure bent over fabric swatches in the atelier. Catinca aka Taz seemed perfectly relaxed. Theo took long, calming breaths. *In an hour, this will be over.* The sound of voices wafted up the stairs, one more strident than the rest. Agnessa Trottiscliffe was in the building.

"... could hardly decide! If I had my way, I'd wear all three. One for the ceremony, one for the reception and one for the evening. Your boss has so much talent and inspiration. It must be terrific fun working here. I mean, it's practically the East End. I used to love Camden, back in the day, but it's lost its edge, you know?"

"I know!" gushed Adrian. "At least the East End is authentic, right? Brick Lane and bagels, Hoxton and hot new artists, plus A-list bars exclusive for those in the know." Theo had no idea what Adrian's accent was supposed to be but guessed it would be described as transatlantic.

"Squeak! Any hints? I'm desperate to find somewhere off the beaten track. The same old gets so same and so old, you know?"

The door opened and in walked the bride-to-be. Theo made his judgement in a second. Lean, blonde and entitled, without an atom of originality. She stopped short on seeing 'Taz', who represented the opposite end of the spectrum. Theo tuned out of the fake greetings and focused his attention on the big man coming through the door. He was overweight but due to his height, carried it well. His suit and shoes stamped him with the hallmark of wealth. He stood on the threshold taking in the room and Theo clocked the precise moment he registered Catinca/Taz.

His posture changed, as if a sleepy lion had just seen a gazelle. Theo zoomed in on the man's face and saw the beginnings of a crooked smile. *That's good*, he told himself. *That's exactly what we want.* But inside, another Theo was rolling up his sleeves and saying, 'you lay a finger on her, you fat bastard, and you're dead'.

Adrian introduced them. "Agnessa, Lord Trottiscliffe, this is Ms Radu's assistant, Taz. I'll leave you in her capable hands. If you need anything, I'll be right over here." He sat down at the computer table in the corner.

Trottiscliffe offered his hand but the redhead merely waved her fingers.

"So pleased to meet you, Lord Trottiscliffe. Did I pronounce Trottiscliffe correctly? Ms Radu tried to coach me but I'm a slow learner." Her voice was lower, borderline torch singer and her smile overpowering.

Trottiscliffe was hooked, that much was obvious. "You said my name perfectly, my dear. Seems to me you're a faster learner than you think." His voice dripped with innuendo.

During the fabric demonstrations, Agnessa's attention was focused wholly on each piece, stroking the material while listening to Catinca's descriptions. Trottiscliffe was wholly focused on 'Taz' and didn't give any of the samples as much as a glance. They'd succeeded in luring him and Theo hated it.

"These three are my top choices and I know they aren't cheap, but then again, this is a once-in-a-lifetime event. Can we have these for my fabulous, head-turning, exclusive dress? Please say yes because I am madly in love with these colours."

Trottiscliffe affected a helpless shrug. "I cannot refuse my darling girls a thing. And they know it. Yes, Nessie, choose the ones you want and I will sign on the dotted line. Excuse me?" He was addressing Adrian. "How about something to seal the deal? I'm sure you have a bottle of champagne on the premises. Or if not, you could pop out and fetch one. No?"

Agnessa threw her arms in the air as if she were about to attempt a cartwheel. "No, Babar, now is not the time. I have an appointment in five minutes anyway, let's just get the job done."

"I'm afraid we don't have any champagne and I need to lock up at five-thirty." Adrian mugged apologetically. "Is it all right if I shut the shop and leave now, Taz? It's just my Zumba class starts at six. Would you like me to walk you out, Ms Trottiscliffe? I can give you the name of that bar I mentioned."

"Double squeak! Yes, please! "Agnessa threw her arms

around her father, kissed him on the cheek and waggled her fingers at Catinca. "Thank you, thank you, thank you, Taz, for your super advice. Have a lovely evening, ciao!" With that, she followed Adrian from the room, closing the door behind her. To Theo's horror and delight, it was show time.

Catinca closed the fabric books and took a file of papers from a drawer. "Your daughter has a good eye. Here are the agreements to enable Ms Radu to purchase the materials. One copy for you and one for Radu Designs. If I could have your signature on both, we're all done."

Trottiscliffe moved around to take his daughter's place beside Catinca. "I never sign any documents without a thorough reading by myself and my lawyer. Why don't you and I discuss this over a drink at my club? You can explain all this and if it makes sense, you can have my signature."

"I understand. You're welcome to take the documentation to discuss with your legal people as and when you're ready. Would you like to take them now or shall I send them to your office?"

"We could cut out that extra administration and I could sign the papers tonight. On condition you come and have a drink with me." Trottiscliffe brushed a lock of ginger hair from Catinca's face.

She moved away. "Sorry, I don't think that's appropriate."

"You girls. All dressed up in Jessica Rabbit colours and fuck-me heels, then you act surprised when men come running to your dog whistles. I'm a sucker for stilettos. Literally." He got down on his knees and crawled towards her legs, grabbing an ankle and lifting her foot to his lips.

"No! Don't touch me!" Catinca yanked her foot from his grasp, gathered all the papers and walked to the end of the cutting table. "I don't mean to be rude, but I think you should leave now. The paperwork can wait."

Theo clenched his fist so hard he thought his knuckles would crack. *Scream now*, he willed her. *No more.*

"It's very painful for a man to part with this much money for something as flimsy as a dress. Perhaps a little something to sweeten the pill would help." He got to his feet and held out a hand. "I think we understand each other."

Catinca backed away. "Lord Trottiscliffe, I don't how much clearer I can make this. I am not interested in any kind of physical interaction. You're making me feel very uncomfortable. Please leave now or …"

"Or what?" Trottiscliffe grabbed her wrist and dragged her into an embrace. His hand grasped the back of his skull. Her wig slid slightly to the left and Theo held his breath.

"No! Please don't do this! Please let me go!"

In a practised move, Trottiscliffe turned her around, bent her over the cutting table, pressed her face into the fabric swatches and scrabbled to open his flies.

Theo was about to bite through his knuckle when her scream echoed around the room.

The door banged open with such force it rebounded off the wall. "TAZ! Stop that! Leave her alone, you filthy bastard! Let go, get off her! You disgusting old pervert!"

"Get out of here, you!" bellowed Trottiscliffe, his grip still tight on Catinca's head.

"You get out of here," roared Adrian, and swung a punch at Trottiscliffe's saggy jaw. The uppercut was badly executed but it connected below the MP's eye with enough force to make him stagger and release Catinca.

Adrian stood there panting as Catinca scrambled to her feet. To Theo's amazement, he remembered his lines. "Did he hurt you? Should I call the police?"

Catinca's wig was askew and her expression impossible to read. "Kick him out. That piece of shit was about to rape me. If he's not out of this building in the next thirty seconds, call the cops."

Trottiscliffe got to his feet and zipped up his flies. "Well, that's a shame. You just cost your boss the commission of a lifetime. I strongly suspect you'll be out of a job by Monday."

Catinca straightened her dress and eased off the redhead wig, wincing as the clips pulled out of her hair. "That's the second time you have sexually assaulted me, Lord Tobias Trottiscliffe. The first time at your rooms in Jeremy's, the second here in my own workshop. No commission in the world is worth suffering sexual abuse at the hands of arrogant arse like you. As for who's gonna be out of a job on Monday, let's wait and see. Now fuck off."

The man's confusion was evident. He glanced from one to the other, then whirled around and stormed down the stairs, with Adrian on his heels. Theo stayed where he was until he heard platform boots enter the room. He switched off his camera, drew back his net curtain and stared at Catinca, unable to stop tears leaking down his cheeks.

She looked from Adrian to Theo, her eyes wide as if in shock. "Did we get him?" she asked in a shaky voice.

Theo showed her the camera in his right hand. "Yeah, we got him."

Chapter 32

It didn't make sense for Catinca to stay in her apartment. If, or rather when the news broke, the first place the press would come sniffing would be her front door. She returned to collect what she described as her 'running-away bag' and went to Theo's place. They both needed to decompress after the stress of the afternoon and if she was honest, she didn't want to let the guy out of her sight. Catinca pulled all the pins out of her hair, scrubbed off her make-up, had a long, warm shower and dressed in pyjamas.

Adrian called to confirm he'd sent his newspaper contact all the footage, photographs and witness statements from Catinca's workshop. The journo said it was an impressive story and potential headline news, Adrian reported breathlessly. She sat on the sofa, messaging Tamsin and Adrian every couple of minutes, checking the twenty-four-hour news and keeping an eye on Theo, who was making pizza in the kitchen. The scent of garlic and dough wrapped itself around her like a comfort blanket. She switched off the TV and came to sit on one of the kitchen stools to watch him work.

He smiled at her as he chopped tomatoes. "Much as I love high-glamour Radu, Catinca in sheep-print pyjamas works for me. Glass of wine?"

"Course! Can't eat pizza without red wine. Can I have an

olive?"

"Help yourself. How are you feeling?"

"Hungry, mostly. A bit nervous, too. I just want to disappear down for a few days, know what I mean?"

"That's exactly what we should do. I'm thinking somewhere in the countryside, a village green with a rustic pub and maybe some friendly neighbours. Go for a walk on the moors, ignore the news and spend some time getting to know each other."

She cocked her head. "You got a plan?"

"Yeah, I got a plan. While you were on the phone to Adrian, Will called. Beatrice has invited us all to Devon for the weekend. Will and Adrian are driving down on Friday and offered us a lift. We could stay in that pub. They have rooms available, I checked."

"Brilliant idea!" Catinca bit into a stuffed olive. "What sort of rooms?"

Theo opened the oven door. "Five minutes and we're ready to eat. The Angel has doubles, twins and singles, depending on what we want. What do you think of the wine?"

Catinca swirled it around her glass, lifting it to the light. "Ripe for drinking, I'd say."

He took off his oven gloves and came to stand opposite, his eyes searching hers. "What you went through today and the time before, it freaks me out. I hate the idea of bugging you with unwanted attention. I'm actually scared to try and kiss you, even though I want that more than pizza and red wine."

She blinked and gave a soft laugh through her nose. "I been trying to attract your attention for years, mate. Why do you think I chose redhead wig? Beatrice told me that yoga bunny you fell for in Mallorca was ginger. Your attention is opposite of unwanted. Yeah, let's go to Devon with the boys. Hey, Theo? Book us a double room."

The first Catinca heard that the news had broken was a phone call at quarter to seven.

Adrian's voice was high-pitched and smiley. "Guess who's trending on Twitter?"

Catinca sat bolt upright. "Me?"

"No, at least not yet. But check out #Trottiscliffe! Why don't you two come over for breakfast? We can conference call with Beatrice and decide how to handle the press."

"Ooh, yeah, great idea. See you soon."

She leaned over a sleepy Theo and kissed his bare shoulder. "Come on, mate, surf's up."

LORD TROTTISCLIFFE CAUGHT WITH PANTS DOWN

Allegations have long circulated around the peer and television personality. Rumours around his treatment of women are rife. Now, exclusive footage obtained by a private detective agency appears to show the MP sexually assaulting fashion designer Catinca Radu at her shop in London. The Trottiscliffe family have yet to comment.

It was all over the Internet. Footage of Trottiscliffe making a sexist joke on *Question Time*, the exterior of Catinca's shop, pictures of PI Beatrice Stubbs whose agency broke the story and the now-viral clip of Trottiscliffe grabbing Catinca, forcing her over the table and fumbling with his trousers. Gossip gold and reputation ruined. Social media was alight.

At Adrian's flat, Will made coffee and Theo took Dolly out to buy bagels. Catinca and Adrian split their attention between TV, Twitter, Facebook and WhatsApp while holding conversations with Tamsin on her sofa, Francisco at the news desk and Ezra at Dionysus.

"Adrian's ecstatic 'cos the film clip includes him punching Trottiscliffe. He can't stop going on about it."

"Yes, a statement later today, Francisco, I promise you. We're having a call this morning and we'll send you the press release before everyone else. You did a brilliant job!"

"Yeah, press conference outside the shop, you know, scene of sodding crime. Free advertising, innit? Just gotta get Beatrice's approval. How's your head today?"

"Until Monday, if you can bear it. I'm sorry, Ezra, but the shop is likely to draw loads of curious rubberneckers now I'm all over the Internet, so get some of the new staff to help out."

When Theo arrived with bagels, excitement levels reached fever pitch. They ate in the kitchen, Adrian and Catinca interrupting each other to share some notable comment from social media, while Theo explained the decision to make this an agency coup. At ten o'clock, they settled on the sofa in front of the screen to talk to Beatrice.

By eleven, they had refined the press statement and agreed, to Adrian's delight, that he was the person to deliver it. After a frantic hour during which he and Catinca scoured his wardrobe for the precise combination of stylish and serious, he was ready to face the media. As agreed, they sent Francisco the press release embargoed until two o'clock. Catinca put on one of Adrian's hoodies so she wouldn't be recognised. Will loaned Theo a suit to play Adrian's bodyguard, complete with sunglasses. They bundled into the Audi and Will drove to Spitalfields Market, where they noticed a pack of journalists half blocking Brushfield Street.

"Whoa," said Catinca. "Look at all of them! Are you nervous?"

Adrian checked his hair and suit. "Nervous, schmervous. I'm a professional performer. Just remember, Theo, the second I finish the statement you bundle me along the street and into the car. I'm taking no questions."

"Got it," said Theo, with an amused grin at Catinca.

Will parked in the alley at the rear of the shop and agreed on a signal to summon the car. Theo and Adrian entered the building via the fire escape, while Catinca sidled off to blend into the crowd. As well as all the journos, the usual Sunday market-goers hung around in expectation of some street theatre or a flash mob. Right on time, the shop door opened and Adrian, flanked by Theo, emerged to face the press. Theo looked so sexy in Will's suit Catinca could hardly contain herself.

Adrian stood at the centre of the furry sound booms, microphones, extended mobile phones and lenses pointing in his direction, unfolding his piece of paper. "Good afternoon, members of the press. My name is Adrian Harvey and I'm acting as spokesperson for the Beatrice Stubbs Agency and Radu Designs. I will be making a short statement jointly approved by both organisations. At this time, I am unable to take any questions. As a result of an incident which took place at Jeremy's in Mayfair, Lord Trottiscliffe's club, Ms Catinca Radu engaged the services of the Beatrice Stubbs agency. The brief was to prove Lord Tobias Trottiscliffe was a sexual harasser. The agency, collaborating with Ms Radu and her team, set up a CCTV network in her workshop. Last night, after a consultation with Lord Tobias Trottiscliffe and his daughter, Ms Agnessa Trottiscliffe, the latter left the room accompanied by one of Ms Radu's assistants. Believing them to be alone, Lord Trottiscliffe made sexual advances towards Ms Radu. Even after being rejected, he attempted rape. With evidence gathered by the detective agency, Ms Radu will be making a full statement to the Metropolitan police and pressing charges against Lord Trottiscliffe. Thank you for your attention."

Theo's hand was on his shoulder before Adrian could even fold away his speech. He used his back to shield Adrian from the intrusive phones, cameras and shouts, guiding him as fast as possible to the Audi. Catinca was right behind them and leapt into the back seat. Will sounded the horn and drove forward. Within seconds, they left the crowd behind, cruising up Bishopsgate.

"How did I do?" asked Adrian.

Catinca gave him a high five and a massive hug, unable to

put her feelings into words.

Chapter 33

Eleven people for dinner would have been a push even with Matthew at his most cooperative. Over breakfast the conversation had been lucid and enthusiastic about the Trottiscliffe triumph, leading Beatrice to believe that he was having one of his better days. They were walking Huggy Bear through the forest when Matthew asked again what had happened in Belgium. She gave him the same reply every time he asked.

"I found out what I could and handed it over to the police," she said, for the fifteenth time. "Regarding dinner tonight, I thought some kind of one-pot dish. Best keep it vegetarian with a few vegan dishes so everyone's happy. What would you say to a Moroccan tagine?"

He did not reply and Beatrice looked over her shoulder. He was pointing at something on the path with that strange slack-faced expression she had come to dread. "Caterpillar," he said. "That's a caterpillar. In a few months' time, it will become a glorious butterfly."

Beatrice moved closer and noticed the snail had withdrawn into its shell to avoid Matthew's finger. "Butterflies to me are heralds of spring. Cabbage Whites and Brimstones fluttering around our garden are a sight to lift the heart. What's your favourite butterfly, Matthew?"

He frowned at her, his face a study of disapproval. "At Exeter, an undergraduate never refers to one's professor by his first name. It's a mark of respect. My title is Professor Bailey and I will thank you to respect that." He bent down to the study the snail and shoved Huggy Bear away as she came to sniff the object of interest. "Take that animal out of here. Dogs should be on a lead in this forest. I blame irresponsible owners."

Beatrice clipped the lead onto Huggy Bear's collar and moved several paces away. His temper flared for no discernible reason these days and was not easily restored. She walked in the direction of the cottage, her heart sinking lower as his mutterings followed. Cooking for almost a dozen was out of the question when he was in this frame of mind. To her infinite relief, Axel's car was parked in the driveway. Matthew snapped at Beatrice and Marianne often, occasionally at Tanya and even Luke but never once demonstrated any aggression towards Axel. It was as if he recognised an authority figure.

The carer was in the kitchen, making Matthew's lunch. "Hello. Good walk?"

Beatrice pulled a face and crossed her eyes while Matthew was still in the hallway, removing his wellies. "Lovely!" she said, brightly. "Butterflies and everything. Can I leave you two alone for half an hour? We have guests arriving tonight and I think we might be better convening at The Angel. I shan't be long."

Axel stirred some pungent herbs and onions in a pan. "Not a problem. I'll save some for you and wait for your return. Hello, Matthew."

"Good morning, Axel. Something smells good."

"Let's hope it tastes that way. I was considering the question you posed yesterday evening regarding identity and I'm afraid I disagree with your parameters."

"How so?" said Matthew, easing into a kitchen chair, his expression alert.

Snatching her opportunity, Beatrice lifted the terrier into the car and set off towards the village. Two magpies flew from the hedgerow in the direction of the wood. Two for joy. She hoped it was a sign.

Susie was more than happy to accommodate the party in the function room upstairs at The Angel as everyone would be out of the pub and on the village green for Bonfire Night. They settled on a menu, agreed a time and Beatrice decided to make the most of her remaining minutes of freedom by taking the scenic route home. Outside the new deli, she saw Tanya coming out with a paper bag. She tooted the horn and pulled over into an empty parking space.

"Lunch at your desk? It's not healthy, you know."

"Hello, Beatrice! I know, but if I eat in there, the kitchen smells make me queasy."

"Oh, dear. I've just booked The Angel for tonight's dinner. Your father's in one of his moods so cooking at home would be trying to say the least. Should I cancel?"

"No, no, I'll be fine by then. Umm, can I get in for a sec?"

"Of course. Is everything all right?"

Tanya got in rather awkwardly with her big coat, handbag and sandwich. "Yes, everything's lovely. I planned to make a family announcement this evening, but now there are so many of us, I wonder if that's a good idea. It might be a bit too much for Dad. You see, I'm expecting. Almost four months gone."

Beatrice gasped and a thrill of pure joy filled her. She hugged Tanya tightly as best she could manage and beamed. "I am SO happy for you! Your father will be delighted, I know it. But yes, you might be better telling him before the crowd arrives. Why don't you come home with me now and have your sandwich with us? I can run you back to the office after you've told him."

"I'd prefer to announce the news when Gabe is there. How about we come over early to tell him and go to The Angel together?"

"Even better. He might be in a more upbeat mood when he knows he's going to see old friends. Have you told Marianne yet?"

"She guessed. I might ask her to come round to yours with us. The more enthusiastic people there are, the better Dad will take it. Is Axel coming tonight?"

"How do you mean? He'll do his usual shift around tea time." Beatrice was puzzled.

"No, I meant coming with us to The Angel. I thought Marianne might have invited him. You do know they're dating, Beatrice?"

"Who's dating? Axel and Marianne? Good gracious! Why am I always the last to know?"

Tanya laughed. "And you call yourself a detective. I'll be round about half six, OK? See you later."

Beatrice drove home in a light-headed state. Even the sunshine seemed pinker and more golden. A little sister or brother for Luke. A boyfriend for Marianne and this one would take none of her nonsense. It was all turning out wonderfully. Five months to go. If only Matthew could stay well enough to appreciate an addition to the family.

When she got in, Axel was washing up and Matthew was doing the crossword at the dining table with a pot of tea. "Thank you for waiting, Axel. Everything all right?"

"Everything is fine. I used the last of your onions in our lunch, so next time you're shopping, please buy white and red ones. I must go now."

"Just a sec. Are you free this evening? The family are having dinner at the pub in the village with some friends. I wondered if you'd like to join us. I'm afraid I was a bit dense the other day when you told me about your date. I had no idea you were seeing Marianne or I wouldn't have mentioned Chez Bruno."

"I'm glad you mentioned Marianne had been there with a previous boyfriend. It's good to be aware of such things.

Information, as you know, is power. Yes, I would like to join you, thank you. What time?"

"Seven-thirty, upstairs at The Angel. As you're having dinner with us, why not skip this afternoon's shift? He won't mind if he knows he'll be seeing you later."

"Thank you, I will. See you at The Angel. Goodbye, Huggy Bear." He went into the dining room and informed Matthew of the change in plans for later that day, which the older man accepted with equanimity.

Beatrice realised with a start that she had blithely invited Axel without giving Marianne a say in the matter. She waited till Axel had driven off, picked up the phone and dialled.

The pregnancy announcement did not go as Beatrice hoped, but neither was it a disaster. Matthew was looking forward to seeing their guests from London and had dressed in a suit, for the first time since Tanya's wedding. Beatrice's greeting hugs were warmer than usual on seeing Gabriel, Marianne and Luke.

Luke whispered in her ear, "I'm going to tell Granddad about the baby."

"Good luck," Beatrice whispered back.

Tanya had stopped hiding her bump and now wore a striped top with smocking detail. She couldn't stop grinning.

"Hello, Small Fry. I haven't seen you in months. Come over here and give your grandfather a hug. There! Good heavens, they're all here. Are we going in mob-handed?"

Tanya sat beside her father and kissed him on the cheek. "You look very smart and you smell nice too. We came round a bit earlier because we have some good news." She pointed at Luke.

"Granddad, Beatrice, I'm very happy to tell you that next year, I'm going to have a little brother or sister." He held out his arms like a showman in the direction of Tanya.

Matthew looked at Luke in confusion. "What? How?"

Tanya placed a hand on his arm. "I'm pregnant, Dad. Due in

the spring."

Beatrice and Marianne gushed and hugged and congratulated them ostentatiously, giving Matthew unsubtle clues about how to behave. He got to his feet but instead of shaking Gabriel's hand, he turned to Tanya, hands on his hips.

"Pregnant? Again! Who's the father?"

Tanya burst into giggles. "Who do you think?" She reached up a hand and Gabriel pulled her up and into his arms. "My husband. He's going to make a superb dad. Almost as good as you."

All the wrinkles smoothed on Matthew's forehead. "Gabriel! Congratulations!" He held out his hand and shook Gabriel's in both of his. "I am delighted for you both." He held Tanya's face and kissed her on the forehead. "I'm very proud of you, my darling." He released her and looked around the room with a broad smile. "This is worth celebrating! At least it's not that bloody Frenchman again."

Marianne snorted and Tanya gasped. Gabriel's shoulders shook with laughter and Beatrice checked Luke's reaction. He'd lost interest since making his announcement and was playing catch with Huggy Bear and her squeaky mouse.

"There just happens to be a bottle of champagne in the fridge," she said. "Gabriel, would you do the honours? There's elderflower fizz for Tanya and Luke."

Marianne linked her arm through Beatrice's. "Come sit down with me and Tanya. She wants our advice on potential names."

After toasting the parents-to-be twice and expressing approval for some of Tanya's ideas – Zachary for a boy and Deia for a girl – Beatrice looked up at the clock and announced it was time to go. Marianne wanted to walk ahead to the pub so she could introduce Axel. Bored by conversations he'd heard before, Luke asked to go with her. Beatrice and Tanya followed at a slower pace, with Matthew and Gabriel bringing up the rear. From one day to the next, Tanya had become incredibly fragile in Beatrice's eyes and she fretted over patches of ice or pot-holes.

They reached the pub without incident and opened the function room door to so much noise it was hard to believe there were only seven people in the room. Catinca flew across the floorboards to embrace Tanya, her delight voluble. Looking around at her favourite faces, Adrian, Will, Theo and Catinca, Beatrice relaxed, releasing a tension she hadn't even registered was there.

Dinner was an animated event, with much to catch up on. Adrian retold the story of the sting operation, skimming certain aspects because of Luke, with a focus on his own fabulous role. Catinca interrupted to share the news that she had received at least four enquiries for wedding and award-ceremony commissions. Axel asked about the resulting prosecution and Will explained that several other women had come forward with similar stories to support Catinca's case.

"How marvellous!" exclaimed Beatrice. "This is my favourite kind of investigation, where the agency is covered in glory and I didn't have to lift a finger. Congratulations to you all!"

At the other end of the table, Matthew raised his glass along with everyone else. Beatrice watched as first Gabriel and Will, and then Axel involved him in conversation. He was in safe hands and she could get on with her own agenda. To her left were the other happy couples. She smiled as Catinca laughed at something Theo said and kissed him. Marianne and Axel were not as demonstrably affectionate, but she observed how Marianne leant against the Swede, that he offered her a piece of his starter and the number of quiet murmurings exchanged.

While Catinca was engaged in celebrity name-dropping with Tanya and Adrian, Beatrice made her move and had a quiet chat with Theo. She caught Will's curious glance as if he'd heard his name mentioned, but Luke's eager questions about the imminent firework display distracted him.

The food was simple but delicious: French onion soup or mushroom pâté for starters, followed by three-bean chilli or Homity pie. Beatrice agonised over her choices and regretted them the minute she saw Adrian's soup and Theo's chilli. They were both generous enough to share a bite of each.

When plates had been cleared and Luke asked permission to leave the table and peer out of the window at the bonfire, Beatrice chose her moment and nodded to Susie, who was hovering at the serving hatch. While Susie started uncorking champagne bottles, Beatrice got to her feet, tapped a spoon against her glass and made her speech.

"It's wonderful to see you all here together, my extended family of choice. I'm especially thrilled that you all seem to like each other too." She smiled at the two couples to her left. "I've asked Susie for champagne because we have a lot to celebrate. The most uplifting news that Tanya, Gabriel and Luke are expecting an addition to the family and Matthew is due another grandchild."

"Hear, hear," said Matthew. "Very pleased with Tanya. I don't suppose you'll ever get round to reproducing," he said, addressing Marianne. "But then again, Tanya is a lot prettier than you."

Beatrice cringed. His social filters were switched off today, but Marianne seemed unfazed. "That's true," she said, smiling at her sister. "And she's never looked prettier than she does at the moment."

Axel twisted in his chair to look at Marianne. He took her chin between finger and thumb, and said, "I'd say pretty is a subjective opinion. I think you are beautiful." He kissed her on the lips.

The entire table made an 'Awww' sound with the exception of Matthew.

"Good God! I didn't see that one coming," he muttered.

Beatrice continued, darting a glance at Gabriel to keep an eye on Matthew. "I'd like to extend the warmest of welcomes to Axel, who has fitted into our family effortlessly and makes more than one of us very happy indeed." Marianne beamed and nestled closer as Axel nodded his head in thanks.

"I'm also deeply impressed by the courage and intelligence displayed by Theo in a sticky situation in Brussels. I couldn't have done it without you. Talking of bravery and ingenuity, I applaud Catinca, Theo and Adrian for taking down that odious boor Trottiscliffe. I am grateful you sold it as an agency triumph and hope it brings in much more work. However, the New Year will bring a change of personnel, when Theo takes over as manager. I feel sure he will choose expert staff who excel in their fields." Her gaze rested on Will.

Marianne leaned forward, grinning. "I know of a pretty good accountant looking for work."

Theo laughed and gave her the thumbs-up.

"The reason Theo is taking over is because I am retiring from detective work for good. No more running around Europe, getting into trouble and neglecting my domestic life. I want to make the most of my loved ones, so from now on, I am staying at home. Raise your glasses, everyone, and let's toast ourselves. To a happy and successful future!"

Candlelight bounced off ten glasses as they toasted one another. Matthew didn't take his eyes off her as she sipped.

"Did you say you were retiring, Old Thing?"

"Yes. I did."

"Humph. Heard that one before," he said, but couldn't disguise his smile.

Outside, the sky exploded into fireworks.

Acknowledgements

With sincere gratitude to Florian Bielmann, Jane Dixon-Smith and Julia Gibbs for their professionalism. Profound thanks to all Beatrice's readers for your comments, reviews, recommendations and generous feedback. For the record, she loves you too.

Message from JJ Marsh

I hope you enjoyed *All Souls' Day*. I have also written The Beatrice Stubbs Series, European crime fiction:

BEHIND CLOSED DOORS
RAW MATERIAL
TREAD SOFTLY
COLD PRESSED
HUMAN RITES
BAD APPLES
SNOW ANGEL
HONEY TRAP
BLACK WIDOW
WHITE NIGHT
THE WOMAN IN THE FRAME

I have also written standalone novels:

AN EMPTY VESSEL
ODD NUMBERS

And a short-story collection:

APPEARANCES GREETING A POINT OF VIEW

For more information, visit jjmarshauthor.com

For occasional updates, news, deals and a FREE exclusive prequel: *Black Dogs, Yellow Butterflies*, subscribe to my newsletter on jjmarshauthor.com

If you would recommend this book to a friend, please do so by writing a review. Your tip helps other readers discover their next favourite read. It can be short and only takes a minute.

Thank you.

Printed in Great Britain
by Amazon